S0-BZO-513

PEGGY WEBB writing as ANNA MICHAELS

The Tender Mercy of Roses

THE
LANGUAGE
OF
SILENCE

PORTER COUNTY PUBLIC LIBRARY

PEGGY WEBB

DISCARDED

Valparaiso Public Library
103 Jefferson Street
Valparaiso, IN 46383

vabfi   VAL
WEBB

Webb, Peggy, author
The language of silence
33410013059607   09/08/14

GALLERY BOOKS

NEW YORK   LONDON   TORONTO   SYDNEY   NEW DELHI

G

Gallery Books
A Division of Simon & Schuster, Inc.
1230 Avenue of the Americas
New York, NY 10020

This book is a work of fiction. Any references to historical events, real people, or real places are used fictitiously. Other names, characters, places, and events are products of the author's imagination, and any resemblance to actual events or places or persons, living or dead, is entirely coincidental.

Copyright © 2014 by Peggy Webb

All rights reserved, including the right to reproduce this book or portions thereof in any form whatsoever. For information address Gallery Books Subsidiary Rights Department, 1230 Avenue of the Americas, New York, NY 10020

First Gallery Books trade paperback edition September 2014

GALLERY BOOKS and colophon are registered trademarks of Simon & Schuster, Inc.

For information about special discounts for bulk purchases, please contact Simon & Schuster Special Sales at 1-866-506-1949 or business@simonandschuster.com.

The Simon & Schuster Speakers Bureau can bring authors to your live event. For more information or to book an event contact the Simon & Schuster Speakers Bureau at 1-866-248-3049 or visit our website at www.simonspeakers.com.

Interior design by Davina Mock-Maniscalco

Manufactured in the United States of America

10   9   8   7   6   5   4   3   2   1

Library of Congress Cataloging-in-Publication Data is available.

ISBN 978-1-4516-8481-0
ISBN 978-1-4516-8482-7(ebook)

ACKNOWLEDGMENTS

M Y DEEPEST GRATITUDE GOES to the people who so kindly helped me with the research for this book. Circus historian and friend Bob Kinney graciously lent me his fine collection of books about the early days of the Big Top: *Mud Show: A Circus Season,* by Fred Powledge; *Circus in America,* by Charles Philip Fox and Tom Parkinson; *Behind the Big Top,* by David Lewis Hammarstrom. Ruth Crosby, executive director of First Light women's shelter in Birmingham, Alabama (www.firstlightshelter.org), patiently answered my endless questions, as did Sonya Hamilton in Tupelo, Mississippi (www.safeshelter.net), and Naomi Duffy, who is associated with Favor House in Pensacola, Florida. Any mistakes I've made in portraying the circus as well as abuse are my own.

This work is entirely fictional, and Ellen Blair's experience in no way reflects the very fine work done by women's shelters across the country. If you are a victim of violence, please seek help in a shelter near you.

In *The Language of Silence* I've tried to balance the nightmare of abuse with the dream of circus magic. Above all, I want to leave you with a sense of hope.

PART
ONE

The tygers of wrath are wiser than the horses of instruction.

—William Blake,
The Marriage of Heaven and Hell

IT WAS THE BLACKBIRDS that first told Ruth something was wrong. At exactly the stroke of noon, they landed in the cornfield and commenced eating her corn as if they'd been the ones to stand in hundred-degree heat and chop the weeds out with a hoe.

In eighty years she'd put up with many injustices, but she'd be damned if she was going to stand in her kitchen mixing corn bread in a stone bowl while a bunch of black-feathered demons deprived her of a whole crop of corn. She jammed on her calico bonnet, then hoisted a soup pot and a clean wooden spoon and raced out her door, spry as any Ozark woman twenty years her junior.

And she'd box your ears if you said different.

Don't ever tell Ruth Gibson she's too old to live by herself. She aims to live to a hundred, all alone thank you very much, and Lord help the man who tries to stop her. Not that one would. The only men she's ever allowed on her farm are her granddaddy, God rest his soul, and Ray Boy Turner, who has been taking care of her place for might nigh fifty years. If Ruth has any say in it—and she plans to have plenty—Ray Boy will be there another fifty.

The screen door popped shut behind her, sounding like somebody had shot off a double-barreled twelve-gauge. But the crows paid the sound no more mind than they did the distant backfiring of Ruth's ancient Chevrolet as Ray Boy navigated down the winding road toward town.

"Shoo!" she yelled at the crows. "Git outta my corn!" A hundred pairs of beady eyes turned on her, giving her the all-overs.

Still, she stalked down the middle of her corn patch banging her wooden spoon against the pot as hard as she could. As the birds beat upward, the sound of wings caught Ruth high under the breastbone and wouldn't let go. Hundreds of blackbirds rose against a sun-bleached sky, pulling her out of her skin so she could look back and see nothing of herself except a pile of bones covered with her bonnet and her blue gingham dress.

Lost in a cloud of dark feathers, borne high by a murder of crows, Ruth found herself dissolving—her thin lips, her gray hair, the pink of her muscles. Finally she was nothing but a wisp of smoke with a beating heart and a pair of sharp blue eyes. Ghostlike, she traveled forward and backward at the same time: backward to the year of the Great Depression where her half sister Lola was forever young, forever fearless, dressed in circus spangles as she subdued golden-eyed tigers; and forward, to see Lola's granddaughter with her neck twisted sideways, blue eyes staring sightless at her bedroom walls.

Ruth fought against the pull of black wings, her silent screams echoing over her cornfields. Her heart strained with the effort to escape the mystical and anchor herself to the solid red clay of the mountains. But the gaping hole inside Ruth ripped wider as the loss of her sister was compounded by the possibility of losing a beloved great-niece who could have been Lola's double.

"No!" Ruth's bellow jerked her down and she found herself sitting in an undignified heap on crushed cornstalks, her bonnet hanging over one eye and her dress hiked up past her garters.

She tested her old bones gingerly to see if anything was broken. Satisfied, she got down on all fours to push herself off the ground. Then she stood in the relentless glare of a June sun, slowly counting to ten till she could get her balance and start back to the house.

This time she'd been lucky. The force of her visions had only thrown her off balance and cost her dignity. Sometimes she lost consciousness. Typically though, the weightlessness that was central to her visions just left her feeling a bit misty-eyed and damp.

"Damn crows," she said. "Next time I'm gonna be totin' my shotgun. See how they like that."

She considered herself fortunate that she'd sent Ray Boy for groceries. If he'd found her wadded up in the corn rows, he'd have called her doctor. If that wasn't enough, he'd have turned right around and called Ellen. Then her great-niece would have driven from Tupelo to way past Hot Springs only to discover she'd made the long drive for nothing.

Lord help her, that girl had enough on her plate without Ruth adding to her worries.

As Ruth trudged back to the house, she tried to figure out the visitation of crows. When her visions came to her whole and clear, she didn't have to ponder. But sometimes the truth was hidden behind a veil and open to all kinds of misinterpretations.

Today, for instance, had she seen harmful intent toward her niece, or merely a terrible accident? Ruth wasn't about to sound an alarm over a veiled vision. She knew the horrible consequences of giving warnings that changed the course of another person's life.

If she hadn't warned her sister about Jim Hall, would Lola have run away from her husband and left her baby in Ruth's care? Would her sister still be alive? Would Jim?

All Ruth's good intentions couldn't justify the end—Lola dead, Jim said to have been murdered, and Josie hating the very sight of Ruth, who had only wanted to keep her safe— three lives forever altered by visions Ruth might or might not have interpreted correctly.

Even though her sister had been gone nearly fifty years, she still woke up every morning with guilt and loss perched on her breastbone, a boulder she had to heave out of the way just so she could sit up in bed and breathe.

The first vision she remembered having was because of Lola. Ruth had been thirteen and under strict orders to take care of her baby sister while their mother hoed the garden. Caught up in her game of hopscotch, Ruth hadn't noticed when the three-year-old woke from her nap on the quilt under the willow and toddled off.

Suddenly the leaves began to fly off the willow tree, though there wasn't a breeze stirring. Ruth got dizzy as the leaves swirled around her, silver as water. And in their midst was a tiny hand.

"Lola?" The quilt was empty, her baby sister gone. The leaves spun so fast they became liquid. "Lola!"

When the leaves collapsed around Ruth, she saw her sister's cap of yellow curls—clear and true—disappearing underwater. She set out running and got to the lake behind their house in time to save her sister by taking a shortcut through the blackberry patch, only the scratches on Ruth's legs to tell the tale.

Some seers read tea leaves and palms, auras or tarot cards. Ruth read her dreams and the world around her, the revelations appearing involuntarily—in the flight of birds, the mystery of leaves, the whisper of stars falling into a river. Even objects as ordinary as a kitchen chair could take on extraordinary form, leaving Ruth with truths to decipher.

Had she read the vision of the crows correctly? When she got back to the house, she called Ellen, as much to reassure herself as to tell her great-niece she should be careful not to trip and fall.

When there was no answer, she went back to her chores in the kitchen, but Ruth's head hurt and she had lost her taste for corn bread. There it sat, eggs and buttermilk already mixed into the stone-ground cornmeal. Ruth couldn't abide waste. She added a pinch of baking soda, some baking powder and salt, then poured the mixture into a black cast-iron skillet and stuck it in the oven.

It was too late to turn on the radio and catch the new show *The Rest of the Story,* and too early to catch the *CBS Evening News,* though she already knew what she'd hear: Nixon and Watergate. Still, Ruth considered Paul Harvey and Walter Cronkite two of the smartest men she knew. Just the sound of their voices reassured her, anchored her to the present.

Skirting the bucket of peas she'd picked earlier in the day before the sun got too high, she left her hot kitchen to call

Ellen again. When there was still no answer, she went into the parlor on the shady side of the house to cool off. Folks nowadays called it a living room, but there hadn't been any living done in this room in nearly fifty years. Not since Lola died.

Ruth turned on a set of Victorian lamps beside a burgundy velvet sofa, then pulled back the faded rose brocade drapes to let in some light. But forsythia bushes had long ago climbed nearly to the roof, and the windows hadn't been washed since Ruth accidentally disturbed a nest of vicious red wasps under the sills. What was it, five years ago? Six?

When Ruth sank onto the sofa, dust rose from the velvet cushions. She fanned it away then reached onto the marble-topped coffee table for the treasures she displayed there—a yellowed newspaper clipping, a small gold brooch, and a grainy photograph made in a booth at the county fair. The photograph showed Ruth and Lola in pigtails, their arms around each other as they smiled into the camera, Ruth taller by five inches and older by ten years, her face defined by the sharp lines that would become hatchetlike over the years, and her half sister already stamped with the golden beauty that would be both her blessing and her curse. And yet there was something fierce inside Lola, too, something that couldn't be threatened out, beat out, or scared out.

Tracing the lines of her beloved sister's face, Ruth stared at the picture so long she became part of the air around her where, suddenly, a lone figure pulsed and swirled, dancing to some unheard melody. Lately, the lines between the physical world and her visions had become blurred and things kept getting mixed up, crossing over. Nothing surprised Ruth anymore, not a crow that could carry you to the sky or a phantom dancing in her parlor.

Half the time she didn't know whether she was on this side or the other. Old as she was, she reckoned she was straddling two worlds and too damned stubborn to give up either one of them.

As disconnected from her own body as dandelions blowing off their stem, Ruth squinted at the dancing vision, trying to assign Lola's face to the woman who sparkled when she twirled. But the phantom turned her back, keeping her secrets.

She found herself back on the sofa, taking off her glasses and wiping them with the hem of her dress. When she put them back on, the photograph had fluttered to the table, and she stared at the headlines in the ancient newspaper from Tarpon Springs, Florida:

The Great Giovanni Bros./Hogan & Sandusky Circus Presents Fearless Female Tiger Tamer!

Her sister smiled back at her, dwarfed by two six-hundred-pound Bengal tigers standing on back paws, licking her face.

Suddenly the brooch sprang to life, a miniature golden tiger turned full grown and fierce, prowling Ruth's parlor, claws extended and teeth bared. Snatched into another dimension, Ruth watched while he circled her rosewood upright piano with its ball-and-claw feet, sniffed behind her drapes, inspected the cushions on the carved mahogany fireside chairs, and sat a spell in front of the swinging pendulum of the grandfather clock.

When the tiger turned to look at her with eyes that could snatch souls, she stared right back.

"You ain't gonna find nothin' here but a skinny old woman with a tough hide. Now, git."

The tiger began to dissolve, first his tail, then his giant paws and upright ears, and finally his glaring, golden eyes. Then he lay back on her coffee table, a harmless brooch that nobody had worn since 1929.

As reality weighed down her bones once more, Ruth squeezed her hands together to stop the shaking. This was the second time she'd seen the tiger. The first had been last week when she'd roused from a nap on the porch and seen it streaking across her yard with Lola and Ellen both on its back.

Lord have mercy. Her sister had been gone all these years with Ruth getting nary a sign. What was the tiger trying to tell her?

She wiped her face with the red bandana she kept in her pocket, then she heaved herself off the sofa, leaned down to fluff up the indentation she'd made in the cushions, walked across the room to close the draperies, and left the parlor.

She had peas to shell, a cake to bake. Last night her dreams had told her company was coming, and she wanted to have a lemon pound cake ready.

By the time she heard Ray Boy chugging back up the mountain, she had the peas cooking, the corn bread cooling, her mixing bowls laid out, and the TV on so she wouldn't miss the news.

When Walter Cronkite signed off by saying, "And that's the way it is," Ruth wished she could be as certain about the messages from today's visions.

It took her to nightfall to get the cake done. She was slower than she used to be. But by the time she went to bed, the pound cake was under its glass dome on the cake plate, plump and proud and fragrant as the citrus groves Ruth sometimes smelled in her dreams, though she'd never set foot in Florida.

Shedding her calico dress, her shoes and garters and stockings, Ruth bathed herself at the washbasin that had belonged to her grandmother, though she had a perfectly modern bathroom. The simplicity of the old ways soothed her. Then she got into a clean white cotton nightgown and climbed into bed. It was taller than ordinary, plantation style with layers of thick bedding, but she had no need for the footstool. Even at eighty she was still a tall woman.

Ruth turned off the bedside lamp, pulled the sheet up to her chin, and lay in the darkness, praying she wouldn't dream. Still, she could hear the black shapes gathering—but it wasn't the rustle of wings. It was stealth with fur and teeth and claws.

Resigned, Ruth closed her eyes and went to sleep in the shadow of a tiger.

THE FIRST TIME HER husband had struck her, Ellen was leaning over the kitchen table putting candles on his birthday cake. The blow sent her face-first into the caramel frosting. Her pale blond hair was saved going up in flames because she hadn't yet lit the candles. Forty of them.

It was the forty candles that set him off.

"Don't you have the sense God gave a billy goat?"

Until he spoke, she hadn't known Wayne had come up behind her. Fixing her face in a *welcome home* smile, she glanced over her shoulder and said, "Hi, hon, wel—"

The blow caught the side of her mouth and stopped her in midsentence. Ellen couldn't have been more surprised if a piano had fallen out of the sky and landed on her head. She pushed herself back from the smashed cake, the taste of blood and caramel in her mouth.

"Wayne?" The man standing in front of her with his face twisted six ways to Sunday didn't even resemble the man she'd married six months earlier at the First Baptist Church in front of God and half of Tupelo.

"Don't think you can sweet-talk me. Here I come home

after a hard day's work expecting a hot meal and a nice glass of wine, and what do I get? A sign on my front porch, a *banner* for God's sake, letting the whole neighborhood know how god-damn old I am!"

He stormed past her into the kitchen and she trailed along behind him, holding her hand over her mouth, every inch of her quivering so hard her teeth knocked together like castanets. The sound reminded her of the rhythm band she sometimes used as a reward with the children in her special education class at Joyner Elementary School.

Was she losing her mind? What had she done wrong?

"Look at you. Put some ice on your mouth." Her husband jerked open the refrigerator door, poured himself a glass of tea from the crystal pitcher that had been a wedding gift from her mother, Josie Hall Westmoreland, Tupelo's leading social maven.

Slumped at his kitchen table, Wayne lifted the glass to his lips and his hands began to shake. He set it on the table, slosh-ing tea all over the white damask linen tablecloth, a wedding gift from his mother, who was reputed to have more money than God and twice the influence.

"Jesus H. Christ, Ellen. Why did you make me do that?"

"I'm sorry, Wayne." She knelt beside him and leaned against his knee, an automatic gesture and one that until today she'd loved. When she felt his hand touch her hair, it was all she could do not to flinch.

"I've got clients who depend on me to be at the top of my game. That takes a young man. Christ, Ellen!" He sighed, then leaned his face into her hair and drew a long breath, as if he might inhale her.

"I'm sorry," she whispered.

"Okay, baby. It won't happen again. I promise."

And it hadn't. Until nearly six months later when she'd for-gotten to put a slab of fatback in his green beans the way he liked them. The patch in the Sheetrock where he'd thrown his chair against the dining room wall would never be the same shade of green as the rest of the room. Too proud to admit the truth, she'd told her mother her arm was black and blue from a fall she'd taken against the side of her Bel Air when her foot twisted on a piece of loose gravel in the driveway.

She tried telling herself he was simply overworked, stressed out, or exhausted. She even tried to figure out every single thing that triggered his explosions so she could avoid the conse-quences. But every time she thought she knew the rules, he changed the game.

Finally, when Ellen didn't know who she was anymore, she'd sucked up her pride and confided in her mother. Josie hadn't shown the least bit of surprise at her daughter's tearful confession.

"For Pete's sake, Ellen. Don't do anything to set him off. You know how moody men can be. You just have to smile and carry on."

So Ellen stopped asking herself *why* and started becoming someone else—deceit wearing a false smile and real pearls, a gift from her heavy-fisted groom.

Now in the middle of June, in bare feet and a hopeful yel-low sundress, Ellen knelt on the floor of the bedroom she shared with Wayne and selected a box marked Red Slingback Pumps. The pumps were satin with rhinestones on the toes. Party shoes. The ones Wayne liked her to wear when he was entertaining out-of-town clients.

The shoes lay on a bed of tissue paper. She lifted them out, paper and all, then ducked her head for the blow she'd anticipated ever since she'd started squirreling away cash beneath the tissue paper. When her hand touched the money—fives and tens and twenties she'd squeezed from grocery money, her school clothing budget, and even, God help her, donations to church charities—Ellen wondered if she was being a fool.

From the country-and-western radio station playing in the kitchen, Tammy Wynette advised her to stand by her man.

In spite of central air-conditioning, sweat beaded Ellen's upper lip. Wiping her flushed face, she reminded herself that Wayne had left for a business trip to Chicago at nine that morning and had already called to inform her of his safe arrival. He would not come home and launch a surprise attack.

She gave herself a little pep talk. What she was about to do was a last resort. She was not in the middle of a fairy tale—unless it was one of those dark stories where the witch was always waiting behind the door—and none of her feverish wishes had come true.

After caramel cake started reminding her of blood, she'd wished that Wayne would fall forward at the supper table, his face in the vegetable soup—a nice, quiet death. She would tell the coroner, "Oh, dear, I never knew he had a bad heart. He was twelve years older than me, you know."

The body bruises and kidney punches brought on visions of Wayne struck down at the intersection of Broadway and Main as he headed to meet investment clients at his office, killed instantly by a speeding car. The cops would be kind to her, a grieving widow. They would say, "He suffered no pain," and everybody at First Baptist would bring casseroles.

Lately, it didn't take any punches at all to imagine Wayne looking out his plane's window at the Sears Tower, then going down in flaming wreckage in the middle of O'Hare. Or picturing him in his sleep mask for the long trip to Japan, plummeting to a watery grave in the Pacific.

Finally she gave up her fantasies. There would be no easy way out, just as there was no way she could fix what was wrong in her marriage. Ellen had tried. Single-handedly, it turned out, because in the eyes of her parents and his—in fact, in the eyes of every woman in the Deep South who still clung to visions of herself as June Cleaver and embraced "Stand By Your Man" as law and gospel—Wayne was the perfect husband: handsome, educated, intelligent, successful.

For nearly two years Ellen had subscribed to the belief that every problem has a solution, and she was intelligent enough to figure it out. But violence defies logic. Defeat destroys hope. And sometimes circumstances can change everything.

Ellen tucked the cash—nearly two thousand dollars—inside the liner she'd carefully ripped out of the cosmetic bag she carried in her purse. Then she got a needle and black thread and sewed the lining back with stitches so tiny even her aunt Ruth wouldn't have noticed.

She would not be her mother, she would not be June Cleaver, and she'd be damned if she'd let a backwoods woman from Tremont, Mississippi, be her hero, no matter how many hit records Wynette had. She wished she had enough courage to be like Gloria Steinem.

Ellen put on her good walking shoes, got her matching summer sweater from the closet, and turned off the radio. Then she sat down on the blue plaid Early American sofa by the telephone to wait for Wayne's call.

It came at three, not one minute after. He was a stickler for punctuality. When the name of her husband's hotel popped onto the caller ID she hadn't wanted and he'd insisted they get because it was the latest gadget, and after all, how could a man look successful if he didn't have the newest of everything, Ellen wreathed her voice in smiles.

"Hello, darling!"

"El, how's it going, baby? You miss me?"

"Like crazy."

His chuckle came clearly over the line, low and suggestive. "Hold that thought. Daddy's coming home tomorrow night."

"Great! I'm going into town to get pork chops for your dinner and I might even shop at the mall, if that's okay with you."

"Buy something lacy for me."

"Will you call tonight?" She forced herself to speak with exactly the right amount of longing.

"Can't, El. I've already *told you,* baby. You know how these meetings go."

"I know." How long should a crushed silence last? She counted to five then perked herself into hopeful. "But I'll see you for sure tomorrow night? You promise?"

"Daddy swears on his big, fat bank account."

She hung up the phone then sat awhile till she could stop her hands from shaking. When she had herself under control, she called Janice Burns, the secretary at First Baptist Church, and spun a tale about needing a ride to the grocery store because her car wouldn't crank and her mother was unavailable.

Then Ellen walked straight to the door without looking

back. Her house held nothing she minded leaving behind. She didn't even take her toothbrush. Her instructions had been specific: *take nothing but the clothes on your back.*

Ten minutes after her call, Janice swooped down Ellen's sidewalk, as full of self-importance flutterings as a flock of house wrens. She talked all the way to the Piggly Wiggly, sometimes waiting for Ellen to answer, sometimes answering herself.

When she let Ellen out at the grocer's double doors, Janice leaned out the window and called, "Are you sure you don't want me to pick you up? It'll be no trouble."

"I'll call Mama from the pay phone. Besides, with Wayne out of town and all, she's expecting me for supper."

By nightfall, Ellen's plans would be all over town. Janice not only took every opportunity to lend a hand, but also to tell about it.

Ellen hurried into the Piggly Wiggly while Janice was trying to turn her Lincoln around. She grabbed a basket and waved at the stock boy as she passed the produce section. While her pork chops were being wrapped, she had to pretend interest in a political diatribe from a butcher obsessed with the Watergate scandal. Trying to act normal.

It galled her to the bone that while women in other parts of the country had advanced beyond the June Cleaver mold, for most small-town southern women *normal* still meant cooking and cleaning and grocery shopping and taking care of the kids if you had any and going to church on Sundays whether you felt like it or not—and smiling, always smiling, even if you didn't have a single thing to smile about. While for men *normal* meant doing any damn thing you pleased, any time you pleased. And that included using your wife for a punching bag.

As she headed to frozen foods, Ellen forced herself not to throw her pork chops at the butcher, though he didn't have a thing to do with Wayne's brutal forms of endearment.

She left the meat she didn't intend to cook in a shopping cart she hated and made her way through double swinging doors that took her through a storage room to the bathroom. Looking into the spotted mirror over the sink, she tucked her hair under the silk scarf she'd had in her purse, donned new Hollywood-style sunglasses, then hurried out of the bathroom and through two aisles stacked high with unopened cartons of Tide. The back door was just ahead. Without looking back, Ellen plunged through.

No one jumped out to waylay her. No one called her name. No one tried to stop her. She felt as successful as Moses parting the Red Sea.

In the blast of summer heat she longed to peel off her sweater, but the fading bruise on her left arm glowed like a dirty yellow headlamp. She started a five-block walk where anything could happen. Someone might spot the yellow sundress she was fond of wearing to church picnics and stop to talk. Even worse, one of Wayne's cronies might recognize her and report that his proper wife was decked out in rhinestone-studded sunglasses and headed in the direction of the bus station.

Scuttling along with her head down would be the surest way to call attention to herself. Ellen lifted her chin at what she imagined to be a haughty angle and walked fast, hoping she looked like a businesswoman who was too important to bother with idle chatter.

By the time she saw the Greyhound sign, she had a stitch in her side and a nearly uncontrollable urge to cry with relief. Still, before she went inside, she scanned the area. The God of Women Who Run Away was smiling on her. Either that or she'd simply been smart to choose the bus as her means of escape. Her circle of friends rarely braved the dingy interior of a bus station where they'd have to wait on hard wooden benches with people who considered antiperspirant a waste of money and a car an impossible dream. Would she soon be one of them?

At the ticket window she said, "One way, Hot Springs, Arkansas." The Ellen everyone in town knew would have said *please.* But she was a new, bold Ellen who didn't give a flip about manners. This Ellen would grow claws and scratch your eyes out if you got in her way.

The rains started when the Greyhound pulled out of Tupelo and didn't let up for six hours. Ellen found the downpour soothing. It drowned out cities and state lines and thought. It blanketed conversations, the Mississippi River, and fear.

She leaned her head against the windowpane and imagined that the fat drops were birds brushing against the bus. She felt herself caught up in a cradle of wings and bird bones, borne toward the mountain where Aunt Ruth, the family outcast, would wrap her in quilts, tuck her into a feather bed, and tell her stories about the grandmother she longed to know.

Ellen was struck by yearning. If only Ruth were younger, she'd move in with her. She could picture how it would be, Ellen learning to trust again and her baby growing up fearless under the care of a tough old mountain woman who would take a shotgun to anybody who tried to harm them. But Ruth was no longer a vigorous woman. Wayne would snap her like a twig.

It was past ten when Ellen got to Hot Springs and another thirty-minute cab ride up the dark mountain. It came as no surprise that Aunt Ruth had lights glowing in every window.

"I been expectin' you." She wrapped Ellen in a huge hug, then led her to the kitchen where the coffee smelled like possibility and the slice of lemon cake on a blue willow plate was as golden as the eye of a tiger.

Ellen didn't ask, *How did you know?* Ruth's *gift* was the reason her mother called Ruth crazy and one of the many reasons Ellen loved her. When Ellen had been seven and told her mother she'd been playing circus with a tiger on her swing set, Josie's split with her mother's half sister became so complete that she let her aging relative sit on her mountain alone, even refusing to invite Ruth to share roast turkey at the Hall family Christmas.

"I can't stay long, Aunt Ruth."

"You ain't goin' nowhere tonight. Eat."

The coffee, thick with cream and sugar, poured energy back into her tired bones so that Ellen felt capable of anything, even leaving behind this aunt she loved so dearly. Aunt Ruth had always been the one she turned to when she needed sympathy and courage.

But the lemon cake tasted like sorrow. Ellen swallowed back the tears.

"I'm pregnant."

"I been knowin' it awhile."

"Is it a girl?"

"I ain't tellin'."

"Then talk to me about my grandmother. What was her life like after she ran away?"

"Lola run away to the circus, a scared little slip of a girl, and turned herself into a woman fierce enough to train big cats. But lions wasn't mean enough for her. Nosireebob. She got in the cage with tigers."

"I don't remember much about her letters." She wished she'd paid closer attention. What might she have learned from her grandmother about survival? "Did she ever mention why she stayed with the circus?"

"She wrote mostly about missing me and your mama. But there was this one letter I remember because it made me feel better about Lola being gone. She said she felt safe there, that the circus family was close-knit and watched out for they own. I'm gonna give them letters to you."

"They're your treasures, Aunt Ruth. I don't want to be a bother."

"Pshaw. Fightin' pesky blackbirds is a bother. You ain't in the same category. In the morning I'll dig out them letters for you." Ruth's look pierced her. "You got your grandmother's grit, and don't you be forgettin' it."

Ellen swallowed another bite of sorrow then had to wash it down with coffee so her voice wouldn't break apart, and her with it.

"I have to go away, Aunt Ruth. I may not see you again for a long time."

"I'll see you in my dreams."

The two of them laughed like women unhinged, kindred spirits who loved music and magic and each other. They laughed till tears rolled into the crumbs of lemon cake. They had to hold the table to keep from falling out of their chairs.

Suddenly something stirred in the night, causing Ellen to jerk upright and stare out the window. Was it Wayne? Had he seen through her elaborate ploy? Was he already on the mountain to drag her home?

"Aunt Ruth, somebody's out there."

"It's just the night owls stirring. Don't pay them no attention." Ruth got up and pulled the curtains shut then took Ellen by the hand and led her to a wide room down the hall. She climbed into bed, sank into a deep mattress filled with duck down, and waited while her aunt pulled a quilt under her chin.

Then Ruth bent close, the moonlight dividing her face into halves, soft and fierce at the same time.

"Now, you listen to me, girl. This here quilt I made from a pattern called Around the World, and it's gonna take you places."

Ellen wrapped her arms around the one person in the world she could trust, then closed her eyes and imagined herself being transported by Ruth's quilt to a place where her grandmother Lola smiled back at her from the center ring over the heads of two trained tigers.

3

IN THE LIGHT OF a pale moon, the Great Giovanni Bros./ Hogan & Sandusky Circus caravan rolled to a stop in an uneven pasture in southern Kentucky. Moving in choreography ingrained from years of bringing circus magic to rural America, the assembly of trucks and trailers took up their spots—the light truck in the side yard on the far right, trucks hauling the midway rides and concession stands in the front, and the cook tent, menagerie trucks, and Airstreams bearing performers in the circus backyard. In the center, in a space larger than several footballs fields, the big top would bloom at dawn like an exotic red and white flower.

Trainers, performers, owners, and roustabouts were soon sleeping, taking advantage of the few hours before the ringing of hammer against metal would make rest impossible. Deep in their dreams of high mountain meadows and green pastures, even the animals dozed—all except the tiger. Lying on a couch in an Airstream that occupied the elite section of the circus yard reserved for owners, the six-hundred-pound Bengal kept his golden-eyed vigil over an old man tossed about by his dreams . . .

The scent of wisteria is strong as I slide through the darkness with my tigers, silent as the circus train beside me, a sleeping dragon on the tracks snaking through another of the small towns where, in a few short hours, we'll pitch the big top and spin magic. Afterward, we'll leave in the middle of the night, thieves making off with the spangles and the wonder, nothing to show we've been there except a crushed grassy lot strewn with popcorn and tufts of cotton candy.

The smokestacks and boxcars are quiet now, the red velvet curtains on the compartments of acrobats and equestrians, of ringmaster and clowns shut tight against the chill of a spring night in the rural Mississippi town. There are no sounds except my footsteps, an occasional call from an owl deep in the woods beyond the train, and the music of chains as the big bulls stir in their elephant dreams.

Suddenly a trumpet alarm that could call down God blasts the deep quiet. Rocket, the big Asian bull who fancies himself watchelephant for the circus.

"It's okay, Rocky," I call toward the chained-off area where the elephants are staked. "It's just me. Razz."

Rocket settles down at the sound of my voice. But he isn't about to let me pass without a bribe. In spite of the fact that I am holding two tiger cubs on leashes, the elephant taps me on the shoulder with his trunk. I settle my tiger leashes into one hand and reach into my pocket with the other.

I'm a soft touch when it comes to circus animals, and they know it. I never go anywhere without pockets bulging with peanuts, carrots, and whatever treat I think my four-legged friends will want.

I offer up a handful of peanuts. "Will that do?" Rocky's lips curl into an elephant smile. "Now, be quiet. I don't want to wake the circus."

We slip through the night, two sleek-coated tigers out for a frolic and a man trying to escape the terror of his nightmares. They are always the same: my Ford Model T touring car going over the bridge, Cynthia screaming my name, me running through the fog, too late to save her and the baby.

As I pass by the stock cars where silver-coated Andalusians are bedded down for the night, I smell their sweet straw and imagine their dreams, white horses dancing, their polished hooves moving to the rhythm of the Blue Danube Waltz.

"Sleep well, beauties." In a few hours they'll be wearing blue and gold spangled blankets, dancing to the cheers of the crowd.

Ahead, in red and gold cages resting on flatcars along the train-dragon's tail, are the rest of my babies, lions and tigers slumbering, and panthers so black they swallow the night. A low rumble from Rufus, the crotchety old lion who hates his sleep disturbed, sends the tiger cubs into a crouch that makes me smile.

Orphaned at birth, they'd been raised on the bottle. Restrained only by leashes, they appear no more fierce than house cats. But unlike man, who will socialize himself so completely he's indistinguishable, a tiger never forgets who he is.

I know this about tigers. And I never exercise them outside the training arena until the circus sleeps.

Born to the circus, I understood the ways of big cats before I could talk. My father and my idol is Ben Hogan, former big-cat trainer and part owner of the Great Giovanni Bros./Hogan & Sandusky Circus, a man who taught his only son the language of tigers, the dreams of lions, and the secrets of panthers.

Pulled by forces I don't understand, I hurry through the meadow. The tiger cubs perk up their ears, the only indication they give that they sense something of interest in the forest beyond. Unlike lions, who signal an attack, a tiger never reveals his plans. Only a man who speaks their language would know that something alive lurks in the forest. Animal or human, I don't know. All I know is the shiver of anticipation that steals through me in the cloudless night.

Beyond them, deep in the forest, wisteria cascades purple from blackjack oaks and gum trees, its scent so sweet it calls up songs and longing. The melodies of night birds send a tremor along the black and gold coats of the tigers, and I find myself dreaming with my eyes open, dreaming of the black-eyed wife I'd once had and the baby with her red hair. Cynthia had been a trapeze artist, as fearless on the wire as I am in the big-cat ring. We were happy as any circus couple you ever saw until a car wreck ended it all.

But it's not the blood and terror of the crash I remember, nor the bargains I'd made with God to rewind time so I would be the one tangled in metal and they would be the ones at home pouring milk into a blue cereal bowl. It's picnics in the rain I recall, lullabies under the stars, a dazzle of pink sequins on a flying trapeze. And love.

A breeze stirs, sending tendrils of scent that draw me toward the forest. I strain my eyes, counting on the moonlight to show me something out of the ordinary. But all I see is a mountain of flowers. They hang in clusters from every branch of every tree, blue as the deepest night. I don't wonder the Native Americans who first settled the land called it Pontotoc, Land of the Hanging Grapes. I half-expect the wisteria blooms to transform to plump, juicy fruit before my eyes, a sleight of hand performed by a circus magician.

Mesmerized, I reach to part the heavy vines, but it's the tigers who see her first. The cubs pounce, bringing a soft screech from the tangle of fur and flowers. Heart pounding, I push through the wall of wisteria. The girl lies underneath the fat, furry tiger kittens, her skin pale as milk, her silvery hair festooned with leaves and flowers, and her eyes an iridescent blue that shivers my soul.

"*Save me,*" *she says.*

"*The cubs won't hurt you.*" *In fact, they seem to have adopted her. Rajah is sitting on her chest licking her face, and Sheikh is stretched beside her with his tail draped over her legs and his head resting on her outstretched arm.*

"*Not from the tigers.*" *Her voice is weak, little more than a whisper, but it holds the sound of bells and meadowlarks.*

I am the last person you'd ask to be your rescuer. It has been only a year since the death of my wife and child, and I still can barely save myself.

"*From what, then?*"

"*From him.*"

The circus is a magnet for men and women running from poverty, violence, or the law. I have no stomach for dealing with her desperation, and no talent for defending her from a determined husband.

She pushes the tiger cub off her chest and sits up. Her dress is torn at the sleeve and her cheeks sunken, as if she'd had her last meal several days ago.

"*Save me,*" *she says again, and then she faints.*

I carry her back to my train car. Any decent man would. I'll give her a meal, give her a bed for the night, and let the authorities deal with her in the morning.

That's the plan I make as I trek across the meadow in the dark, carrying the woman who is so small I'd first thought her to be a girl. Inside my compartment, I place her on my bed. In the glow of gaslights, her hair looks like fallen stars. Temporarily enchanted, I don't notice the bruises blooming under the collar of her dress, along her arms, down her calves, until Sheikh starts licking her face.

Leaning over to inspect her, a man full grown and robust in spite of my skinny legs and a face nobody would call handsome, I cry.

Razz was still crying when he woke up from his dream. Sitting up with the covers pulled to his chin he studied the huge red and gold circus poster hanging on his bedroom wall. Circa 1929, it featured the golden-haired goddess of his dreams with two tigers kneeling at her feet. Sheikh I and Rajah, fully grown, posing beside Lola Hall.

The dream clung to Razz as he got out of bed and dressed. When he passed into his living room, a six-hundred-pound Bengal tiger lifted his massive head and stared at him with eyes that held deep green jungles and tall savanna grasses, wide streams and vaulted blue spaces.

"Good morning, Sheikh." Razz treated all his cats with respect, especially this one, Sheikh IV, a descendant of the tiger he always thought of as Lola's. Sheikh II and III had lived ordinary circus tiger lives, but IV had been orphaned as his great-grandfather had.

Razz scratched behind the tiger's ears then continued his journey to the bathroom. Bits of his dream were as vivid to him as the tiger on his couch, but he didn't question why he was still dreaming of events long gone for nearly fifty years.

He believed in love that neither time nor death could destroy, in the loyalty of friends, and in the heavenly spirits who took a personal interest in all God's creatures. But most of all he believed in the red and gold magic of the circus.

As long as he had breath, he was determined to keep the magic alive. From the looks of things, that might not be too much longer. The bathroom mirror reflected a face pitted as a walnut shell, bare arms jagged with claw-shaped scars, legs bowed with age, and a head covered by a Yankees ball cap.

"Old coot." He was too old to travel all over the country

eight months out of the year. What he ought to do was retire to Florida before the cats took the rest of his scalp and him with it. "Stubborn old fart," he muttered, knowing he would fight anybody who suggested he was too old to travel with the circus.

He pulled the bill of his cap lower. Razz had worn a baseball cap everywhere he went since Congo, a five-hundred-pound African lion, took umbrage at jumping through a ring of fire and decided to rip off a portion of his trainer's scalp. It had been stitched back on, of course, but the hair would never grow back.

Razz stepped outside and listened to the songs of the circus. It didn't matter that he was on the ugly side of Kentucky, the lot was full of cockleburs, and the smells coming from the cook tent meant breakfast would be bologna fried in grease that wouldn't set well in his digestive system. His beloved big top was going up, and he was smiling.

The canvas men chanted as their sixteen-pound sledgehammers rang against metal, five men to a stake, the staccato rhythm of their strikes so well coordinated that if one man missed a beat, another's brains would be scattered over the ground. Asian elephants—both male and female called *bulls*— rattled their chains and swayed in lumbering dance as they hauled the poles that would hold the red and white striped tent in place. The lone African bull, big-eared and mean enough to throw a man down then roll over him for the sheer pleasure of it, lifted his massive trunk and trumpeted.

From the menagerie tent, the cats—tigers and lions and leopards—greeted the morning with roars, while the monkeys and bears and camels and llamas and goats and exotic birds of every feather complained with hoots and growls and bleats and chirps.

Underneath it all was the thundering music of horses' hooves. Straining his eyes into the pearl-colored morning he saw twelve Andalusians prancing in a wide circle, their white coats ghostlike, their tails arched and manes tossing as a lone rider leaped from horse to horse, flying through the air as if he had wings attached to his feet.

"Luca."

It could be no other, for only this grandson of Razz's friend and business partner, Alfonse Giovanni, possessed the magic handed down from Mario Giovanni of Rome through six generations of the finest equestrians in circus history.

Razz set off in the direction of the big top. As he wound his way through the melee that would soon be transformed into one of the greatest shows on earth, he was caught in a net of time, his arthritic legs limber again, his body light enough to sidestep a raging lion, his heart strong enough to do two performances a day then load his big cats into a circus train at midnight and set out for the next town.

He missed the trains, the groaning of couplings between the cars, the long, lonesome hoot of the whistle, the rhythmic clacking of wheels against rails as the circus hurtled through the night. It was the favorite lullaby of a true showman. Nowadays, the few circuses that still performed under canvas used trucks to haul animals and equipment, while performers followed in trailers..

Razz followed the scent of grease around the big top to the cook tent. Alfonse Giovanni was already there, his gnarled hand wrapped around a mug of coffee Razz personally thought tasted like axle grease, his wide girth taking up enough room for two. Razz made his way toward the table reserved for owners, sat down beside his old friend, and piled his plate with bologna and biscuits, grits floating in butter.

"The bear struck again last night," Al said.

"What'd he take this time?"

"Indian Joe said he took his stash of poker money."

"Did he see anything?"

Razz and Al had been trying to find out who the bear was ever since they'd started the circus season, back in March. Since they hadn't had a problem with theft for the last two seasons, both of them believed the bear was one of the new people they'd hired, more likely a roustabout than any of the Chinese tumblers from their new act.

"He didn't see a thing." Al buttered another biscuit, a sure sign he was ignoring the advice of his doctor as well as his wife, both of them predicting a heart attack and urging retirement.

"I guess it's a good thing he didn't, Al. Joe would have taken the bull hook to him."

Indian Joe was the elephant trainer. Nobody remembered his last name, or why he was called Indian. He didn't have a drop of Native American blood. Pale and freckled, Joe had so much busy red hair his head looked like the business end of a mop. He was known for his quick temper with men he disliked, his kindness to the elephants he called *my babies,* his fondness for gambling, and his ability to get every elephant under his care to do his bidding. Every elephant, that is, except Betsy.

"I guess you're right." Al drained the last of his coffee and stood up. "I'm going to watch Luca. He's trying out a new triple somersault."

"Maybe that'll draw a straw house."

Razz fell into step beside Al. Any act that would guarantee a crowd big enough to fill the bleachers and spill over onto the straw laid down on the hippodrome track had his full attention. The circus had been in jeopardy long before Sandusky died last year of lung cancer. But buying Sandusky's share of the circus from his heirs, one a lawyer in Atlanta, the other a doctor in Chicago, and neither with an interest in running a show, had strained a budget already under stress from dwindling crowds that preferred the razzle-dazzle of a show under air-conditioning to the authenticity of circus magic under a canvas big top.

Razz and his cats were still the major center-ring attraction, but how much longer could an old man losing his teeth draw a circus crowd big enough to keep the show alive?

As they passed the trailers in the circus backyard, a door flew open and a dark-haired child catapulted out. Luca's son. With a face solemn as a judge, he caught up to Razz and Al, put his tiny hands in theirs, and fell into step.

"Good morning, Nicky. Can you say good morning to Papa?" The hope in Al's eyes wrenched Razz's heart. The four-year-old hadn't said a word since his mother toppled from the Andalusians and was trampled underneath—a long year of dashed hopes and failed attempts with various child psychologists.

Al swooped his great-grandson onto his shoulders and the little boy giggled.

"I keep telling everybody, this boy will talk when he has something to say. Right, Nicky?"

As Razz walked with Al toward an open field beyond the

big top, the little boy's laughter flew out behind them like the tail of a kite. They didn't stop until they were close enough to see chunks of earth flying up around the hooves of twelve white Andalusians. The volume would have been deafening to an ordinary man. But they were genuine showmen, two of the last, born under canvas and planning to die there. If God was good.

And in spite of a circus season where the winds had ripped the big top out of its moorings in Oklahoma, the balance sheet was staying stubbornly in the red, and all his old friends urged him to fold up the canvas and take his show indoors like Ringling, Razz believed in the grace of a generous God who knew exactly the right moment to produce a miracle.

"May it be soon." Razz crossed himself, then watched as Luca executed a perfect triple backward somersault, flying from the back of the lead stallion and landing atop the back of the white stallion three horses back.

Luca guided the horse out of the circle, cantered toward them, and scooped his son off Al's shoulders. Then in a voice that sang of rushing wind and whispering rivers, he gave his command and the Andalusians began to dance. Though it was hours before the brass band would strike up for the matinee, Razz could hear the melody of the Blue Danube Waltz.

With the sun now beating down on him as yellow and warm as melted butter, Razz's happiness grew so wide it spread beyond the pasture and into the green trees where birds transformed it to song.

ELLEN WOKE UP TO the sound of calliope music. Lying under the canopy of her aunt's quilts, she waited till her spangled dreams faded and she was firmly planted in the Ozarks once again. The calliope metamorphosed into a John Phillip Sousa march blasting from Ruth's console stereo in the dining room.

Her first thought was that after today it was possible she'd never see this aunt who always wore garters with her stockings, saw things no one else could, and played circus music before breakfast. Ruth was old, and anything could happen while Ellen was hiding in a shelter for abused women.

What her life would be like there, she couldn't imagine. All she knew was that she couldn't continue with the life she had. It was unthinkable that she might one day say to a daughter with three broken ribs, "You just have to smile and carry on."

Pressing her palms over her abdomen, she whispered, "I never will. I swear to you."

Did a child in the womb hear its mother's whispered promises? Had her own mother ever whispered to her, only to discover that the world was too hard and breaking promises too easy?

Suddenly she was six, sitting at a shining mahogany table with turkey and dressing on her plate and spilled milk on her taffeta skirt, her face flaming as her father dished out a tongue-lashing. After he stormed out, her mother announced from the far end of the table, "If you would just behave, your father wouldn't have to act that way. Now go wash yourself off, then march back in here and eat. And please try not to embarrass me to death."

Blindsided, Ellen pulled the covers up to her chin. Why was she unearthing memories long buried and forgotten? To hear her mother tell it, she'd been raised with a silver spoon.

The smell of coffee brewing pulled her out of dark memories and into the sun-drenched house on the mountain whose only inhabitant would whip wildcats for her. Or at least try. It always came as a shock to see how Ruth had aged. Though she was still fierce, she was no longer capable of fighting off all predators.

Determined not to let anything spoil her day, Ellen threw back the quilt and raced barefoot into the kitchen. Ruth was standing at the stove tending bacon in a cast iron skillet.

Grabbing her aunt's waist, Ellen danced them around, keeping time to crashing cymbals and thumping trombones until the bacon started to smoke. Ruth jerked up a pot holder to rescue their breakfast and Ellen fell into a chair, her face flushed with heat and triumph.

"Do you realize I'll never have to see my husband again? Just think about it. I'm free!"

Ruth got two plates from the cupboard and began piling on food, bacon a bit scorched and biscuits fat as hydrangea blooms.

"You gonna need a good breakfast."

"Pile it on. I'm so hungry I could eat a bear."

When Ellen had imagined her last moments with her great-aunt, she pictured time growing big as an ocean, the two of them sitting on its endless shores basking in long embraces and perfectly worded good-byes. Ruth would condense eighty years of wisdom into pithy quotes Ellen would remember years later when her own daughter would be leaving for college and needed words to live by.

There would be tears when her aunt finally waved to her from the door, but not the kind that made your eyes swell and your nose turn red. They would be tears tinged with the joy of beginnings.

Instead, Ellen was still dressing when the taxi arrived. While the driver honked his horn, she gave her aunt a quick hug, said, "I love you," then hurried outside before he raced down the mountain without her.

It was not until the taxi was around the bend where Ellen couldn't look back and see the house, no matter how hard she tried, that she realized she hadn't had time to get her grandmother's letters. And now she might never have the chance.

She refused to begin her new life with regrets. Instead, she wondered about Ruth's understated enthusiasm at the prospect of a Wayne-less future.

Did Aunt Ruth know something she wasn't telling? Had she experienced another vision, one so horrible the thought of sharing it over bacon and biscuits subdued her?

Even Ruth's last words to her on the porch had been somber.

"You be careful now, you hear?"

Before Ellen could work herself into believing that something as simple as a farewell contained hidden warnings, she made herself think about where she was going: Haven House, tucked into a corner of northeast Mississippi near Holly Springs. A shelter where women like her could escape from husbands who had promised to be loyal till death, and then set out to serve it up in small slices.

When she'd asked the director of the shelter in Tupelo to recommend a place farther away, she'd been told, "Typically, a woman goes to the shelter in her own hometown."

"My husband is well connected. I need a place to hide where he can't find me."

"Shelters are not merely a place to hide. They are a place to heal."

While Wayne was in Chicago expecting pork chops when he got home, she'd be getting to know a roommate whose bruises might already have faded. While he was tearing through his wifeless house, wondering why supper was not on the table and trying to convince himself she couldn't be far because all her clothes were still in the closet and her car in the garage, she'd be having her first session with a counselor.

"Being a victim is learned behavior," the director had told her. "We teach you how to break the cycle."

Well . . . Wouldn't Josie be furious to hear she was part of a cycle?

Ellen almost giggled as she got out of the cab and paid the driver. Across from the bus station she found a small corner café that reminded her of Dudie's Diner back home, a favorite hangout during her teens when reality was colored by innocence and the future was spun of dreams.

As Bruce Springsteen crooned through the scratchy speakers of the jukebox in the corner and two men in faded overalls argued over whether President Nixon should resign, a hole opened up inside Ellen's heart and her courage began to drain out. Was she doing the right thing? Could a woman ever run far enough to escape her past?

She plugged the hole with memories of her aunt. Ruth had made sure Ellen knew the names of trees and stars. She'd pointed out migratory birds and taught Ellen their flight patterns and winter homes. And as long as Josie had allowed Ruth to be part of the family Christmas, Ruth's gifts were the best, always something made by hand—an album with pressed leaves, each one dated and identified; a little pink quilt Ellen had finally outgrown and used for her dolls; Christmas ornaments made with pinecones and glitter.

When she pulled herself back together, Ellen bought a ham sandwich and three fat dill pickles to save for later. A celebration lunch, she decided.

Besides, the small café might be her last chance for food till she got where she was going. She didn't know if she'd get to stop for lunch after she made the transfer from bus to police cruiser. Probably not. The cop's job would be to escort her to the safe house, not indulge her cravings.

Clutching her purse and her sack lunch, Ellen went into the station, bought her one-way ticket, and sat down to wait for the bus. It was right on time, and she was the first on, settling in a window seat near the front so she could watch for the Mississippi River. Once she got to the river, the biggest part of her journey would be behind her.

She'd eat her celebration lunch then, including all three pickles.

The other passengers started filing in. Though the crowd was small and the bus wouldn't be nearly full, a rumpled woman with fuzzy gray hair and faded blue eyes heaved herself into the seat next to Ellen. She settled a flowered satchel under her feet and an overstuffed plastic bag from Fred's Dollar Store in her lap.

"You going far, honey?"

Ellen had always thought the best part of travel was not arriving at the Washington Monument in Wayne's black four-door Cadillac DeVille, but enjoying small talk with the strangers she met on the journey—a sweet old couple sitting in a diner sharing a piece of apple pie, for instance, or a friendly service station attendant with pictures of his kids, or a harried woman in the public restroom wondering aloud if her lipstick was the wrong color for a job interview.

Wayne never talked to strangers. He said it was a waste of time and even dangerous. Until today, Ellen had thought he was wrong.

Now here she was, trapped. A woman enamored of truth trying to manufacture a lie her inquisitive traveling companion would believe.

Ellen cleared her throat and said, "Not far."

"I'm going to visit my cousin in Holly Springs. Haven't seen her in fifteen years. She's probably put on weight." The woman shifted her bag. "You got somebody waiting on you?"

Ellen had a sudden vision of Wayne turning red in the face as he stormed through their empty house.

"No," she said. Her ears burned with the lie. A woman on the run had to do better than that.

"Well, that's too bad. A pretty little thing like you. My

niece . . . she's not half as pretty as she thinks she is, and she's already had two husbands." The woman whose religion was small talk eyed Ellen. "I don't believe in divorce. Do you?"

Wayne didn't believe in divorce, either. He believed in the sanctity of marriage and fists.

"Will you excuse me? I have to eat now."

The lunch intended for celebration became one of rescue. Ellen ripped into the wrappings then tried to see how far she could stretch a sandwich and three pickles.

Far enough, it turned out. By the time she finished, her companion was dozing and the Arkansas-Tennessee Bridge was far behind them. Ellen had a stomachache brought on by anxiety or pregnancy, she didn't know which. All she knew was that she wanted nothing more than to lean over a toilet bowl and be sick.

Still, she had a long way to go and only the dress on her back. Closing her eyes, she prayed without words, a battered soul straining toward the promise of mercy.

IT WAS DUSK WHEN she got to Haven House via a network of strangers, secret cars, and finally a police cruiser. Ellen was so exhausted and scared she couldn't even get out of the car.

"Ma'am, we're here. Have yourself a good evening now."

Did being out of reach of flying fists constitute a good evening?

Ellen thanked him, and when she got out of the car the dusk closed around her like a security blanket. She felt safe in the dark. Anonymous. Just another woman walking in shadows.

Ellen counted the steps to freedom. Thirteen. As the cruiser pulled away from the curb, the door cracked open.

"Hello." Ellen smiled at the woman in the dimly lit room. Did they keep the lights low so the enemy couldn't see inside? "Mrs. Rakestraw?"

"I've been waiting for you, darling." Wayne stepped out of the shadows behind her, and suddenly the air was too thick to breathe. There was nowhere to run, and no mercy left in the world.

As helpless as a peeled egg, Ellen stood beside her husband while he kissed her on the cheek, then took hold of her arm.

To the casual observer he was just a loving husband making sure his wife didn't fall in the dark. His thumb dug into the crook at her elbow hard enough to bruise but not deep enough to make her scream. What would happen if she did? The cop had long gone and the woman standing on the other side of the door was empty-handed, no gun, no knife, not even a brass lamp to defend the battered women in her care.

But then, wouldn't a weapon have made starting over a farce, just a contest to determine the biggest bully?

"Mrs. Rakestraw, my wife changed her mind and called me to pick her up. Ellen, tell Mrs. Rakestraw you're sorry you wasted her time."

"I'm so sorry."

The words rasped over a tongue gone dry, but Ellen was too scared to see if Mrs. Rakestraw believed her. She was too defeated to notice whether the director of Haven House was fooled by Wayne's smooth manner and false charm.

"I can call the cops, dear."

And then what? Obviously one of Wayne's cronies in the

Tupelo Police Department had tipped him off to her plans. She didn't think the cop who had delivered her was part of it, but how would she know? She was trapped in the wide net of Wayne's influence.

"Oh, no . . . please, Mrs. Rakestraw. My husband and I had a little tiff and I got carried away. Everything's fine now."

The darkness that only moments earlier had felt safe now felt as if it had claws and teeth. Though clouds obscured the stars and the moon, Wayne waited till he was around the corner of Haven House before he twisted her arm behind her back. His black Cadillac waiting at the curb made her think of a hearse.

As Ellen was marched to the car and shoved into the front seat, her trick of becoming someone else no longer worked. Without the domestic props of her blue-tiled kitchen where she always kept a conciliatory pie in the pantry, she was laid bare, a featherless bird caught in a net of bad fortune.

Wayne leaned close to buckle her in, his mouth sharklike against her cheek.

"Did you think I'd let you go?" he whispered.

Even if there had been a miracle on this street whose name she didn't know, beside a house where she couldn't hide, her lips were too dry to speak.

He grabbed a fistful of hair and her head snapped back.

"Well, did you?"

"No."

"That's my girl." His smile didn't touch his eyes, and the way he smoothed her hair was more threat than caress. "I'll always find you."

Long ago she'd lost her faith in miracles, and now she lost all hope of escape.

Wayne went around the car, slid behind the wheel, and drove away from Haven House, whistling.

For nearly an hour there were no sounds except tires swishing against pavement and her husband's eerie, tuneless whistling.

Wrapping her arms around herself to hold back her shivers, Ellen told herself the worst was over. Her husband had blown off steam and now they could go home where she would swear on the Bible and her Betty Crocker cookbook that she'd never run away again. She didn't know what got into her, she'd tell him. *Really*, she hadn't realized how good her life was.

The white steeple of Belden Baptist Church in a small community on the outskirts of Tupelo rose against a sky angry with a fast-approaching storm. When Wayne made a sharp right into the empty parking lot of the church, the first premonitions shivered through her. And when he stopped the car and flung open his door, a killing wind howled across Ellen's soul. In a parking lot suddenly grown as vast as the Sahara, there would be no one to hear her scream.

5

NIGHTMARES ARE MADE OF sharp knives and vicious voices and places so dark it's impossible to see a soul trying to rise. Ellen lay in the hospital bed with her eyes shut and waited for the darkness to swallow her whole. Complete annihilation would be preferable to a place where she'd be patched back together and sent to live with a man determined to love her to death.

When she heard her husband, so close she could reach out and touch him, she cringed back against the sheets. Had he kicked the baby from her womb?

At the thought, Ellen began to turn herself to ice. Instead of being a woman made of glass who shattered when you touched her, she would become a woman made up of glaciers you'd need a sledgehammer to break apart.

"She's going to be all right, Josie," Wayne was saying over the telephone. "Just a few cuts and bruises from the wreck, that's all."

After the beating he'd deliberately driven his car into a telephone pole before picking up that god-awful bag phone he'd had installed in his car. *I'm bleeding and my wife's hurt,* he'd said. *I lost control.* They thought he meant control of the car.

Ellen squeezed her eyes tight against the remembered nightmare, hoping he wouldn't notice that she was fully alert. But he was too quick for her. He rammed the receiver into its cradle, reached over the bed railing, and grabbed the hand that was not hooked to tubes.

"I see you." He squeezed. Hard. "I'm here. I'll always be here."

She tried to disappear into the darkness behind her eyelids. She tried to vanish into the emptiness of a mind gone numb to everything except pain. But his deadly promise made escape impossible.

She was trapped in a place where everything was colored gray—the walls, the clock, the curtains, her spirit. Even the random thoughts she tried to marshal into order.

"What you don't seem to understand, Ellen, is that I believe in the sacredness of wedding vows."

"To love and to cherish?"

The audacity of such a question coming from her after she'd been choked so hard her voice was no more than a croak shocked both of them into silence. Obviously, the defiant wife frozen as solid as a polar ice cap was tougher than the old Ellen.

Secretly, she celebrated her small victory.

Wayne's faced reddened, and he raised his fist.

"Go ahead. Finish me off. I don't care."

Would he do it? Even with witnesses outside the door?

She waited. But instead of a blow she felt his warm breath on her cheek.

"You're talking out of your head, darling. Let me straighten your pillow."

"Mrs. Blair?" A man in a white lab coat entered the room and headed toward them. When Wayne started patting her hand, Ellen wanted to reach up and claw his eyes out. "I'm Ben Carlson."

She'd never seen this doctor before. He looked far too young to have finished medical school, let alone to understand how a woman could sleep with a man who equated love with violence.

"I want to assure you the baby is okay."

"The baby?" Wayne's face turned a shade darker. Surprise topped with rage. "You're pregnant?"

She closed her eyes, hoping her husband saw a wife too weak to talk instead of a desperate woman praying to become a smooth liar. Would God even listen to such a plea?

"My periods were never regular." When she opened her eyes, she saw Wayne nodding his head. Ellen tried not to let her relief show. It had worked to her advantage that she had a husband who paid attention to every little thing she did. "I didn't know I was pregnant, either."

"I see." Dr. Carlson looked into her pupils and down her throat. Then he turned to Wayne. "Mr. Blair, I'd like a word alone with Mrs. Blair."

"She's my wife."

"She's my patient. You can wait in the hall."

Ellen wondered what it cost Wayne not to storm out when he left.

"Mrs. Blair, your injuries are not consistent with a car accident. Is there anything you'd like to tell me?"

If Haven House couldn't help her, nor the network of police who had planned to deliver her safely there, how could she

48 PEGGY WEBB

expect to be saved by a doctor who looked barely old enough to shave?

"No," she said.

He patted her hand. "I'm here if you change your mind."

ELLEN NEVER SAW HIM again. Her husband had gotten wind of Dr. Carlson's treachery and had him transferred off her case. Too soon she was moved home, to a bedroom with the curtains closed and either her mother or Wayne constantly at her bedside.

Today her watchdog companion was Josie, offering up a smile and milk through a straw.

"Drink this. It'll be good for the baby."

Ellen drank half of it because her mother was right about at least this one thing.

"Mama? Did Daddy ever hit you?"

"Don't be ridiculous. Sim has never laid a hand on me. Or you, either."

That was Ellen's recollection, too. But couldn't a closed door have hidden raised fists as surely as it hid the marriage bed? Though Ellen couldn't remember ever seeing bruises on her mother or seeing Josie wear long sleeves in summer.

"I know. I was raised with a silver spoon."

Bristling, Josie set the milk on the bedside table then stood with her hands propped on her hips while she studied Ellen. What did she see? Matted hair and discolored skin and enough stitches to hold together a patchwork quilt? Was even a small part of her seeing a daughter who deserved better? Or had she worn blinders for so long she could only see a daughter who didn't know how to toe the line, obey the rules?

Finally, her mother sighed. "I swear, Wayne's right. You hardly know what you're saying anymore."

Ellen didn't have enough strength for every battle, so she chose not to fight this one. Anyhow, if Josie hadn't already acknowledged what was happening to her daughter, one more argument wouldn't convince her.

Still, she wasn't about to lie there swaddled in bandages and addled with painkillers and meekly confess that *no,* she really wasn't in her right mind.

Josie chewed on her lower lip while Ellen stared at her, unyielding. Finally, her mother said, "You look a mess," then marched to the dresser.

Picking up a brush, she walked back to the bed, sat on the edge, and started to pull it through her daughter's hair. But Ellen noticed that in deference to injuries that were all too real, Josie used a light touch.

"Ellen, maybe you ought to get a cute feather cut like Mia Farrow."

"I don't want to look like Mia Farrow."

"She looked darling on the cover of *People.* Besides, it would be so much easier to care for when the baby comes."

A few more beatings like this and there would be no baby. But it would do no good to say that to Josie, who chose to remain blind and deaf to Wayne's dark side.

"My poor baby," is all she said. "You've got to get a grip, hon. Pregnancy drives some women around the bend."

"Who?"

"Your grandmother, for one."

"Because she ran away?"

"You tell me. She left a fine husband worrying himself to death and me, a helpless little baby, in the Ozarks with a crazy woman."

Ellen had heard the Hall version of this story many times. According to them, Jim Hall had been a fine upstanding man—mayor of Tupelo and a deacon in the First Baptist Church—hitched to a flighty woman who abandoned her baby in the Ozarks and ran off to cavort with circus riffraff. After Jim went looking for Lola, he vanished and was never seen again. If you asked any one of his Hall relatives, including his daughter, Josie, they'd tell you Lola had killed him, then buried the body and gotten away scot-free with murder.

Aunt Ruth's version was another thing altogether. *Your grandmother was a good woman married to a no 'count man who beat her black and blue,* she'd said when Ellen had gotten old enough to wonder why Lola ran away. *She left Josie with me, knowin' I'd take my twelve-gauge to the first fool who come lookin' for her.*

"Aunt Ruth's not crazy."

"Seeing animals and people who aren't even there? She ought to be locked up. If I hadn't come back here to Daddy's people when I was fourteen, I'd probably be crazy as a loon, too."

"Different is not crazy." Ellen might not know how to stick up for herself, but she'd go to the mat for those she loved. Aunt Ruth. Her baby. "Sometimes I have visions, too."

She didn't know if that was true, but it sounded like a convincing argument.

"You do not!"

"Do you remember that tiger on my swing set when I was a little girl? It wasn't make-believe. It was as real as you are."

"Good lord, if you're not careful, Wayne's going to have you committed."

Sometimes when you think all hope is gone, you'll see a spark tiny as a firefly on a summer night, and the wings you thought were broken will start to unfurl. You'll look around for an updraft that might keep you afloat until your wings have grown strong and you can fly again, until you can soar straight toward freedom.

Ellen saw the idea of commitment as the breeze that would keep her aloft until she was safely tucked inside some institution where she could rest until she was strong enough to convince a doctor that she wasn't crazy but abused.

"Ellen? Did you hear what I said?"

"Yes, Mama."

"You'd better mind your p's and q's."

"I will."

"That's my girl." Josie hugged her lightly, then pranced across the room to put the brush back in place. "I told Wayne I'd raised a daughter with plenty of sense. You just need time to adjust to your pregnancy, that's all."

"You're right. I'm in a period of adjustment."

Josie clapped her hands, a childlike gesture she was fond of. "And getting better every day."

"In every way." Ellen located the smile she'd perfected before she ran away, when she still thought being compliant might save her.

"That's settled then." Josie began to gather her purse, her *Southern Living* magazine with recipes she'd clipped while she watched over her daughter, and her yarn and knitting needles. Already she was knitting bootees for the baby. Blue, because Wayne was determined to have a boy. "Now where did I put my car keys?"

Flustered, Josie hurried out. While her mother searched the house, Ellen realized that if she were committed, they'd take her baby. Besides, Wayne had said, *I'll never let you go.* He might kill her, but he'd never commit her. Then she'd be out of his control.

Quickly, she abandoned the idea of commitment as escape. Ellen's baby couldn't afford for her to make the mistakes of a desperate woman. If her child was to have any chance, she had to keep filling herself up with ice until she could walk across nails and never feel a thing, until she was so cold her tears froze before they could fall.

"Ta da!" Triumphant, Josie posed in the doorway with her keys held high. Then she bustled over and kissed Ellen on the forehead. "You be sweet, now. I have a ton of stuff to do for the barbecue."

"What barbecue?"

"Lord, of course, you've lost track of time. Next Thursday's the Fourth of July. Sim will be barbecuing ribs in the backyard, as usual. Wayne said if you weren't strong enough to walk, he'd bring you in a wheelchair."

"I can walk."

The day she let Wayne push her in a wheelchair would be the day the sky fell.

Ellen lay in the bed under the covers, docile as a rag doll till her mother left the room and she heard the front door slam. When she got out of bed, her rubbery legs almost didn't hold her upright. Gritting her teeth, she held on to every available surface—first the bedpost, then the nightstand, next the dresser—as she made her way to the bathroom.

She switched on the light and teetered over the sink looking at her ghost self in the mirror. Blue eyes looked back at her, deep as two holes punched into a face devoid of a single expression. Not even fear.

Opening the medicine cabinet above the sink, she found bottles of pills meant to take away pain, banish soreness, and encourage sleep. Pills that would keep her in the amenable haze Wayne apparently craved in his wife.

She twisted open the caps and dumped the pills into the toilet. Then in a gait that grew steadier with each step, she went into the living room and sat upright in a plaid wing chair where she watched the clock, counting the minutes till the enemy came through the front door.

HIS KEY TURNED IN the lock, his briefcase bumped against the shelf in the hall closet, his footsteps echoed on the tiles. Ellen waited till she knew Wayne was almost in the living room but still could not see her.

"How was your day, sweetheart?" The endearment tasted like persimmons. She wondered that her mouth didn't pucker.

"Ellen? You're up." Beaming, Wayne hurried across the room and knelt beside her chair. Though her belly was flat as a pancake, he laid an astonishingly gentle hand against it. "How's my little man in there? Hmm. How's he doing?"

Ellen called up snowstorms and icicles and crop-killing frosts. She hoped his fingers froze and fell off.

Still squatting, Wayne smiled up at her. "Can I get you anything, baby? A cup of milk? A snack?"

"Nothing, thank you."

"Can't have my girl wasting away. The doctor said you were underweight."

"I'll eat something later. Right now, there's something I need to ask you." She hoped she'd captured exactly the right tone. *Wife asking permission.*

"Anything my little mother needs. You just name it."

"Who's coming tomorrow?"

"My mother."

"If Wanda feels up to it, I wonder if she could drive me to the library?"

"You need to stay in the house where we can take care of you." It didn't take much effort to make her lips tremble. "Now, baby, you've got everything you need right here. If you want something, just ask and Daddy'll get it for you."

The finishing touch was lowered head and tears. *Pregnant wife defeated.*

"Aw, come on, baby. Why the library? Why not the park? Come to think of it, a little fresh air and sunshine might put some color in your cheeks. Maybe an outing to the park would do you good."

Head up. Tremulous little smile of gratitude. She should get an Academy Award.

"That's a wonderful idea," she said. Wayne could now take credit for an outing designed to help his wife get her color back. "Maybe your mother could drive me there afterward. But first I want to do a little research on child care. Maybe check out a few books you and I can look at together."

When the crease between Wayne's eyes turned smooth once more, Ellen knew she'd won. She let herself be led into the kitchen and deposited in a chair while a husband who thought his wife was coming around heated the soup Josie had made, and served her first.

THAT NIGHT WHILE WAYNE slept, Ellen lay on the other side of the bed, plotting. This time, her plans would be as carefully mapped out as the invasion of a small country.

Tomorrow she'd cover her tracks with child-care books. But it wasn't Dr. Spock that drew her toward the Lee County Library. It was the stacks of newspapers from places all across America—Bowling Green and Nashville and Huntsville—newspapers with entertainment sections that followed the excitement as the circus moved from one small town to the next.

Apparently her unborn child would give her a reprieve from Wayne's beatings. She'd seize that time to gain her strength and fine-tune her plans.

"Coming Soon!" the newspaper ads would say. "Hoxie Brothers; Ringling Brothers and Barnum & Bailey; the Great Giovanni Bros./Hogan & Sandusky."

Ellen had the kind of mind that could recall the meanings of words nobody else had ever heard of. She could keep an entire grocery list in her head and come home from the Piggly Wiggly with every item. She could quote the names of all the great players on the Yankees baseball team, tell you their batting averages and the dates of their home runs. It would be no leap for her to keep the schedules of several traveling circuses in her head.

There would be no paper trail for Wayne to find, no one to call and warn him of her plans.

When the time was right, she'd run to the only place she knew where a woman could vanish so completely there was nothing left of her except a yellowed newspaper clipping, a gold tiger brooch, and enough conflicting stories to keep three generations guessing.

BETSY ROLLED TOWARD RAZZ like a gathering gray storm cloud, with Indian Joe striding alongside, making sure his baby was at the front of the line for the Fourth of July circus parade. In her pink spangled blanket and headpiece, the huge elephant dazzled. Watching her, the crowd would remember the dreams of their childhood, and remembering, would follow the pink spangled circus star into the big top in hopes of recapturing magic.

But the elephant brought different memories to Razz . . .

"Please don't send me away, Razz."

It has been three days since I found Lola Hall in the wisteria, three days of lying to the cook about why I'm eating so many snacks of peanut butter sandwiches and milk, and making excuses to everybody who comes to my train car about why they can't come in.

"The cats are fierce today," I say. "They might claw you." "I've got a virus you don't want to catch." "It's a mess in here. Let's visit outside."

And now here she is, fragile as a long-stemmed rose, prettier than any of the girls in the lineup for the Grand Spectacular, the bruises on her throat gone and the ones on her arms covered with one of my long-sleeved shirts, begging me for something I know I'm going to give.

"You'll have to earn your keep."

"I'll do anything. As long as I'm hidden from view of the public."

"Can you cook?"

"Fair to middling."

"That's better than what we have. I'll see what I can do."

I don't let on that I'm the son of one of the owners, that I can do pretty much whatever I want as long as it's not selfish and is good for the circus. She's told me nothing of herself except her name, and I've told her not much more. My first name and that I am the cat trainer. I trust her because the tigers do, and they never lie. But I'm not a man to go about spilling my business.

I've asked myself a thousand times why I let her stay, but the only answer I can come up with is that Lola Hall looks like she belongs. She seems as much a part of the circus as the doves Magic Melinda uses in her bird act for the matinee and later releases in her fortune-telling tent when she wants her customers to see the spirits of the dearly departed.

Besides, what would it hurt to get Lola a job in the cook tent? An improvement in food is always a morale booster for a traveling circus with too many problems and never enough money.

Lola's first day in the cook tent, she's bundled up in a head scarf I'd borrowed from Magic Melinda, my long-sleeved white shirt, and a pair of my pants, rolled at the hem and gathered around her slender waist with a length of rope. It's impossible to tell she's pretty and hard to tell she's even a girl.

Whether or not she can cook is another story. I pay particular attention for a week, but I don't see any noticeable improvement in the food.

Word gets around, as it always does in a close-knit circus family, *that she's living with me. I don't bother to explain that she's in my bed and I'm on the couch. I know the story elevates Lola's status.*

As a matter of fact, I'm the one that put out the word. "The little blonde is mine." That's all I had to say. On the Q.T. from Lola, of course. I don't know what she'd do if she ever found out.

But if this motley crew of men thought Lola was on the loose, they'd have her in the cooch tent before I could even find my whip.

Her second week on the job, I'm late to lunch because Sheikh had a bellyache and made a general mess of the trailer. By the time I got it soaped down and mopped out, and the two disgruntled tigers settled down, I was in no mood for the fracas that greeted me in the cook tent.

"This soup is horrible," Magic Melinda yells at me. "Razz, get your skinny arse back there and tell Cookie I won't put up with slop for lunch."

"Yeah!" Burning Beulah, the fire-eater, takes up the hue and cry. "What's the matter, Cookie? Can't you tell garbage from food?"

"You trying to poison us?" Burning Beulah's husband, Tim the Tattooed Man, spits out a mouthful, then stands up and pours the offending soup on the ground. "I ain't eating pig swill."

Cookie emerges from the back wielding a butcher knife, his Irish temper in full force.

"I'll carve up the lot of ye."

I step between Cookie and the sideshow performers, figuring I might as well get a few cuts to go with the claw marks.

"Get out of my way, Razz." He waves the knife under my nose. "I swear, I'll cut ye."

"If Rufus can't scare me, you think you can, Cookie?" He has the good sense to look chagrined. "Get back to the kitchen. I'll handle this."

I scan the cook tent for Lola, but she's missing. I nearly go crazy. Burning Beulah doesn't simply eat fire—when she's mad, she also spits it. If she's already turned her temper on Lola, somebody's going to pay.

Forcing Lola from my mind, I pour myself a bowl of soup, take a sip, and have a hard time forcing it down. Cookie is no five-star chef, but he generally serves edible food.

"Forget the soup." I grab a loaf of bread and peanut butter off the shelves, and plenty of knives for spreading, then fling it all onto the wooden tables. "Have something that will stick to your ribs."

The sideshow crew is a pretty swell bunch of people and I don't pull rank very often. But the idea of what this kind of riot in the cook tent could do to Lola has me puffing out my chest and lording it over them. A reminder that I'm the son of one of their bosses.

"If I hear so much as a peep out of the lot of you, I'll be back and you'll be sorry."

Melinda laughs. "What'll you do, Razz, growl? You're just a big pussycat."

The rest of them have a laugh at my expense, but as long as they're back in good humor, I don't care.

With the sideshow bunch satisfied and Cookie back at the stove grumbling, I hurry out of the cook tent to find Lola. She's in my train compartment, dressed in the blouse and skirt I'd bought for her, tying her hairbrush and toothbrush, her gown and underwear—also my purchases—into Magic Melinda's scarf. Rajah cavorts around her, tugging at her skirt.

"I'll send Magic Melinda the money for the scarf," Lola says.

"What's going on here?"

"I put soap in the soup." The way she ducks her head and looks at me as if she expects a blow makes me want to smash my fist into the wall. "It was an accident."

"Of course it was. Everything's okay now."

"No, you have to tell Cookie . . . I dumped the soup into a sieve and washed it till it stopped making bubbles. I guess I didn't get it all out."

By the time she finishes with her story, I'm laughing so hard my sides hurt. Finally, Lola starts laughing, too. That's when I see her for what she is, the North Star that guides me home. And yet, I don't reach for her, don't tell of my heart's longing. She's a wounded canary, far too fragile to add the weight of love to her fear and sorrow.

"They can always use another hand in the costume tent. Can you sew?"

"No better than I can cook."

"What can you do?"

"Plan a tea party, play two songs on the piano so the mayor can call me accomplished, smile and keep my mouth shut while the mayor introduces me as his 'pretty little wifey.'" *Lola sinks to the floor and Rajah pounces, hoping for a wrestling match. "Not today, Rajah."*

She pulls the cub into her lap and gentles him with her hands while she tells me the story of a wife the townspeople called pampered and the powerful man who usually hit her only where the bruises didn't show, of the baby girl she'd birthed then left in Arkansas with a fierce sister named Ruth.

"I have no talent for anything, but I will never again put myself in the position of being any man's pretty little plaything. I have to be strong and independent, so that when I go back for my daughter, nobody will dare mess with me."

Seeing Lola's ferocity for the first time, I believe anything is possible, that a man who remains upright in spite of desire melting his bones can rise above his own limitations and become the hero this woman needs. "We'll think of something."

Razz's memories dissolved as Indian Joe hustled Betsy to

the front of the parade line. Why that particular memory, he couldn't tell you, except that the circus cook had served cabbage soup for lunch.

Unfortunately the soup didn't contain much cabbage. Lately somebody had been stealing the cabbages, and Razz was pretty certain it wasn't the bear, who favored costume jewelry and loose change.

Judging by all the signs, this was going to be a circus season plagued by theft and red ink. Not to mention folks blowing the show. Razz didn't know how they'd replace the trapeze artist and the circus teacher who had left in the middle of the season, but he was hoping the parade would help stem the flow of red.

It would be the first parade for the Great Giovanni Bros./ Hogan & Sandusky Circus since the African bull got loose in Tallahassee five years ago and uprooted twelve palm trees before they could capture him.

Razz had wanted to continue the tradition anyway, but Al and the sensible Eric Sandusky, God rest his soul, had argued that they still had the Grand Spec so why take the risk? Somebody could get hurt and sue. Razz had argued that watching the circus performers and animals parade in a sedate circle under canvas in the Grand Spectacular—except when Edna, the perpetually disgruntled llama, occasionally broke ranks to spit in somebody's eye—didn't hold the same excitement as marching the entire show along the streets where little kids raced along beside the clowns and an occasional husband on the run from his wife or the law threw down his hoe and signed up to travel with them as a canvas man.

But he'd lost, two to one.

Now he and Al were bringing the parade back. Neither of them mentioned desperation as the cause.

"It's in the true spirit of the circus," Al had said when they'd discussed the parade last week in Nashville.

"And America," Razz had told him. "What's more American than a circus parade on the Fourth of July?"

As far as Razz knew, the little mountain town of Lebanon, Tennessee, where the circus caravan was parked, didn't have a single palm tree. Besides, the African bull would not be allowed to march in the street parade.

Resplendent in shiny black boots, a tall black hat, and a blue jacket with gold braided trim, Al walked over to join Razz. Suddenly Al's top hat went sailing into the air.

Towering above the two old showmen like a gray storm cloud, Betsy curled her trunk backward and deposited the top hat on her own massive head. Then she drew back her mouth in a gleeful elephant grin.

"Now, you stop that, Betsy." Pretending an outrage he didn't feel toward his favorite bull, Indian Joe tapped Betsy's trunk with a silver-tipped cane. "Give the boss back his hat."

Betsy turned a startlingly intelligent-looking eye in Razz's direction. Then she snatched off his baseball cap.

After giving him a mischievous wink that displayed impossibly long eyelashes, the elephant put the baseball cap on Al and the top hat on Razz.

Laughing, they exchanged hats, then held on to their respective headgear as they walked the length of the sequined and tasseled line to inspect the circus performers and animals.

Vintage circus wagons that held the most reliable cats were being hauled into line by the workhorses. Sturdy Percherons, they were so used to being near their mortal enemies that they no longer required blinders to haul the big-cat wagons.

In the lead car, Sheikh IV turned his majestic head and gave Razz a golden-eyed stare. If you didn't know better, you'd think the tiger in the sunshine was harmless.

"Al, I've been thinking of trying to get Sheikh on Betsy."

Razz's biggest disappointment was that he had not yet matched the dazzling performance of the handsome young German circus star over at Ringling. Gunther Gebel-Williams rode a tiger on an elephant. In a stunning departure from the Clyde Beatty era of trainers who subdued their cats with cracking whips and pistols loaded with blanks, Gebel-Williams' performance showed the amazing feats you could do if you treated wild animals with respect.

"Why would you want to copy Ringling? You're the best big-cat act in circus history. Forget it, Razz." Al straightened the top hat he'd put on crooked. "Let's go see the horses."

Al would never say *You'll break your old fool neck trying such a stunt.* Razz trotted along beside him, grateful for the small mercies of friendship.

Besides, for all Betsy's easygoing nature and love of frolic, she would not be inclined to make friends with a tiger. Razz was secretly relieved that he didn't have to try.

Up ahead, the Giovanni equestrians were lining up the Andalusians, four abreast.

Razz glanced down at the lot. This one was flat, which had made it easy to set up the big top and the three rings.

But early this morning the lot had also been scattered with stones, not unexpected in a town tucked into what the townsfolk called hills and Razz described as mountains. Under Luca's critical eye, the ground had been raked and smoothed until not a single stone remained in the ring to cause problems for his stallions. A stone in a lot in Georgia last year had caused Luca's wife Daniela's horse to stumble, a stone no bigger than a fist that sent her tumbling to her death. A circus tragedy Razz hoped he never had to see again.

Now, all Al's grandsons, in the traditional Giovanni blue and gold, were getting ready to mount. All of them except one.

"Where's Luca?" Al asked.

Luca's older brother, Antonio, squat, sturdy, and reliable as Al himself, nodded beyond the Andalusians toward the clowns.

"Back there."

Al nodded, then told Razz, "I'll be right back. I want Nicky to ride."

Razz was already atop one of the white stallions when Al returned with Luca's son dressed in the blue and gold Giovanni colors. He swung Nicky onto the horse, then mounted behind him.

"Ready?" Razz asked and Al nodded.

They let Nicky give the signal, the band struck up a march, and the Great Giovanni Bros./Hogan & Sandusky Circus began their Fourth of July parade. Amid balloons and streamers and cheers, circus magic unfolded on the streets of Lebanon, Tennessee.

Halfway through the parade, a baggy-pants, big-shoed, sad-faced man reeled from the ranks of clowns and lurched toward the Andalusians. Luca, in the grand hobo tradition of the famous Emmett Kelly. Women and children screamed as he tried to lunge onto a stallion, only to hang at such a precarious angle it appeared his head would be crushed under the flying hooves.

In one drunkenlike pratfall after another, Luca bounced

foolishly from horse to horse while Nicky's smile grew wider and wider. Only Razz and the great Giovanni equestrians saw the expertise it took for Luca to safely navigate the thundering line of Andalusians in the parade while repeatedly losing his seat, his footing, and his floppy hat with the big yellow sunflower.

As usual, the parade drew a straw house. With the big top bleachers filled beyond capacity, canvas men laid down straw for the overflow crowd.

Long after the evening show where Razz rode Sheikh—though not atop an elephant—after the last rigging was empty, the last kernels of popcorn were swept from the big top, and the blue flicker of television lights shone through the windows of performers' Airstreams in the circus yard, Razz sat in a lawn chair outside the marquee sharing a glass of Scotch with Al.

"Another straw house tomorrow night will put us closer to the black, Razz."

"From your mouth to God's ears." Razz clicked his glass against Al's.

With talk drifting around him like smoke and Nicky and the other circus children playing in the pool of light from the cotton candy stand nearby, Razz counted his blessings instead of his losses.

Someday even the Giovanni/Hogan canvas would fold. The red and gold magic would fade into a pale imitation of its former glory. The circus would be boxed up and commercialized and sterilized and sold as a small show you could view from the comfort of your living room.

But for now, Razz gave thanks for circus parades, straw houses, and good Scotch as he and Al sipped their amber liquid and gazed at the stars.

7

UNDER A CANOPY OF stars as big as baseballs, Ruth surveyed the crowd. Everybody within a ten-mile radius had come up her mountain with their picnic baskets of pickled peaches and black-eyed peas and fried apple pies and jugs of sweet tea to celebrate the Fourth of July at Ruth's annual hog roast.

Though she wasn't the sociable sort and was rarely seen in town except when Jesus and the pilgrims dictated her attendance at services—she'd sooner tie herself to the railroad tracks and wait for the four o'clock train than stop the tradition started by her beloved granddaddy Gibson. Every year he'd slaughtered three hogs on the Fourth and put on the biggest barbecue in the Ozarks.

As long as she was breathing, Ruth aimed to keep it up. And if you had even half sense and one eye, you'd best not try to stop her.

Standing near the pits, Ruth inhaled the scent of sizzling fat from three spit-roasted hogs. Feeling a mite hot, she turned her face toward the copse of evergreens bordering her yard, their branches swaying as if the mountain played music only trees could hear.

She reckoned the Ozarks offered up the night breezes as an apology for the boulders. They hid rattlesnakes that would kill you if you didn't have sense enough to take a gun when you went walking on the mountain. And if you wanted to have a garden you could tend without breaking your hoe, you'd best be hooking up a mule strong enough to drag the stubborn rocks out of the earth.

Still, the harsh old mountain produced folks as sturdy as ninety-year-old Letty Hennesey, Ruth's quilting buddy, who sat on the front porch drinking iced tea from a Mason jar. Ruth thought about joining Letty just to cool off. The young children chased fireflies in the front yard while the older ones played a game of horseshoes. It would be nice to sit a spell and watch the young folks having fun, but the Coca-Colas were rapidly vanishing from the zinc tubs and she had to find Ray Boy and tell him to ice down some more.

She was scanning the crowd for him when the smoke over the roasting pits grew so thick Ruth couldn't see the stars. As smoke spiraled around her, deceitful and black as snakes, the barbecue sauce spilling over the sides of split hogs turned to blood.

The power of her bloody vision hit Ruth so hard she almost passed out. Fighting to stay upright, she backed away from the terrible truth she saw in the roasting pits.

Hands grabbed at her. Voices echoed through a mind spinning into cotton wool.

"Miss Ruth? Miss Ruth? Are you all right?"

Weightless as a bird, she drifted among them, everything tethering her cut away. Drawn upward by a vast darkness that had dropped over the full moon, Ruth was nothing more than brittle bones held together by a wisp of stocking and a dress bleeding red polka dots. Filled with a sorrow so deep you could fall in and never find your way back out, Ruth waited for the visions to claim her. Soon she wouldn't be part of the mountain at all. She'd be a ghost of herself adrift in a bloodred sea.

She had to reassure her friends and neighbors while she still could.

"I'm fine," she managed to say. "Just need some air."

The darkness boiled so hard through her she could no longer tell whether her feet were on the ground or in the air. She couldn't tell whether she was in this world or in the next.

Her vision was filled with blood. On the walls, in the baby crib, puddled beneath long blond hair. The vision shimmered, then turned as clear as a reflection in a mirror. And through it all, Ruth saw *him,* his face twisted with triumph and remorse.

She stumbled and almost fell. Up ahead, she could barely make out Ray Boy, his thinning gray hair slicked back, his overalls pressed, and his face a question mark of concern.

She reached blindly through the fog.

"Miss Ruth!"

As she toppled, she felt herself borne up by Ray Boy's work-toughened arms and callused hands.

"Is she dead?"

Yes. Soon she would be dead, and no one would bear witness to the crime.

"WHERE ARE THE ONIONS? By God, Josie, this potato salad has no onions!"

Trying to shut out the sound of her daddy's voice, Ellen

bent her head over her plate of wet barbecue, southern style, and silently recounted the circus schedule she'd discovered at the library: Hagenbeck/Wallace, Fourth of July, Salem, North Carolina; Ringling, Fourth of July, New Orleans, coliseum; Giovanni, July Fourth and fifth, Lebanon, Tennessee.

"Don't get in an uproar, Sim," Josie said. "It's not good for your blood pressure. I left the onions out because I didn't want to give your pregnant daughter heartburn."

"Ellen's strong as a horse. My God, woman, what do I have to do to get potato salad in my own house the way I like it? Beg?"

Ellen, strong as a horse, concentrated on her iced tea while she ran through the list of Yankees players inducted into Baseball's Hall of Fame, starting with the most recent, Whitey Ford and Mickey Mantle in 1974, Yogi Berra and Lefty Gomez in 1972, and ending in 1937 and 1936 with Lou Gehrig and Babe Ruth.

"Just hold your horses, Sim. I'll whip you up a batch in a jiffy." With a careful smile on her face, Josie folded her Fourth of July paper napkin featuring stars and stripes next to her Chinet plate on the picnic table where candles melted down in fat brown beer bottles. "Excuse me, folks. I'll be right back."

She pranced back to the house, acting sassy as a fire-cracker, while her husband patted a dribble of barbecue sauce off his lips.

"Now that's the way a man gets things done." Sim winked at his son-in-law.

Wayne laughed while Ellen thought of *s* words she hated: *smirk, supercilious, sudoriferous.*

"Ellen?"

Subservient. Her eyes flashed as she glanced at her husband. *Smug.*

"Why don't you help Josie in the kitchen?"

"Of course."

"And while you're in there, turn on the outdoor lights," Sim said. "Josie and her damned candles. I can't see a thing on my plate."

Ellen was only too glad to go to a place where she didn't have to breathe the same air.

When she got inside, water was boiling in the pot and Josie was already chopping onions. Ellen picked up a knife and began peeling potatoes.

She saw it all so clearly now. Her father didn't have to lay a hand on Josie. He wielded a sword of words.

"Mama, why do you let him talk to you like that? He treats you like a bug under his shoe."

"I'm sure I don't know what you're talking about."

"It's not right."

"It's a new gold shag carpet on the living room floor and an extra two hundred dollars on my after-the-Fourth shopping spree. And what do I have to do for it? Nothing, if you ask me. What's a little onion?"

Josie's knife made sharp tapping sounds against the avocado-colored Formica countertop as bits of onion flew out from her blade.

How many times had her daddy bought her mother's acquiescence for two hundred dollars? Or had the price gone up over the years? In the beginning, had she settled for twenty-five?

"I swear, Ellen. You could learn a thing or two about getting along with a man." Josie dumped pieces of sweet Vidalia onion—the only kind Sim would allow her to buy—into a yellow Fiestaware bowl. Next, she turned on the radio, then attacked two fat red tomatoes. "Take a lesson from my book. That's what I say."

Ellen already knew that lesson. How you close your ears to words hurled like stones. How you look at the rubble collecting beneath your feet and fool yourself into seeing summer grasses and woods violets and moss so soft you could fall down face-first and not get hurt. How you give yourself over to pretense, and smile without mirth, all the while shutting off the outraged bellowing of a trampled spirit trying to rise.

It's the art of silence, and Ellen had learned it all too well.

But she didn't share her insight with her mother, who was listening to Stevie Wonder on the radio singing "Tell Me Something Good." It might as well have been Josie's theme song. She never wanted to hear the truth, only some sugar-coated version that wouldn't change one iota of her life.

Suffocating, Ellen flung open the window over the sink and studied the backyard where night-blooming flowers, white as buttermilk, opened their faces to a full moon. A net of stars over the darkening sky glowed like Fourth of July sparklers. The straggling roses, heat-distressed and naked of leaves from black spot blight, put on one last effort of red blossoms while crickets sent their harp-leg songs into the evening.

It was the kind of night where everything was silvery and revealed—mockingbirds quenching their thirst in the birdbath, wind chimes hanging silent in the still air, and a hurt so big there was no place to escape the pain.

In her mind, Ellen was already gone from this place. If Wayne got down on his knees and begged, if he swore on a stack of Bibles, even if he signed in blood that he would never touch her again, Ellen would not stay.

Words spoken in rage can never be taken back. Fists delivered in hatred can never be forgotten. And once the fabric holding two people together is torn, every move they make leaves behind a tattered edge of sorrow.

Ellen covered her sorrow with potatoes, placing them in the pot with a spoon so she wouldn't splash herself with boiling water. Then she started mixing mayonnaise, mustard, and sweet pickle relish. Just the way her daddy liked it.

"Ellen? Penny for your thoughts?"

When she glanced at Josie, Ellen saw a woman she dared not become. She saw a woman who would forever play her assigned role in a marriage turned to farce. She saw a mother she would leave behind.

She put her arms around Josie and hugged her. Her mother, slightly uncomfortable in the embrace, soon pushed herself back and patted at her hair.

"My goodness, Ellen. What was that for?"

"I was just thinking that I might dream of this night for a very long time."

"That's sweet. I will, too, hon."

By the time Josie and Ellen got back to the picnic, Sim had long ago finished his barbecue and was ready for dessert. Nobody remarked when he had potato salad with his apple pie.

And certainly nothing was said of the incident on the drive back to Madison Street in the black Cadillac DeVille with the newly repaired right-front bumper.

Though the front porch light was on, Wayne took Ellen's arm to help her up the sidewalk. Two years ago she'd have been ecstatic that the man she'd dragged to the Ozarks and introduced to her aunt Ruth as "the man of my dreams" treated their marriage like a package marked "Handle with Care."

But a box can contain all sorts of things that should be marked "Handle with Care"—rattlesnakes, hand grenades, and distrust so fierce it will scorch you if you linger too long.

For Ellen, the question was *how long*? How long did she have to plan before she took action? How long before Wayne's self-satisfaction at fathering a child turned to anger because that same child robbed him of the lithe body he saw as his personal playground?

They were barely inside the door before he ripped off his shirt and reached for her blouse. Besides her, his weakness was barbecue. Her only hope was that the huge amount of pork fat he'd consumed would make him sluggish and quickly satisfied.

Where she had once seized such moments with the joyful abandon of a woman walking on stars, Ellen filled her veins with ice water and her heart with stones as she marched a hopeless trail to the sheets she'd hung on the line because Wayne liked his linens to smell like sunshine. With her hair spread across the pillow and her eyes trained at a reflection of the streetlight on the ceiling, she imagined a pickax trying to chip a glacier. She called up icy blue waters and frozen tundra and an indestructible force of nature that went so deep under the ocean only its dangerous jagged edges were visible. And then only to an eye that could see the truth.

Wayne was blind to the truth, deaf to anything except the endless tooting of his egomaniacal horn.

When the phone rang and he rolled off to answer, she had to cover her mouth to hide her sigh of relief. Wayne would no more let a phone go unanswered than he would drink tea without lemon, wear a shirt that wasn't starched, refuse to beat a wife who deserved it.

"This is he . . . Yes . . . How bad is it?"

Something in his tone jerked Ellen upright, huddled her on the bed with the sheet wrapped around her. She was so cold she couldn't even feel the tips of her toes, the ends of her fingers, her baby's heartbeat.

"What is it?" she asked.

Wayne covered the receiver with his hand. "It's Ruth. She's in the hospital. Ray Boy Turner says she's dying."

She covered her mouth with her hand, but even the fear of her husband's quick retribution couldn't still her distress. Sound burst from her like water from a crumbling dam. Her wails peeled the paint off the walls. She screamed so hard the sound ricocheted off the ceiling and rained all around her astonished husband.

Still screeching, she leaped off the bed, dragging the sheet behind her as she ran toward the closet and started throwing clothes into her suitcase.

"Ellen." Wayne slammed down the phone and grabbed her. "Stop that."

Oh, God . . . She knew what he would do, feared the threat of his unchecked rage as if it were a grizzly bear in the room. She rammed a fist into her mouth, trying to stop her wails of loss.

"Good God, Ellen. What will the neighbors think?"

Astonished and shaking with relief, she swiped her hand across her face, smearing mucus and tears. There could be only two explanations for Wayne's newfound restraint: her pregnancy and their interrupted intimacy had temporarily softened him up.

"If Aunt Ruth dies and I'm sitting here like some silly prom queen, they'll think we're white trash."

Wayne's faced reddened. "Baby, listen to me. We can't strike out to Arkansas in the middle of the night."

"I've got to go, Wayne. Let me go."

"We'll call the hospital. Talk to the doctor." He caught her upper arms. "She's tough, Ellen. I'm sure it's not all that bad."

"I'm going to see her, no matter what anybody says." She slapped his hands away and started hurling shoes into the suitcase on top of her slacks and blouses.

Wayne watched awhile, then walked into the kitchen, pulled down a pan, opened the refrigerator door, and slammed the pot onto the stove, probably heating milk. When the sounds filtered through to Ellen, identifiable as the most domestic of all chores, a husband taking care of his pregnant, hysterical wife, Ellen had to muffle her mouth with a sweater to keep from giving way to laughter.

When she got herself under control, she found her purse—the one that held her cosmetic case with her freedom fund sewn into the lining—and set it beside her suitcase. Next, she lined up her good driving shoes on the floor. Then she added pajamas, toothbrush, toiletries.

"Baby?" Standing in the doorway holding on to a glass of milk, Wayne looked like any other husband befuddled by bad news and an unreasonable woman. For such a big man, he hardly made a sound as he walked across the floor naked as a plucked ostrich. "Here. Drink this. Maybe it will help."

She drank half the warm milk in one slug.

"You might as well unpack, Ellen. We're not going to the Ozarks."

"I can wait till morning. Morning's okay, Wayne."

"Masa will be here tomorrow night."

"Masa?"

"For Christ's sake, Ellen. My client. Masa Shimayoka. From *Japan*."

"I'll go by myself."

"You're not strong enough to drive. Mother's certainly not capable of driving that far. And I can just hear what Josie would say if you asked her to take you all the way to Arkansas to see Ruth Gibson."

It didn't take any effort at all for Ellen to open her mouth and start screaming again. It didn't take the least bit of acting for her to squall until her face crumpled like an American Beauty rose tromped on by careless heels.

"Christ, Ellen! Will you just stop it?"

Her increased decibels measured on the Richter scale.

"Jesus!" Wayne patted her arm, ran his hands through his hair, paced to the bed and back, patted her shoulder, and trotted once again to the bed. Finally, he sank onto the mattress, a battleship torpedoed.

"You can leave in the morning then. But you have to call me every day at three o'clock. Have you got that, Ellen? That call from you doesn't come in at three o'clock and I come looking for you, I don't care who's dying and who's here from Japan."

"I'll call. I promise."

Ellen knelt beside him and put her head in his lap. A really good woman might have been truly grateful. The only gratitude she felt toward Wayne was for teaching her the power of hysteria and sex.

WHEN ELLEN BARRELED OUT of her Bel Air trailing suitcases and tears, Ruth would have felt guilty except for her Fourth of July vision: Wayne Blair was going to kill his wife and baby. Sooner rather than later. Ruth Gibson had already lied to stop it, and if she had to she would cheat and steal.

"Git out there and help her, Ray Boy. I don't want the shock of seein' me alive to finish her off."

She watched from behind the curtain while Ray Boy took Ellen's suitcase, then bent down and spilled the beans, a tall, earnest man trying to put the best spin on his employer's deceit.

Ellen listened with her head cocked and her tears drying up. Then her face split into a grin and she ran up the steps calling Ruth's name.

It could have gone either way. Ellen could have been upset she'd come all this way for nothing.

Ruth trotted out to meet her niece on the front porch. The sight of Ellen up close—nothing but bones and bruises and stitches—made her so mad she could have walked all the way to Mississippi just for the pleasure of hearing the pop when she slapped some sense into Wayne Blair.

Still, this wasn't about her. As she drew Ellen into a hug, she got ahold of her anger. She even managed to wink at Ray Boy over her grandniece's shoulder.

He winked back as he set off toward the garden. The roasting ears were in. By nightfall he'd have two tubs full cooling on the back porch, waiting for shucking.

When Ellen held her at arm's length and inspected her from head to toe, she felt like a dried-up old fossil. Women her age didn't bear close scrutiny.

"When Ray Boy called, I was scared to death, Aunt Ruth."

"I'm sorry. I didn't know of no other way to get you here."

"Are you sure you're okay? Ray Boy said you did have a sinking spell. You look a little pale."

"I ain't pale. I'm old."

It wasn't her own appearance that concerned her. Ellen had lost at least ten pounds since Ruth last saw her, and the yellowing bruises and scars told their own story. Not only was Ruth's vision true, but Wayne had already started the process. He was bent on doing the job, whether he killed his wife piece by piece or in one fell swoop.

She'd seen him as he was the first time Ellen brought him to her mountain. There was a shadow stitched to that man's soul that wouldn't detach itself, no matter how much love a good woman like Ellen heaped on him. It was the kind of darkness a man could keep hidden for only so long before it started seeping through the cracks, escaping through the seams. And finally, when not even the constraints of society could hold it back, it would overflow and annihilate everything in its path.

Telling herself that everybody has a dark side, that she had not seen whether Wayne would control his or turn it loose, she'd dismissed her worries as needless. That she hadn't warned Ellen was one of her many regrets.

"Set. I kept lunch warm for you."

When Ellen sank into a straight-backed kitchen chair, Ruth checked to make sure her ankles weren't swollen. A long drive like that and her pregnant and hurting, to boot. For two cents, she'd fill Wayne Blair's britches full of buckshot.

Ruth reckoned the good Lord knew what he was doing when he'd left her on that mountain and put Josie and Ellen too far away for her interference. Even without her visions, Ruth wasn't one to tolerate nonsense, and she sure didn't cotton to meanness.

For years she'd stuck her head in the sand and let matters take care of themselves. But that was over and done with. If anybody dared raise a hand against hers again, she'd shoot him. And she didn't care who bore witness.

She watched while Ellen dug into her peas and corn bread, her fried chicken and potatoes, her heap of coleslaw, all made with vegetables fresh from Ruth's garden. When she'd eaten everything on her plate and a second helping of peas and corn bread, besides, Ellen scraped her plate over the garbage pail, then started toward the sink.

"You need to rest," Ruth told her. "I'll wash up."

"I am a little tired. It was a long journey."

"We ain't even started yet."

"What do you mean?"

"Wayne aims to kill you. And the baby in the bargain. I seen it clear." Ellen paled. "You got to git outta there."

"I know. I know I have to leave. But I haven't figured it all out yet."

"You ain't got time for figurin'. We gotta run. Now."

"We?"

"I'm goin' with you, and there ain't no use arguin'. I done packed."

"Do you think Wayne's just going to let me go? He'll come after me, Aunt Ruth. I can't put you through that."

"What you think's gonna happen if he finds me settin' on this mountain and you done struck out to Mexico?"

She saw the picture flash through Ellen's mind—Wayne beating the truth out of an old woman, his rage destroying his judgment until it was too late, until there was nothing left of Ruth Gibson but crumpled bones and a bonnet filled with blood.

"Besides, what have I got to set on this mountain for? Ray Boy will tend to everything till I die, then it'll belong to you and the baby. But you got to promise to let him stay in the caretaker's cabin as long as he lives."

"I promise, Aunt Ruth."

"Good. I don't know what I'd a done all these years without Ray Boy."

Leaving Ellen with a fresh glass of iced tea, Ruth marched to her dining room and took an atlas out of the bottom drawer of the china cabinet. Ever since she'd had Ray Boy call Ellen and tell a pack of lies, she'd been marking routes. Though she'd happily go in any direction Ellen wanted, including Canada, she was hoping for someplace warmer. She imagined living the rest of her days in a sunny spot where she could have some relief from her arthritis.

When she plopped the atlas onto the table in front of Ellen, it fell open to Georgia. A woman who saw signs in the evening flight of blackbirds, the glitter of Japanese beetles beneath the stars, and the shadow of tigers under a moon knew how to read this event.

Ellen would be heading south. When and how, Ruth didn't know. All she knew was that she'd be along to keep her niece safe.

Ellen bent over the map, tracing Georgia back roads. With her finger on Fort Benning, she said, "This is where we're headed, Aunt Ruth."

Ruth didn't like to question her niece, who was smarter and better educated, but she couldn't sit still and let them end up in a place so close to home that catching them would be like picking off sitting ducks.

"I'd a thought we'd go farther than that."

"We will, eventually. But this is where I think we can catch up to the circus."

"The circus?"

"I thought I might be able to disappear there." Ellen massaged her temples as if the effort of thinking was about to explode her head.

Ruth wet a dishcloth and held it to her niece's hot face. "Breathe deep."

"I'm scared, Aunt Ruth. I tried a shelter and look what he did to me. The circus sounded like an answer to my prayers when I saw their tour schedule, but now I just don't know."

One of Ruth's greatest sorrows was that she hadn't run away to the circus with her sister. If she had, Lola might still be alive. But Lola had insisted she could travel faster without

Ruth and Josie, she could escape detection easier. Lola had begged her sister to keep the baby safe on the mountain.

And now, here Ruth was, an old visionary so tough and ornery nobody could stand to be around her except Ray Boy and Ellen. She'd never expected to get a second chance.

Still, she was not the consideration here. And she couldn't afford to mix her own desires into Ellen's trouble. She shut her eyes, trying to call a vision that would give her an answer.

"Aunt Ruth? Are you all right?"

"I was just rememberin' your grandmother." Ruth took off her glasses and wiped her face. She had to buck up. Now was not the time for her to start acting like a sentimental old fool. Or to be waiting around for a vision, either. They didn't come like a dog when you whistled. "If we go someplace Wayne might not expect, say Pittsburgh, we still couldn't get jobs without spreadin' around a bunch of private information."

"That's what I was thinking. And we'd be in one place, which would make it easier for any decent detective agency to track us."

"We'd be sittin' ducks, two women alone in a strange city without a soul to care if some man come along and killed us. Wait right here."

Ruth went into her parlor and rifled through a packet of letters till she found what she was looking for, then returned to the kitchen.

"Look at this." She handed the letter from Lola to Ellen, then traced the line with her finger and read aloud. "'Circus people are suspicious of outsiders. They don't tell anybody anything, especially about their own. I'm one of their own, Ruth. Safe, for now.'"

Visibly relieved, Ellen got up and draped the wet dishcloth over the sink. "It's settled then."

"I'll tell Ray Boy soon as he gets back with the roastin' ears."

"We can't tell anybody our plans. Especially not Ray Boy. He's the first person Wayne will question."

"Ray Boy's done lied to him once. He'll do it again."

"We have to keep him in the dark for his own safety, Aunt Ruth. Tell him you're going back home with me. Then maybe you can send him on a vacation for a few weeks."

"He won't go. But he ain't about to get caught with his britches down, neither. Ray Boy knows everybody who comes up this road. I'll tell him if he sees that jackass you're married to, he needs to light out."

"Where can he go that Wayne can't find him?"

"Roy Boy can disappear in them woods behind his cabin and ain't nobody gonna find him unless he wants to be found."

Ellen glanced up at the clock on the kitchen wall and turned whiter than Ruth's bleached sheets.

"I've got to call Wayne."

"In God's name, why?"

"If I don't call and check in at three, he'll be up here before the night's over."

"If you need me to act like I'm in the hospital dying, put me on the phone. I ain't above lying."

"I think it's best if I just talk to him myself."

Ellen pulled her chair closer to the kitchen phone, and Ruth went to her screened-in front porch for a breath of fresh air.

Winded for no reason she could think of, she sat for a while in her favorite rocking chair. She liked to come out on the porch and watch the birds in the feeder Ray Boy had put in her front yard. Sometimes she'd bring a book or her sewing and enjoy the breeze coming off the mountain. Sometimes she just rocked while she scrolled through her memories.

Last year, she'd even had Ray Boy install a telephone out here because she didn't like being cooped up in the house yapping at somebody. Being in view of birds and trees and the flowers she'd tended over the years—and sometimes neglected—made her more likely to be civil over the telephone.

She leaned her head back. She needed to rest a spell.

It was her own snores that jerked her awake. Light as autumn leaves adrift in a brook, Ruth found herself falling straight into the eyes of a blackbird. Perched on her birdfeeder scaring away the warblers, he sucked Ruth into a maelstrom of darkness and evil, the scent of trouble as sharp as brimstone.

The present merged with the future as Ruth was held captive by the vision of feathers. When she felt her bones resting in her chair once more and her feet on the ground, she saw the immediate future, true and clear.

Ruth got out of her chair, went into her house, and set her shotgun beside her suitcase. She'd be a fool to ignore the message of blackbirds and leave home without it.

SITTING IN THE KITCHEN as the hands on the wall-hung clock inched past three, Ellen prayed. But it wasn't the pale prayers of comfortable Christians safe in their own homes that passed her lips. Ellen prayed in the gaudy colors of the slapped-down, the stomped-flat, and the fed-up.

She imagined her husband looking at the clock, already

steaming at a wife who didn't have sense enough to be punctual. Her fingers shook as she dialed.

"You're three minutes late, Ellen."

"I just got back from the intensive care waiting room. I got held up in traffic."

"Advance planning would have solved that problem."

"I'll do better next time."

"How's Ruth?"

"As well as can be expected."

"Good. You need to come on home."

"I can't just leave. She needs me."

"Christ, Ellen. I don't need this. Shimayoka will be on the eight o'clock flight tonight, and tomorrow I'll be driving him down to see the facilities in Jackson."

The answer to prayer takes all kinds of forms. Wayne's travels would give her some lead time. Ellen closed her eyes and silently said *thank you.*

"Tomorrow I'll call your car phone."

"At three, Ellen. No later. I'll leave Shimayoka with a cup of coffee and be in the car waiting for you."

"I'll call promptly, Wayne. I promise."

"You know better than to mess with me. Right?"

"I know."

"Good then. Tell Ruth I've put her on the prayer list at church."

Was it only when you were already leaving something behind that you saw it true? Was it only after you'd put two states between yourself and your husband that you saw the black net of deceit he'd woven around himself, thin as a spiderweb, invisible on the front seat of a church pew, impossible to see in a brightly lit restaurant where wealthy clients grateful for his financial guidance thought he walked on water, undetectable to neighbors who judged him by his neatly clipped lawn and his new car?

"I'll tell her, Wayne."

Ellen was shaking when she hung up the phone.

It was amazing how you could grow up with your life all mapped out, only to discover yourself being consoled by an aging aunt who took one look at your face and knew you'd ended up on another road entirely.

"How'd it go?" Ruth asked.

"We're safe for now."

"Good. I've got to shuck them roastin' ears."

Without maps or compass, without any clear idea of the future and only an eighty-year-old woman to care whether she was going in the right direction or whether she ended up in a husband trap with her neck twisted sideways, Ellen followed her aunt onto the back porch where a big tub of corn was cooling in ice.

As Ruth and Ray Boy began to shuck, corn silks drifted across Ellen's feet. "Aunt Ruth, do you have any scissors?"

"In my sewing basket. By my suitcase in the bedroom."

Ellen marched into a bedroom as spare and neat as a hotel room. Her aunt's sewing basket was made of willow branches, twisted and dyed by hand, stuffed with knitting needles, crochet hooks, yarn, embroidery thread, packets of needles, a handmade pincushion shaped like a heart, and a pair of pinking shears.

Before she could change her mind, Ellen grabbed the pinking shears, ran into Ruth's bathroom, and sawed off her hair. She paid no attention to the long strands collecting at her feet, bright as a pile of stars. She tried not to flinch as she emerged shorn, her hair sticking out all over her head like the angry feathers of a startled baby bird.

Wouldn't Josie be surprised? She now had her Mia Farrow hairdo, but it didn't look like anything that would attract the likes of Frank Sinatra or André Previn.

"Ellen?" She turned to see Ruth standing in the doorway, holding on to a small gold brooch. Without a single comment about her whacked-off hair, her aunt pinned the tiger to Ellen's blouse. "This was Lola's. It'll bring you luck."

She closed her hand around the brooch, hoping for a fistful of courage.

"We need to leave, Aunt Ruth. Now. I don't know how long it will take us to catch the circus. And I don't know how long before Wayne gets suspicious. But I want as much of a head start as I can get for when he comes after me."

"Ray Boy's waiting for word to pack the car."

For the next hour, as they selected and packed all the items they might need, Ellen tried to focus on the positive aspects of her journey with Ruth. But when her aunt marched toward the car with a shotgun, she felt the full impact of a life gone so far off the tracks there was nothing to do but leave it behind.

"Aunt Ruth, do you know something I don't?"

"All I know is this journey ain't gonna be easy, and I aim to be prepared." Ruth hugged her. "Don't you worry none. This thing ain't for show, and I ain't scared to use it."

If Wayne had insisted on packing a shotgun for a trip, Ellen would have refused to get in the car. But this was Ruth. She hugged her aunt, and finished sorting through the quilts, deciding which ones to take.

Finally, loaded with their suitcases, sheets and towels and washcloths, Ruth's sewing basket and her shotgun, three of her handmade quilts, and a cooler filled with fried chicken, ham and biscuits, fresh tomatoes, and enough peanut butter and crackers and Almond Joys to keep them out of roadside diners, they said good-bye to Ray Boy and set toward the Mississippi River.

Without the weight of her long hair and the possibility that she ever had to go back to the house on Madison Street, Ellen felt light as a dandelion. Even after her long drive to Aunt Ruth's, she drove through Arkansas as alert as a wide-eyed tourist, drinking in every loblolly pine and log cabin roadside stand selling genuine southern pecan pralines.

The setting sun was made up of colors she'd never seen, the stars more spectacular than usual, the moon so huge she seemed to be driving straight toward it. And she might as well have been. She was running away to the circus, a place as exotic as the moon and twice as bright.

With Ruth dozing in the passenger seat, Ellen ran through the Great Giovanni's schedule. His tour was taking him straight south from Nashville to Huntsville, Alabama. From there he'd trek an easterly direction through the state till he hit Georgia. If Ellen was lucky, she'd catch up to him there.

Meanwhile, it was past ten and she'd been on the road off and on all day.

"Aunt Ruth, there's a Motel Six ahead. It's not fancy but it's clean and cheap."

"Suits me. I ain't fancy, neither."

Ellen checked in and paid cash for the night, twenty-five dollars parceled out from the small stash in her cosmetic case.

Their room had two single beds, a straight-backed chair, a fourteen-inch TV, two coat hangers, and not much else. Ruth looked for roaches while Ellen put on the night latch and wedged the back of the chair underneath the doorknob.

If Wayne broke in, the chair crashing to the floor would wake her up, give her time to run.

Just in case, she slept with one foot outside the covers.

RUTH HADN'T SLEPT WELL, worrying that foretelling dreams would howl through her all night or a brown recluse spider would crawl out of the corner in their nasty motel room and bite her niece. To her great relief, she woke up without a single new prediction to worry over, and her niece was already sitting on the edge of the bed.

For a shimmering moment Ruth caught a glimpse of her sister, smiling at her from the hayloft where they once played make-believe.

The image dissolved as fast as ice cream on a summer's day, leaving behind a niece with shorn hair holding two ham-and-biscuit sandwiches wrapped in tinfoil from Ruth's kitchen.

The sight of Ellen without the long, silky hair, so like Lola's, made Ruth want to weep. But she'd bite her tongue off before she'd say anything negative to her beloved niece, who already bore more wounds than Ruth had accumulated in a lifetime.

"I didn't even hear you leave the room."

"I didn't want to wake you." Ellen handed her a sandwich.

"I've got to find a place to swap the car. When Wayne comes looking, he'll be trying to find my Bel Air."

"Then let me quit lollygagging and git dressed while you eat. I can have my breakfast in the car."

In the Bel Air, headed east, the road curved before them and the sun broke into a thousand stars. A good sign. Ruth glanced to see if her niece had noticed, but the only indication that Ellen saw the silvery trail spinning across the sky was the way she rummaged in her purse and took out a pair of oversize sunglasses.

All along I-40, ordinary travelers lowered visors and reached for sunglasses to cut the glare. Only Ruth, educated by the mountain and tuned to signs, knew the glare came from a pair of eyes, golden as the sun from which they emerged.

They stared at each other, a tiger who refused to show more than his eyes, and a stubborn old seer who refused to faint. She grabbed the door handle and hung on, anchoring herself in the reality of a battered niece with nothing between her and a raving madman except a mountain-toughened old woman with a shotgun.

Still, she felt herself falling into a whirlpool of gold, and just when she thought she might drown, a voice jerked her back.

Don't be afraid, Ruth. His name is Sheikh, and he's nothing but an overgrown pussycat.

It was the miracle Ruth had been waiting for: the voice of her sister, echoing through the years. A million questions popped into her mind, but she knew better than to ask. A vision tells you what it wants you to know. Best you can do is get still and listen.

From the time I entered that circus train, the tiger was mine. Before he got so big he could break the bed, he slept beside me with his head and one big paw on my chest. You'd think a country girl who'd never seen anything wilder than a coyote would be scared, but I wasn't. It was strange, Ruth. There I was sleeping beside a terrifying beast, and I'd never felt safer.

The voice and the eyes began to dissolve, and as hard as Ruth tried, the only thing she could hear was a faint echo. *Be safe.* It might have been Lola or it might have been the wind.

Then the voice vanished entirely and the eyes faded piece by piece until there was nothing left to show they'd ever been there but the buttery sunlight pouring through the windshield.

"Wayne will eventually figure out that I'll ditch the car," Ellen was saying. "The first thing he'll do is check the dealerships. Be on the lookout for a vehicle for sale on the side of the road, Aunt Ruth."

Shaking the last of her vision from her head, Ruth tried to act like she hadn't just seen a tiger's eyes and listened to a voice from beyond the grave.

"Any particular kind?"

"I probably won't have much choice."

Ellen pulled into an Esso station under a sign advising motorists to Put a Tiger in Your Tank.

Ruth's tiger was partial to staring out from the sun and showing up in shadows. She'd bet her shotgun—and her not even a betting woman—that her tiger wouldn't take too kindly to being put in somebody's tank.

"I'm headin' to the toilet," she told Ellen.

"Take your time."

What did she need time for? Even if she spent two hours at

her morning ablutions, she'd come out the same dried-up old fart.

The toilet could use a good scrub brush and some Dutch Boy, and she didn't tarry long. Coming back out, she saw a rack offering free color brochures. Since she was traveling farther than she'd ever been from home, she figured she might as well take a few pamphlets to study the sights she would have seen if she and Ellen hadn't been running for their lives.

By the time Ellen finished paying for the gas, Ruth was back in the car with a brochure open, wishing she could stop by Ruby Falls. She knew she was in a car leaving the Esso station and weaving back into the endless thread of traffic, but she was hearing the rush of water over rock, feeling mountain-cooled breezes against cheeks still too hot from her morning visions.

"I'm thinking we need to find a place that sells fake IDs, too." The pull of Ellen's voice was strong, and Ruth found herself not at Ruby Falls but on the front seat of the car. "Probably Chattanooga. In your wildest dreams, did you ever think you'd need a fake ID?"

"Reckon that fake ID can take fifty years off my age?" Ruth got a blue bandana out of her purse and wiped the dampness off her face.

"You can be any age you want."

"Wouldn't do me no good to be thirty. I done forgot everything I know about courtin'."

Ellen's giggles were the sweetest sound Ruth had heard in a long time. If she wasn't good for anything else, maybe just making her niece laugh once in a while would be enough.

After they first got on the road this morning, they'd talked about their plans. Ellen had said she'd take a south-

erly route all the way across Tennessee till she got to Chattanooga, probably late in the afternoon, depending on how
many stops she had to make. From there she'd cross south
into Georgia in the hopes of catching up to the Great
Giovanni Bros./Hogan & Sandusky Circus sometime the next
day or the day after that.

Ruth wouldn't be any help behind the wheel. She didn't
see well enough to drive, and even if she did, her reflexes
weren't what they used to be. Still, she reckoned she wasn't
bad company. Though her formal education didn't extend past
the eighth grade and she'd never traveled farther than Tupelo,
Mississippi—and that was back in the days before Josie started
treating her like she had leprosy—she hadn't gone through
eighty years of life with her eyes shut.

She could tell you things they didn't teach you in school.
How you could tell by studying a man's eyes whether he was
telling you the truth. How to make a biscuit that would stay
soft and fluffy all day. How to make dye from the berries on
her mountain and quilts with stitches so precise they looked
machine-made. How to live with your heart and your mind
wide open, and how to know who to trust.

Ellen could do worse than have a cantankerous old country
woman at her side. Especially one who had just spotted a car
for sale.

"Ellen, look on your right."

A double-wide trailer sat in a treeless yard on an empty
stretch of highway. The best Ruth could tell, they were halfway
between Olivehill and Lawrenceburg, Tennessee. Two vehicles
sat in the front yard, pretty as you please. One was an old
pickup truck that looked like it had seen its best days. It had

probably once been red, but now it had so much rust it was hard to tell the color.

The other was a 1965 Ford Fairlane, sky blue with a hard white top and angled tail fins. The car was jaunty and brave looking, just the kind you'd want if you were running away to the circus.

"Go for the car, Ellen. That old truck's on its last leg."

"My thoughts exactly, Aunt Ruth."

Ellen turned into the driveway, grabbed her car title out of the glove compartment, and bailed out. Ruth rolled down her window to get some fresh air. She wasn't about to complain, but being cooped up in a car all day was harder than she'd imagined.

She'd get down on her creaky old knees and ask the Lord to hurry up and let them find the circus if she didn't know he had bigger problems than hers to solve.

She searched around till she found something to fan with— one of the flyers from the gas station, a full-color advertisement that read "See Rock City."

Outside the window, sweat was soaking the back of Ellen's sweater as she haggled with the owner of the car, a man nearly as old as Ruth, wearing overalls and a straw hat. Ruth wanted to go out there and knock some sense into him. Couldn't he see he was dealing with a woman who'd had all the stress she could take?

"Old turd," she muttered, but she stayed in her seat and kept her mouth shut. It wouldn't do Ellen any good for Ruth to go around picking fights with everybody she considered a bully.

By the time they drove away in the Ford Fairlane, Ellen looked frazzled as a sparrow that has just tangled with a tomcat. Still fuming but trying not to act like it, Ruth turned up the air-conditioning and fanned her with the Rock City brochure.

"You done good back there, Ellen. I'm proud of you."

"I ended up trading even. My car was worth far more."

"If you worried about money, I got some."

"I can't take your money."

"I ain't askin'."

"Aunt Ruth, I don't know what I'd do without you."

"Don't worry. You ain't fixin' to find out."

She didn't aim to go anywhere before she'd helped fix this mess Ellen was in. If the Grim Reaper came after her before she saw her niece safe and the baby born, he'd better come with plenty of reinforcements.

THE ROAD STRETCHED ENDLESSLY before Ellen, every black car a threat and the wide open spaces as terrifying as if she were a sitting duck in a shooting range. Aunt Ruth was napping, her head leaning sideways against the upholstery and her mouth open in loud snores.

Ellen glanced at the clock. Two hours till she had to call Wayne. She couldn't chance one minute later.

Sweat beaded her upper lip and she suddenly felt the fatigue of a pregnant woman who only weeks earlier had been beaten half to death, and then had spent the last day and a half behind the wheel of a car.

She almost wept when she saw the sign for Walgreens drugstore. Easing into the parking lot, mindful of her sleeping passenger, she cut the engine.

Ruth sat straight up. "Where's my shotgun? I'll shoot 'em."

"We're at Walgreens, Aunt Ruth." Had her aunt been dreaming, or was she getting senile? *Please, God. No.*

"I can see that. I ain't blind."

Thank God. "I thought we'd take a break."

"I hope the toilet's clean. Ain't no excuse for dirty toilets." Aunt Ruth set her glasses straight. "I'll get us some good cold drinks."

"That sounds wonderful. I need to find a few things. Meet me back at the car."

The store that was a haven for shoppers coming in from the heat presented another side to Ellen, a hunting ground where any minute somebody might recognize her from posters Wayne would have scattered through six states or an interview where he sat in front of TV cameras sobbing about his wife who had gone missing.

Trying to hide her urgency, Ellen approached a photo counter where a young man with "Carl" embroidered on his blue smock was sorting pictures.

"I wonder if you can tell me the location of the nearest welcome center and whether it has a pay phone."

"The closest one is five minutes," he said, "but all it has is a toilet."

Ellen hoped her panic didn't show. "Do any of the Tennessee welcome centers have a phone?"

"There's a big one less than an hour away that's got everything, toilets, phones, picnic tables, walking trail that allows dogs. Have you got a dog?"

"Not yet."

"I like Labrador retrievers. They act like pussycats, but

if somebody threatens you, they'll scare the bejesus out of him."

"Thank you. I'll keep that in mind."

Was there something about her that told a stranger she might need a large dog that could scare the bejesus out of anything that would do her harm?

Alarmed, Ellen hurried away. The sight of her reflection in the mirror over the display of sunglasses showed a pale-faced woman wearing bell-bottoms to cover the still-healing wounds on her legs, a pink sweater to cover the ones on her arms, a pink scarf around her neck to hide Wayne's fading fingerprints, and too much foundation to mask the yellowing bruises from her recent beating and the fresh scar that ran from eyebrow to hairline where he'd smashed her face into the windshield. Even with her hair in jagged blond spikes all over her head, she still looked like Wayne Blair's wife.

She needed a disguise. Something that said she was the kind of woman who would not be a victim, the kind who expected to be treated right.

Ellen whizzed toward the cosmetics counter and bought lipstick and mascara that might make her look older, more sophisticated, and less like the special education teacher some of her newer colleagues mistook for a girl who had recently graduated from college. Next she selected a shade of Clairol that promised dark auburn hair, a common enough shade certain to let her blend in with the crowd.

When she got outside, her aunt was waiting beside the Fairlane with two Coca-Colas, the cans so cold moisture condensed on the side.

The skinny woman standing on hot asphalt, her throat

working as she alternately sipped her drink and told Aunt Ruth her plans, was not the Ellen who had sung "Eternally" at her own wedding and imagined herself growing old surrounded by her husband and grandchildren in the same town where she grew up. The dream she'd believed in had evaporated. In its place was the clawing uncertainty of a woman empty of everything except desperation.

They got back into the car and headed east. When they pulled into the welcome center just before two o'clock, Ellen parked under the shade of a blackjack oak beside a picnic table and a public phone. According to the clock on the dashboard she had an hour before she called Wayne. She double-checked her watch, just to make sure. Then she helped Aunt Ruth spread the quilt called Around the World, and trotted to the restroom with her Walgreens purchases and two of the towels they'd packed.

Imagining how the auburn shade would camouflage the jagged edges of the whack job she'd done on her hair, and how it would attract sunlight and little children who trusted sturdy colors, Ellen continued the process of transforming herself.

With her head wrapped in a towel while the color soaked in, Ellen applied her new makeup. The plum-colored lipstick made her look like somebody had slashed her mouth. She decided it was the contrast to the white towel. The darker shade would look better when she unveiled her new hair color.

She approached the mascara with caution. Ellen had thick eyelashes, darker than those of most blondes. Without mascara they were perfectly suited to her conservative image as a public schoolteacher and the wife of a prominent businessman and civic leader.

She pulled the wand from the tube. "No more three-piece suits for me," she said.

A middle-aged woman in khaki walking shorts just coming into the restroom gave her a funny look then hurried into the toilet stall as far away from Ellen as possible.

By the time the woman emerged, Ellen looked as if two spiders had taken up residence above her eyes. Disdain flitted briefly across the stranger's face before she averted her eyes and turned quickly to the washbasin.

Ellen congratulated herself on her transformation. Nobody had averted their eyes from Wayne's wife. In fact, on more than one occasion, he'd accused her of flirting simply because she drew admiring stares.

When she took the towel off her hair, she nearly fainted. Her head looked like a fire engine. What had gone wrong? Either hair that looked like stars didn't soak up color exactly the way it should, or Ellen had left off a step.

Bending over the sink, she scrubbed vigorously with Prell shampoo. Finally, she lifted her head and saw herself in the mirror.

The good news was that she no longer resembled a fire engine. The bad news was that her hair rivaled the color of a mean old rooster's comb. She was now a blazing redhead with purple lips who would stand out in any crowd.

Ellen scrubbed off her lipstick and mascara and sent a silent prayer winging upward that repeated washings would tone down her hair. Still, looking on the bright side, nobody would mistake her for Wayne's golden-haired wife.

She gathered her supplies and started back to her car. In the distance, her aunt was curled on her side on the quilt, napping, her head pillowed on a book.

Aunt Ruth's snores drifted her way as she stowed her bag and towels in the car, then leaned against the public phone booth checking her watch until the hands said two minutes till three. She dialed Wayne's car phone.

"Hello, Wayne?" She sounded rushed and nervous, even to herself. She made herself slow down, take a deep breath. "How are you?"

"More to the point, how are *you*?" Wayne sounded calm, unhurried.

She prayed that was really true. Her husband practiced many forms of cruelty. One of the most diabolical was seething anger disguised as bemused tolerance.

"I'm fine. The baby's fine . . . And Aunt Ruth's getting better every day."

"I'll just bet."

Ellen's hopes toppled like doves shot down in a baited field. Still, she had nowhere to go except forward.

"The doctors say she might even get to come home soon."

"Is that right?"

There was no correct answer for Wayne's question. Ellen thought about love that turns cruel, and desperation that makes you stand in a distant welcome center with hot asphalt melting under your feet as you lie to your husband.

A woman in yellow pedal pushers that matched her hair trotted down the path with her Pomeranian on a pink leash. The little dog bowed up his back and started barking.

"Is that a dog I hear?"

She couldn't very well lie to Wayne about that. "Yes."

"Where are you, Ellen?"

"It's the neighbor's dog. I'm on Aunt Ruth's front porch."

"Are you sure?" Silky smooth—Wayne's question—and dangerous as the warning of a rattlesnake. "That's where I am. Parked right outside Ruth's front porch."

Ellen dropped the receiver. But she could still hear Wayne screaming her name while the little dog strained on his leash, barking at the phone swinging back and forth on its silver cord.

ELLEN TORE THROUGH TENNESSEE as if feral dogs were after her. On the passenger side of the car, Aunt Ruth had the look of a woman you'd have to blast with dynamite to get her away from her niece.

As perceptive as she was staunch, Ruth hadn't asked a single question when the commotion at the wayside telephone woke her. She'd assessed the situation with one look, then grabbed her quilt, her book, and hurried to the car.

Ruth was the one true thing in Ellen's life, the compass she would use to steer herself and her unborn baby to freedom.

Everything else was illusion—the marriage held together with lies and false smiles and long sleeves to cover the bruises, the mother who lived her own fantasies in a house built of stone words, Ellen's future in a community wearing blinders.

Until she swore off caramel cake forever, Ellen had been in blinders, too.

The first time she'd ever noticed Wayne, she'd been starstruck. He was on the football field and she was in the bleachers with her parents. She was the smartest student in the first grade and he was the Tupelo High School football team's best running back. He was also a senior, and totally out of her league.

The first time he'd ever noticed her was years later at the mayor's reception for participants and sponsors of the annual Christmas parade. Ellen, in full Mrs. Claus regalia, was flushed with the effort of keeping her special students—all dressed as elves—from running wild through the mayor's party.

Wayne walked right up to her, and without even introducing himself, he said, "I've been watching you."

Not that he needed an introduction. Everybody knew Wayne Blair, premier sponsor of the Christmas parade and the best catch in town.

She'd thought it a miracle that he chose her, a nice girl, pretty enough if you liked the understated type, but one so quiet she'd be the last person you'd notice in a room. Wayne could have had any girl in town. He was so popular dogs crossed the sidewalk so they could run alongside him, and songbirds turned up the volume of their music when he passed by.

When Ellen was younger and drunk on dreams of being Mrs. Wayne Blair, she couldn't get to her future fast enough. Now she wished she had wings to fly away.

Twenty minutes passed before she could trust herself to speak—twenty miles of unfamiliar places and interstate highway taking her to a future where she might sit in an open-air café sipping tea without lemon and wearing silver bracelets on bare arms marked only by the sun.

Ellen glanced at Aunt Ruth, sitting straight and fierce in the passenger seat.

"Wayne's already at your house. I didn't think he'd get wise to me this fast."

"He probably called the hospital and found out I ain't been near the place."

"I must have done something to tip him off."

"No use thinkin' like that. He was comin' after you no matter what you done."

Now Ellen didn't dare stop in Chattanooga to purchase fake IDs. Spread enough money around and people will tell you all kinds of things, including that Wayne's wife is now a redhead.

She wouldn't put it past Wayne to have detectives in every state checking motels.

"Aunt Ruth, I'm driving as far as I can tonight. Do you think you can sleep in the car?"

"Don't you worry none about me. I can sleep on a rock. And I'm totin' a gun. In case anybody comes messing around my redheaded niece."

It was Ruth's first comment about her hair, and it opened a pressure valve that let all sorts of things escape—tension, fear, and laughter so unexpected that once Ellen started, she couldn't stop. She laughed till the road blurred and everything in her path turned the watery blue of dreams.

Wiping her face with the back of her hand, Ellen saw how there was no such thing as coincidence. Events you'd once thought were random will twist themselves together until they become an arrow pointing straight to your future.

She followed that arrow with a single-minded purpose that would have astonished Josie, stopping only long enough to grab pieces of fried chicken out of the cooler in the trunk. As she whizzed through Chattanooga and turned south toward Georgia, where endless pines were punctuated by an occasional fruit stand, Ellen wondered if she'd taken a wrong turn, if she'd somehow driven in a circle and was even now speeding back home toward disaster.

"Check the map, Aunt Ruth. Is this the right road?"

Ellen flipped on the overhead light so her aunt could see in the dark. She wished she'd insisted on driving on the car trips she and Wayne had taken to D.C. to see the Washington Monument and the White House, out west to take pictures of each other standing in the Painted Desert and posing at the Grand Canyon.

He hadn't even let her drive when they went to New Orleans to hear Pete Fountain play his clarinet in the French Quarter. Only a five-hour drive, and he'd said she was too skittish in heavy traffic on major highways; it would be best if she navigated.

And she hadn't protested, hadn't seen his refusal to let her drive beyond the usual rounds—to the grocery store, church, work, and Josie's house, plus an occasional trip to the Ozarks to see Aunt Ruth—as just another way for Wayne to control her.

"We goin' in the right direction, Ellen. You need to quit worryin'."

"Be on the lookout for a welcome center or a wayside rest area. We'll stop for the night."

"If it's got a pay phone, I reckon I might call Ray Boy."

Though Aunt Ruth acted casual, Ellen knew there was nothing casual about Ruth's love for the caretaker who had seen her through unexpected snows so deep they drifted halfway up the henhouse walls, crops that curled up and died from blights with names nobody had ever heard of, a bout of pneumonia that nearly snatched Ruth over to the other side.

"That's a good idea, Aunt Ruth. Maybe Ray Boy knows about my husband's bad intentions."

When Ellen finally stopped, she picked a place surrounded by woods, with a small entrance you'd barely notice at night. It was not a full-fledged welcome center but a small rest spot on the side of the road, one outdoor light on a lone telephone pole beside a telephone booth and a primitive toilet. Two picnic tables sat in the shadows of the trees.

Her Fairlane was the only car in the small parking lot.

"Wait here, Aunt Ruth."

Grabbing their flashlight, Ellen stepped from her car. Instantly she knew she was not alone. Somewhere deep in the woods a branch snapped. The shivers rippling down her spine told Ellen she had a watcher.

She didn't mind being watched by woods creatures with wings and claws. What scared her was the thought of a two-legged watcher with obsession in his soul and violence in his heart.

Terrified to get too far away from her car, she leaned against its side and swept a beam of light through the trees.

"Who's there?"

A pair of eyes stared back at her.

When you've been slapped and shoved, choked and kicked, you learn to sense disaster before it arrives. You can gauge the degree of hurt by the thumping rhythms of your heart and the chill that rises along the back of your neck, by the sound of angels whispering in your ear, *run, run, run*.

Ellen waited for all the signs. When nothing came except the faraway rustle of water over rocks, she sagged with relief. Still, she'd learned caution the hard way.

She took only one step away from the car, but it was enough to startle her watcher. Wings beat the air as a night owl rose from his perch and flew toward deeper shelter.

Ellen slid back into the front seat. "There's a phone by the toilet, Aunt Ruth. We'll go together."

"I aim to take my gun."

"I won't argue with that."

As they headed toward the telephone booth, Ellen smiled at the idea of traveling with a personal guardian angel, one with a slightly crooked halo and a twelve-gauge shotgun.

Aunt Ruth didn't like telephones and she didn't like beating around the bush. It didn't take her long to find out what Ray Boy knew.

"Ray Boy's fine," she said when she returned to Ellen.

"Thank goodness. Did he hide in the woods while Wayne was there?"

"He said he ain't the hidin' kind. He met up with that husband of yours."

A meeting with Wayne could turn deadly for many reasons or no reason at all.

"Don't you worry none." Ruth added, "That man of yours is meaner than a copperhead, but he ain't gonna mess with nobody as tough as Ray Boy."

"What happened?"

"When Ray Boy said me and you had gone back to Tupelo, Wayne said he was gonna tear the place apart till he found you. Ray Boy dared him to try."

Ellen could picture Wayne's rage curdling under Ray Boy's ways. Like the mountain that sheltered him, Ray Boy gave the impression of a man who could withstand the violence of both man and nature and come out the other side still solid.

"Does Ray Boy have any idea which direction Wayne went or what he planned to do?"

"No. Wayne left and come back up the mountain with Tracker Joe and that bluetick hound of his that can sniff lost souls clear to hell."

Chilled by the image of an obsessed man with a tracking dog on nodding acquaintance with the devil, Ellen took her aunt's arm and led her back to the car. She had to insist that Ruth take the backseat where she could stretch out. And then Ellen curled onto the front seat and covered herself, but she kept one foot outside the blanket in case she had to run.

RUTH DREAMED OF CITRUS groves again, the smell of orange blossoms so mouthwatering a drizzle of saliva ran down the side of her mouth. It was spring, the weight of bloom heavy on trees whose branches made a canopy as they touched the ground. Ruth and Ellen were underneath the canopy, and other people, too, people she didn't know, men and women and children dressed in clothes as colorful as the poppies Ruth grew around her front porch.

Beyond the fragrant white canopy, his coat gleaming in the sun, the tiger stood on all fours, the white and orange fur turning his face into the shape of a heart and the golden eyes sending beams of light so powerful you could see through flesh and bone, see intentions and promises and hope.

And if you followed the light, if you looked far enough, you could see the future. Ruth strained toward the light, aching to see what lay ahead. She didn't know how much time she had left, and she was impatient to find out if she'd live to see Ellen's baby born.

Ruth felt the sunlight touch her hair, move down her face, and warm her chest.

"Aunt Ruth."

Ellen was leaning over the front seat, her alarming red hair sticking out like she'd stuck her finger in a light socket.

"I hate to wake you. But the sun's up and we need to leave."

Ruth sat straight up. She was tough as a buffalo hide, and usually up at dawn. She set the blame for her lollygagging squarely on that devil Ellen had married.

"It won't take me but a minute to do my business." She had a crick in her neck, but she wasn't about to let on to Ellen. As she hurried toward the washroom, she made herself act as spry as a woman who'd been sleeping in cars all her life.

By the time she'd finished in the toilet, Ellen was standing at the basin brushing her teeth. The scent of orange blossoms swirled around her in clouds that drifted to the ceiling, curled around the toilet stalls, and seeped through Ruth's skin deep down where secrets are kept.

Ellen paused, her toothbrush in midair. "Aunt Ruth? Are you okay?"

"Fit as a fiddle." She never had told everything she knew, and she wasn't about to start now. "Let's get this show on the road."

If you were sitting in the backseat of the car and happened to look out the window, you'd see a streak of black-eyed Susans as blurred and golden as melted butter. But if you were a woman who sees beyond the facade and into the deep heart of things, you wouldn't be at all surprised to find yourself being followed by a tiger.

ELLEN HARDLY KNEW THE woman she was becoming, hurtling down an unfamiliar road, scaring up red-winged hawks as she sped through pines as tall as skyscrapers. Still, she kept an eye on the speedometer. A speeding ticket would be just one more way Wayne could track her.

She turned on the radio and found Gladys Knight, backed by the Pips, crooning "Midnight Train to Georgia." Ellen imagined herself on that bluesy soul train, heading toward a better future.

"Aunt Ruth, do you know if my grandfather ever found my grandmother at the circus?"

"Them Halls says he did, but that's hearsay. All I know is that Jim Hall went looking for her and was never heard of again. Lola run away at eighteen and was dead at twenty-three."

"What happened?"

"Her possessions was sent back to me by a man named Razz. He said she died of TB."

"Razz who? What did he do?"

"He didn't say. Lola mentioned him in her letters. *My dear friend,* she called him, but that's all she ever said."

As the rain beat against the car, Ellen imagined what her grandmother's life might have been like. Her own research revealed that circus performers came from all over the world, that within the circus family you'd hear so many languages you'd mistake the place for the United Nations if it weren't for the lions and the elephants, the popcorn and cotton candy, the big top and the three rings filled with wonder.

Searching through the windows for signs of circus posters, Ellen fingered the tiger brooch. She was startled to find not the cool of metal but the heat of something alive, a force made up of claws and hope.

She was in rural Chattahoochee County now. Hunkered between sharp green hills and soft valleys were the farms dug out of Georgia clay and carved out of pine forests. Chattahoochee's backbone. And on that backbone rested Ellen's future.

"Look a yonder!" Ruth's hand shook as she pointed to a sign on a whitewashed fence post: "The Great Giovanni Bros./ Hogan & Sandusky Circus. Three rings of dazzling entertainment. One night only!"

Underneath was an arrow pointing straight ahead.

Their laughter filled the cab, floated out the window, and transformed itself into something sturdy you could hold on to, an umbrella buoyed by the wind of hope, one that would lift you across state lines and embattled marriages and wide tragedies then set you down safely on the other side.

PART TWO

Every day was circus day.

—Merle Evans, bandmaster, Ringling,
in *Behind the Big Top,* David Lewis Hammarstrom

Tyger! Tyger! burning bright
In the forests of the night.

—William Blake,
"The Tyger," in *Songs of Experience*

11

THE FAINT SOUND OF the calliope lured Ruth and Ellen toward an open pasture where vehicles were strung out for a quarter mile along the side of the road and parked in uneven lines in a large grassy pasture. The car shimmied as Ellen headed straight into the thick of things.

"We'll be like 'The Purloined Letter,'" she told Ruth. "Hidden in plain sight."

"Ain't no danger here." Not yet, at least, but Ruth kept that to herself.

Ellen had finding a job on her mind, and that was enough without Ruth telling everything she knew, including that the tiger who had followed her all the way from her mountaintop was now vanishing by bits and pieces. First his tail flew into the blue summer air, then his white underbelly and the black and gold stripes of his back. Next went the legs and his massive head until there was nothing left except his eyes. Finally, those, too, disappeared.

Ruth couldn't say she was sorry to see him go. She hadn't heard a peep from her sister since the day Lola told her the tiger's name, and she was sick and tired of putting up with an old tiger who did nothing except make her feel light-headed.

Ellen looked into the rearview mirror and wiped a smudge off her cheek, then grabbed her purse.

"Aunt Ruth, I don't know how long I'll be. Do you want to go with me?"

"I think I'll just mosey over to that big oak tree and set a spell."

"That's probably best. I don't know how far I'll have to walk."

Ruth could still walk up a mountain, spry as that old goat Ray Boy brought home last year to clean up an overgrown patch he'd been aiming to claim for the garden. The only trouble was now she had to do it in spurts with plenty of rest in between.

She headed to the shade tree where she could revive herself with some fresh air. She couldn't say she was sorry to have some time to herself. There were things she wanted to do without worrying Ellen.

The oak tree was spitting distance from the car—and her shotgun, if she needed it. Ruth knew she didn't—not now, anyway—and so she took her time settling under the tree with the biggest root as her backrest. This was her first up-close look at the circus that had harbored her sister, and she wanted to savor it.

A red, white, and blue ticket booth strung with colored lights stood in the gap of the chain-link fence that surrounded the pasture. Beyond the fence, a sea of humanity rolled through the midway—farmers in pressed overalls, housewives with straw purses, teenagers in miniskirts and the thrall of puppy love, and barefoot children of all sizes, their skin burnished by a hot Georgia sun, their fists caught tight in their mamas' hands. If you looked carefully at the circus goers, you'd see they were so light with joy their feet didn't even touch the ground. Is that the way Lola had felt while she was here?

A sudden image came to Ruth of Ellen's baby, cradled in the arms of the circus, surrounded by the night songs of crickets and the sounds tigers make when they dream.

And in that way of knowing that came as clear as water drawn from the artesian well on her mountain, Ruth understood how the jewel that was Lola had found the perfect setting in the circus. She knew that if she walked the midway, she'd see her sister, memories imprinted on the place.

She needed to stretch her legs, and besides, she was hungry. The smells of popcorn and cotton candy and corn dogs deep fried in sizzling oil reminded Ruth that she'd had nothing to eat for lunch except a Baby Ruth Ellen had snagged out of the cooler.

She might as well have a hot dog, and while she was at it, some cotton candy. It took a while to get her old bones off the ground, and another eternity to get them moving.

Finally she was at the ticket booth paying to enter the midway. A few more steps, and Ruth was swallowed up by the universal fantasy of sawdust and greasy food and small canvas tents where dusty teddy bears with blank plastic eyes were hanged by the neck.

Visions pushed at her mind, sent black spots spinning behind her eyelids. Ruth ducked into a large rectangular tent under a sign that screamed "Sword Swallower! Fire Eater! Elephant Man! World's Fattest Lady!"

A tall, skinny, middle-aged man with slicked-up hair and a

goatee leaned close. "Ticket?" Ruth passed her hands over her eyes and blinked till she was clearheaded. "Ma'am, do you have a ticket?"

"No. I just come out of the heat to cool off a bit."

"Take your time, ma'am. Do you need a chair?"

"No, thank you just the same."

Food. That was what she needed. Any fool knew going around with an empty stomach was just asking for trouble.

She paid twice what the hog dog was worth, and instantly decided against cotton candy. No telling what the going price would be. There was no use spending money Ellen and the baby might need.

The cacophony of the circus pulsed through her like a drumbeat—carousel music, the patter of the barkers, the excited screams of children.

The carousel music swirled in Ruth's head till she got dizzy. Thinking it might be her digestion in an uproar, she looked around for a quiet spot to eat.

Ruth. Ruth.

It wasn't carousel music at all, but her sister in a spangled costume, standing in front of Ruth as clear as the overpriced hot dog in her hand.

I used to wake up to the smell of spun sugar. Razz didn't care a flitter for it, but I longed for it the way a little kid will long for a new bicycle. Before anybody knew I was hiding out in the circus, Razz would sneak cotton candy into our train car three times a day. When Al Giovanni caught him, Razz said he'd developed a sweet tooth.

Her sister didn't say another word, but floated along beside Ruth as she hurried back to the cotton candy stand. So what if it cost an arm and a leg? She didn't aim to miss out on a single thing Lola had loved.

With a towering cone of pink spun sugar and her hot dog, Ruth struck out opposite the midway rides toward a series of canvas tents without banners. Anybody watching would never know Ruth was following along behind a sister as shiny as a star in her spangles.

Ruth came suddenly upon the elephants, a giant wall of gray swaying to the music of their clanking leg chains. Did they imagine themselves running through jungles and spraying their backs with water from deep blue lakes?

"I ain't gonna bother you." She gawked at a sight she'd only seen in dreams, and the elephants went still, studying her with eyes more human than animal, eyes that held a thousand secrets.

"You're good with elephants." A young man with flaming red hair appeared out of nowhere, toting two buckets of water.

"Me and animals understand each other."

When he set the water buckets down and doffed his hat, Ruth saw a balding patch on top of his head. He was older by a good ten years than the twentysomething she'd first thought.

"I'm Indian Joe, and these are my babies."

"Them's some mighty big babies."

His smile showed two gold teeth. "I'd offer you a chair, but I don't have one handy. Best I can offer is a bale of hay." He nodded toward bales stacked out of the reach of elephant trunks.

"Don't mind if I do." She didn't say her name, didn't know if Ellen wanted her to change it or not, but he didn't seem to mind. Like Ray Boy, he went on about his business so she could eat her hot dog in peace.

Not many people would call the roar of big cats and the cacophony of monkeys from a tent somewhere beyond the bales of hay peaceful. Nor would they cotton to the idea of an ephemeral woman in spangles dancing in a patch of sunlight. Of course, Ruth was the only one who could see Lola, but she'd bet her britches she wasn't the only one around here who knew her.

After fifty years of waking up with a stone on her chest, after half a century of wondering what had happened to Lola and Jim Hall, Ruth was now at the same circus where her sister had died. She didn't believe in coincidence. She believed the universe always carried you where you were meant to be, and if you kept your eyes and ears open, you'd find out what you needed to know.

She could start by asking Indian Joe some questions— mainly if a man named Razz was still around—but jump the gun and she'd arouse suspicion. First she'd settle in, win friends, and when the time was right, people would open up and talk to her.

As she bit into her hot dog, the image of Lola dissolved until there was nothing for Ruth to see except sunshine glinting on the hay. With circus magic and possibility seeping into skin and blood and bones, Ruth finished eating, then made her way back to the oak tree, stopping only to buy food for Ellen. She didn't aim to start the first day of their new life worrying her niece.

RAZZ'S AIRSTREAM MADE HIM feel cramped. It was hardly big enough for him, let alone the tiger on his couch.

As if the six-hundred-pound Bengal knew what Razz was thinking, he roared, shaking the trailer and showing teeth that always sent circus fans into a screaming frenzy.

"I know, baby. Are you reading my mind, or do you have another toothache?"

He leaned close to inspect the tiger's mouth. The newbies, circus workers who had joined midseason and didn't know better, called the Bengal *Razz's pet*.

A tiger never allows himself to belong to anyone. He tolerates socializing to get what he wants, and he'll nurse a grudge for years, waiting for the right moment to exact his revenge.

Razz glanced at the clock, then scratched behind Sheikh's ears.

"Stay."

He rammed on his Yankees baseball cap. If he hurried, he had time before the matinee to talk to Al. Razz planned to keep Sheikh out of the show until he could get the circus vet to check the big cat's teeth.

He stepped out of the trailer, and that's when he saw the woman. Standing at the end of the midway beside a cotton candy stand, she had a pale face shaped like a heart and eyes a shade of blue Razz would never forget.

Lola.

His head spinning, Razz wondered if he was having a stroke or going senile. At his age, it could be either. He thought about going back inside to lie down, but damned if he'd start taking to his bed in the middle of the day. The tiger had the couch. Even if he hadn't, it now sagged so bad Razz would just as soon sit on the floor.

He took a whistling breath through lungs that had been punctured twice by a black panther who went rogue and had to be taken off the show. Razz never blamed his cats. That particular night, a storm had caught them unaware just as they prowled into the center cage and Razz was trying to get the unnerved cats to *seat*.

"Excuse me." The female voice brought him crashing back to the damp straw under his feet, the smell of spinning sugar, and the unhappy notion that he'd been caught staring.

Even worse, he was now trapped between his trailer and a woman whose red hair stood up all over her head as if she'd had a bad fright.

The woman reached out as if she meant to grab ahold of his arm. Up close, he felt himself being sucked into eyes that held both heartbreak and hope.

Razz stepped out of her reach. He'd rather tangle with a rogue tiger than get mixed up with a woman who wore desperation as carelessly as a summer shawl.

"I'm sorry. I didn't mean to startle you." The woman's voice was soft, a bit uncertain. "I'm looking for someone. A Mr. Giovanni?"

"I'm heading that way. You can follow me."

Now look what he'd done. All because the woman had bruises she was trying to hide under makeup and a voice like one he'd heard before.

The woman fell into step beside him. She didn't tell her name and he didn't ask. He didn't want to know. In seventy-nine years on this earth, most of them ones you wouldn't want to repeat, he'd learned there was no such thing as second chances. What life took, you couldn't get back, no matter how hard you tried, no matter if you stayed on your knees three years straight begging for a different outcome.

ELLEN WISHED SHE HADN'T told Aunt Ruth to wait. She wished she'd found somebody to lead her to Mr. Giovanni besides a taciturn old man with a face as pitted as a walnut shell and scars all over his bare arms. The only thing she liked about him was his Yankees cap.

She started to ask him the name of his favorite player on the team, but one look at his face told her that any conversation she tried to start would be one-sided.

Instead, she focused on the circus around her. There was a ticket booth on her right, an exact replica of the one at the entrance. Beyond that the big top, a sea of red and white striped canvas, was far larger than Ellen had imagined. It was at least the size of a football field.

Growing up, she'd never been allowed to go to the circus, which was not surprising considering Josie's hatred of anything associated with her mother. After Ellen had grown up, she'd been too busy getting an education, a job, then later, being married to Wayne, to think about the circus.

Now, she would have been excited if she hadn't been so scared—even though anybody looking for a neat, blond housewife whose mantra was obedience would never come to a place where unshaved men in muscle shirts hawked chalk Kewpie dolls for a dollar. And if he did, he wouldn't look twice at a rumpled, jazzy-haired woman who looked like she fit right in.

Still, the prospect of asking for a job from somebody who had *Great* before his name made Ellen weak-kneed.

Up ahead, the silver trailer was set apart from the others. It had a roped-off yard big enough for two plastic lawn chairs and a child's plastic swimming pool. Red and gold lettering on the side proclaimed "The Great Giovanni: World-Renowned Equestrian and Showman Extraordinaire!"

Ellen decided to take the child's pool as a good sign.

"What do I do now?"

"Whatever you want." The man, who hadn't said a single word in the five minutes it took to walk from his Airstream to the ostentatious trailer of his boss, turned and walked off.

Ellen mounted the steps and knocked on the door.

"Mr. Giovanni?"

"Who's there?"

The question was spoken from inside the trailer in a tone more bellow than polite inquiry. Ellen refused to cringe.

"I've come to talk to you."

"Then you'd better be the queen of England."

The Great Giovanni still hadn't shown his face. If she were in her classroom telling the story to her students, she'd say, "I felt like Dorothy meeting the Wizard of Oz."

"No, sir. I'm Eve." The name just popped into her head, and it seemed exactly right. A brand-new woman in a brand-new world. "I'm looking for a job."

"What? What!" The door to the trailer burst open. An ancient, white-haired, shaggy-looking beast of a man stared at Ellen with eyes so black they allowed for no light. "Are you a trapeze artist? I need a trapeze artist."

Somewhere between hearing Giovanni's first bellow and realizing she was standing in the presence of a circus icon, Ellen had lost her courage. All she could do was shake her head.

"No? A human cannonball? A clown?" She dwindled under Giovanni's scrutiny. "A fortune-teller? A dog trainer? No? No? *No?*" His face blazed red. "Speak up. What do you do?"

Somewhere behind them a band struck up a lively, brass-filled version of the Blue Danube Waltz. On Ellen's right, twelve Andalusian stallions appeared, dazzling in their white coats and their blue and gold spangled blankets.

On the backs of the horses, their legs spread wide, their muscles taut, stood a human pyramid. At the very top was a black-haired man whose head touched the sky.

A whirlwind that was the Great Giovanni blew past Ellen.

"I don't have time for you. My grandsons are getting ready to perform."

Giovanni vanished in the direction of the big top, leaving Ellen in the sunshine where twelve white horses began to dance.

Was this how her journey ended?

As the horses pranced toward the big top in perfect time to the music, Ellen thought about Ruth waiting in the car, an aging aunt who had given up everything for her. She thought about her unborn child, cocooned in the womb, listening to his mother's heartbeat and dreaming that she would always keep him safe.

And what about her? Ellen had left her hair in Arkansas, her car in Tennessee, and her husband in Mississippi. She wasn't about to give up now.

As she took off running after the Great Giovanni, wet straw kicked up from her heels. And if you knew where to look, and how, you could see trailing along behind her a wake of stubborn hope.

As Ellen raced after Giovanni, an ancient woman with her eyes lined in black and her hair dyed yellow leaned over the ticket booth and reached out her arm.

"Hey, miss. *Miss!* You can't go in there without a ticket."

"Press!" Ellen said, never checking her speed.

A woman subject to inquisitions over everything from arriving home from a teacher-parent conference five minutes later than she'd said to forgetting to put starch in his shirts learns the salvation of believable lies.

Unhindered, she entered the big top, where magic swirled over the watchers in a silver cloud and dreams were as possible as twelve white horses dancing the waltz. Lights suspended from the rafters shot stars from the spangles on riders and horses, and cheers from the crowd mingled with the cacophony from the brass band and the spiel of the ringmaster.

"The stupendous Giovannis!" he said. "Amazing! Breathtaking!"

But it wasn't the spiel Ellen heard, it was the sound of her own heart, beating to the remembered song of her dreams.

Standing in the damp straw with the scent of cotton candy, hot dogs, and popcorn making her stomach lurch, she clung to the almost-forgotten song and yearned toward her future like a sunflower trying to follow the light.

All her hopes were condensed into two words. *Please, God.*

She spotted Giovanni in the front row of the bleachers, a section cordoned off with heavy red velvet rope, his white hair gleaming under the lights. Beside him sat a petite woman with her silver hair in a coronet of braids on top of her head, and beyond her, a handsome middle-aged woman with a dark-haired little boy in her lap.

Getting to Giovanni meant dashing across the track and not getting kicked in the head by twelve galloping stallions. Ask any woman who had lived life at the hands of a husband with flying fists: Ellen was an expert at walking a thin line between safety and a blow to the head.

She waited for the stallions to round the corner, then made her move. Heart pounding, she dashed across the track until she stood in front of the Great Giovanni.

"I'm standing right here till you give me a job."

"Good God, woman!" Giovanni snatched her up like she weighed no more than a rag doll, then shoved her onto a seat beside him. "What in the name of all that's sacred do you do?"

"I teach."

"Why didn't you say so in the first place?"

"Does that mean I have a job?"

"God help me, yes. What's your name?"

"Eve." Casting about for a last name, Ellen scanned the big top, her gaze moving upward where the canvas ceiling, filled with suspended lights, gleamed like a summer night sky. "Star," she added. "My name is Eve Star."

"You will be the circus teacher."

"Papa," the dark-haired woman said, but the old man acted as if he didn't hear her.

"You will teach my great-grandson how to talk."

"Thank you, Mr. Giovanni." She was so relieved not to be kicked out of the only safe haven she knew she'd have agreed to wrestle live alligators.

The woman holding the child gave Ellen a glance that would wither potted petunias. "I'm leaving the show, Papa, taking Nicky to a specialist."

"Nobody's leaving, Clarice. I will not subject my great-grandson to another doctor who doesn't know what he's doing. Now be still and watch the show." His glare in Ellen's direction meant he'd included her in the command.

Still limp with fatigue and relief, she watched as the man she'd seen at the top of the human pyramid sailed through the air and catapulted through a ring of fire. She was so close she could hear the soft thump of his feet landing on the back of another horse.

Ellen wondered what it would be like to face Wayne Blair without fear, to jump straight through the blaze of his rage and come out on the other side unscathed. Is that why her grandmother had learned to train tigers? So she could become a woman so fierce no one would dare lift a hand to her?

Horses and riders left the big top, blue and gold gods floating on a snow-white river. The audience, full of the magic of horses that danced and equestrians with wings on their feet, rose to pay homage. Almost unnoticed, six roustabouts stole into the center ring. Under cover of cheers, they hastily erected a steel cage, the bars strong enough to hold back disaster.

But there was no haste about the lone man who stepped into the cage. Dressed in black leather from his brimmed bush hat to his high-top boots, he appeared to be out for a stroll. You might mistake him for a man planning to dine at one of the large round seats the roustabouts had arranged around the cage except for one thing: the leather whip coiled in his right hand.

In the distance, a tiger roared.

When they stalked into the big top trailing their black and gold tiger dreams behind them, the tigers took on a mystical quality, as if you were seeing them through the tunnel of time.

Mothers worried over teenagers sporting Beatles hairdos and smoking pot were transported back to carefree days of poodle skirts and riding in convertibles with the top down. Fathers worried over a president called Tricky Dick and the U.S. Army Corps of Engineers' plans to flood two hundred acres of good farmland to save fifty remembered a better day when public servants were honorable and the government stayed out of a man's business.

Fingering Lola Hall's tiger brooch, Ellen traveled forward instead of back, seeing a time when she could walk anywhere she wanted without looking for trouble over her shoulder.

12

THE EARLY THUNDERSTORMS HAD unsettled the cats and they were restless. The lions would come in uncooperative; Lucifer, the black panther, would be sulky, but the tigers would be looking for somebody to blame. Razz would be the first thing they'd see. They'd fix their golden eyes on him, trying to gauge if they could take a swipe and get away with it. They loved the sound of tearing. Let one of them get a claw into leather and he'd have a hard time keeping order.

They were already quarreling with each other in the tunnel. Today could be Razz's day to die.

That he viewed his own demise so dispassionately told him it was time to hang up his hat and hand over his whip. But something kept him going—a stubborn streak, a desire to die under canvas. Or maybe he was just a crazy old man waiting for something he hardly dared to hope for. Was it too much to ask that the universe give him something besides tigers in his old age?

Beyond the cage, in his roped-off section, Al Giovanni sat forward in his chair, his posture suggesting that he knew Razz would be performing for his life today. Razz fixed him with a look that said, *Don't even think about stopping the cat act.* Al glared back, but Razz was no longer staring at his old friend and partner. He was seeing the fragile-looking woman beside him.

So she'd stayed, had she? Why was she here? And why couldn't he look at her without thinking of Lola . . .

I should have known better than to let her stay. After the soup disaster, I should have known better than to let Lola help out in the menagerie tent.

"I can help feed the animals," she'd said.

It seemed like a good idea at the time. She'd be where I could keep an eye on her, make sure she would be all right. I figured she'd get a kick out of tossing birdseed to Magic Melinda's doves. Little did I know she'd gravitate toward the cats. Even more astonishing was the way the cats reacted to her, especially the tigers. When Lola was near, they put on their best manners. Instead of the disgruntled snarls that said to me, Come in here late with my meat again and I'll take a chunk out of your leg, *they rubbed their shaggy bellies against the bars when Lola was near.*

"I could train them," she said, and I told her, "You will not."

The next thing I knew she and my whip had both disappeared. I found her out behind the cook tent practicing, tangled up in leather coils and oblivious to the marks she'd made on her arms and legs.

I wanted to cry at the angry red welts, but circus people learn to go through bad performances and bad food, hostile crowds, no crowds, weeks without pay, loneliness so bone deep you think you'll go crazy and even worse without letting feelings get in the way. Nothing is allowed to steal the magic of the show.

"Give me the whip, Lola. You're going to hurt yourself."

The way she looked at me, with eyes that had seen so many tragedies she'd never live long enough to forget, made me ashamed.

"All right, then. Let me show you how."

She didn't say a word, didn't speak about stout fists and blows that didn't show, didn't talk of anger so deep it can burn through a woman till she's nothing more than skin and bones and determination. She simply stood aside and watched every move I made; watched and learned.

It took her a week before she figured out how to snap the whip without getting hit by the backlash, and another before she could make it crack.

"I did it!" She came running full tilt, and I grabbed her up in a bear hug. We reeled around like two crazy drunks until she became aware that I was holding her, or maybe how much I liked it. Suddenly shy, she walked off.

I didn't follow her. I needed time to cool off, and I guess so did she. A woman broken and a man still unable to find the ground beneath his own feet have no business starting anything.

I found her later that evening in our railroad car, curled up on the bed with Sheikh and Rajah. Though they were big enough now to be turning dangerous, Lola showed no fear . . .

Cats can smell fear. The first lion slunk out of the tunnel growling. The kids and women in the bleachers screamed. They didn't know that lions are big showoffs. They growl to say, *Look at me. I'm the king of the jungle.* They also growl before they attack, but Razz could look into a cat's eyes and see what he was thinking. This cat was in a snit, not a murderous rage.

Cracking his whip, he yelled, "Seat!" and the massive lion he called King jumped onto his perch, still snarling.

The tigers who came in next, shoving with their shoulders to see who could get through first, had different ideas. Unlike the lions, they never broadcast their intent, preferring instead the element of surprise. One look into the endless gold of their eyes told Razz they were up to no good. He sidestepped just in time to avoid the claws of Jezebel.

He had to give the seat command twice before the tigers decided Razz meant business. Seeing how the cats were going to test him on every trick, he considered ditching the most dangerous segment of the show. But he was too proud to turn in a performance that would be compared unfavorably with the one over at Ringling, and he'd worked with cats too long to give them the idea that they could get the upper hand.

Besides, there was a woman in the owner's box who reminded him of Lola. When his Lola had watched, Razz always put on his best performance.

Razz warmed his cats up with the simple tricks first—balancing on gigantic balls, teetering on a lion-size seesaw, jumping through hoops.

When he circled his whip over his head and yelled, "King, march!" the still disgruntled lion leaped off his stool and began to circle the cage. "Jezebel, march!" He cracked the whip in her direction and she slunk off to follow King.

One by one, Razz got his cats lined up and going around him in circles. This was Lola's act, one of the many that had made her famous. Though Razz now had only ten cats, she'd worked with sixteen tigers, all circling until they were so close their fur brushed against her white leather jumpsuit. She'd give the command and they would miraculously divide into groups of two, eight going in one direction and the other eight going opposite.

She hadn't learned the act from him, and she certainly hadn't learned it from anybody else on the circuit. She was the only one doing it. Seeing a little slip of a woman standing unarmed in the middle of sixteen tigers had been an awesome sight. Watching her, women used to faint and have to be carried out on stretchers.

What the audience didn't know, of course, was that Sheikh and Rajah had been with Lola since they were cubs. They'd frolicked with her on the floor of Razz's train car, all around the winter quarters in Florida, and on the beach in Galveston where Razz and Lola and the tigers loved to stay when they needed to get away from the circus. They'd even slept in the bed with her.

Unlike the cat trainers of old, Lola used the reward system, a trick she learned from Razz. Cats will do just about anything if they know they'll get a bloody piece of meat for their troubles.

Still, Lola had a magic touch all her own and could get the tigers to do anything. But that didn't mean the tigers were domesticated. You can never tame a tiger. You can never count on being in his good graces. Get too complacent around a tiger, and he'll sink his claws to the bone just to remind you of who he is.

Now, Jezebel was eyeing Razz with malicious intent, and King wasn't so much walking as slinking. Razz gave the signal to his cage man and ended his act five minutes early, something he almost never did. Maybe he was tired. Maybe he was old. Or maybe he just wanted to get out of the cage in one piece and find out about the young woman who still sat beside Giovanni, her face as pale as milk and her pull on him so strong you'd think she'd attached a string to his heart.

By the time he got his cats back into the tunnel and himself out of the steel cage alive, one more time, the band had struck up the last song and the woman was gone. So were Clarice and Nicky and Al's wife, Angelina.

Razz made a beeline for the owner's box.

"Who's the redhead?"

"Eve Star."

A false name if he ever heard one. Still, it didn't surprise Razz. Half the people working the show had names they'd snatched from billboards and comic books and even the label on a bottle of whiskey. Jack Daniel was in charge of the midway rides.

"What's she want?"

"A job."

"You didn't give her one?"

"We need a circus teacher, and she fell into our lap. It's a good sign."

Unlike Razz, who stuck to common sense and the things he learned from the school of hard knocks, Al believed in new moons that can change your luck and the migration of birds that can point the way to a better future.

"Besides, she's going to teach Nicky to talk."

"I sure hope so." Razz would have chewed off his own arm before he'd destroy the hope he saw in his friend's face. For all Al's bluster, he was like a big housecat, happiest soaking up sun and enjoying his optimistic dreams.

But something was in the air, something that made Razz's skin tingle. Whether it was the sight of the young woman or a premonition, he couldn't have told you. Nor could he have said whether the feeling he got was anticipation or fear. All he knew was that it was up to him to keep his eyes open.

WHEN ELLEN LEFT THE big top, she hardly knew her feet were touching the ground. Filled with the spangled visions of the show and excitement over her new job, she went in search of the trailer bearing a sign marked "The Great Giovanni Bros./Hogan & Sandusky Circus, Manager."

The Great Giovanni himself had said it would be parked in the circus backyard, an area she quickly determined was off-limits to ordinary circus goers. Beyond the midway and behind the big top were trailers lined in neat rows with wading pools, lawn chairs, and grills in the front yard. In the slant of afternoon sun, children played a game of tag.

Ellen would have thought she was in any neighborhood in America until she saw a clown on stilts and a woman in a pink sequined dress tossing white doves into the air. They flew around her head in a circle then formed a perfect heart in midair.

"Come, my pretties," she said, and they landed along her outstretched arms so that she looked as if she'd sprouted angel wings. She waved when Ellen passed by.

But the children dashing about paid her no attention. Nor did they seem to notice that a large woman in a billowing silver caftan walked by with an ocelot on a leash.

Even better, no one except the bird trainer paid attention to a woman with a bad dye job, a make-believe name, and too many scars to count. She'd be willing to bet her life that no one here knew Wayne Blair or cared about his standing in Tupelo, Mississippi. No one would be running to the telephone to tattle about his wayward wife. Ellen stood in the circus backyard breathing, simply breathing.

And then she found the trailer marked "Manager" and knocked on the door.

"Do come in." The voice belonged to a pleasant-faced middle-aged man with graying temples, green eyes, and a wide smile. "And won't you sit down?"

"There's no need for her to sit down." The black-eyed woman from the owner's box had appeared from the back part of the trailer to glare at Ellen. "This woman, whoever she is, won't be staying. I won't let her near Nicky. He's been through enough."

"Clarice, this is not your business."

"My grandson is always my business. And he should be yours, too, Mark."

Oh, God. The little boy who couldn't talk was this formidable woman's grandson. Ellen's dreams were dying right before her eyes. She pictured herself slumping back to Aunt Ruth to tell of her defeat. But no. With one more deep breath of circus air, she filled herself up with the kind of blazing arrogance it would take to face down a tiger.

"I'm Eve, the new circus teacher." Ellen lifted her chin just a notch as she slid into a chair with a blue and gold satin cushion. "The Great Giovanni sent me."

When Mark laughed, he threw back his head. "You don't have to call him Great, but sometimes it helps." He held out his hand. "I'm Mark DeChello—call me Mark—Giovanni's son-in-law." He smiled again. "But the only circus trick I've ever performed is marrying the astonishing Clarice and fathering Luca, the greatest equestrian in the world." He smiled toward his wife. "Clarice, this is Eve."

"I have ears." Clarice stomped out of the trailer, and for a while Ellen and Mark simply stared at each other with the slammed door still echoing between them.

Seeing her newly born freedom going up in smoke, Ellen tried to call up the thundering white horses and the courage of the riders who rode them without toppling, but all she managed was a timid question.

"Is Luca the one who jumps through a ring of fire?"

"Yes. Among other things. All of them amazing."

Though Ellen knew little of the circus and even less about equestrians, she'd agree that Luca was amazing. But astonishing wasn't the word she'd use for Clarice. Formidable, maybe. Even a bit scary.

Still, under the kindness and easy grace of a man named Mark, she saw her future unfold as someone who could take afternoon tea with a woman who wore doves on her arms and another who strolled with an ocelot. She would be someone who could eat cotton candy every day and watch magic unfold under the big top, someone who would blend in with the eccentric circus family, unnoticed and out of range of flying fists.

"We'll be here another day," Mark was saying, "which will give you time to check out the school supplies and get settled in. Tomorrow we'll pitch the school tent, and I'll show you the ropes."

"Thank you."

"If you need it, I'll have someone help you move your trailer to the circus backyard."

"That won't be necessary. I'm very self-sufficient." What she didn't know about taking care of herself, she planned to learn. Besides, what would he do if he knew she slept in a car—and why? Would he take back his kindness? His offer to help? Her job?

"There'll be some paperwork, of course," he said. She hoped her alarm didn't show, nor her relief when he added, "But we can get to that before payday. Around here, nobody gets in a hurry."

Ellen thanked the circus manager again, but as she made her way back through the laughing children and the doves who were now flying about their pink-sequined trainer in figure eights, Clarice intercepted her.

"You might have fooled my father and my husband, but you don't fool me," she said. "I know your kind. Little opportunists who weave spells by batting their pretty blue eyes."

"Mrs. DeChello, I'm sorry if I've offended you in any way. I'm just here for a job."

"My job is to keep the men in my family from suffering for the mistakes of their soft hearts." She glared at Ellen in a way that seemed to see straight through her lies to the bruises and even the husband she'd left behind. "Make no mistake about it, *Eve*. I'll find out who you are and why you're here."

Clarice walked off without another word, leaving Ellen to dread that Clarice might spot her face on a missing flyer. *Lost* it would say, *Wife and Mother-to-be. If spotted, call Wayne Blair.*

It would bear a picture of her, blond and smiling, the Peter Pan collar of her dress hiding bruises he'd made when she cooked bacon instead of sausage for breakfast. Or maybe he'd post his favorite, a picture of Ellen at the beach in Biloxi, a striped caftan covering her swimsuit and the black and blue marks on her arms and legs where he'd beaten her because the lifeguard smiled in their direction.

Gone was the freedom she'd felt in the circus backyard. Now she hurried along, scanning the faces of strangers waiting in line at the carousel, searching for a tall, dark-haired man among the ones lined up to knock over a weighted cat and win a teddy bear, looking back over her shoulder for a long-armed man who knew how to catch you unaware and punch before you could even say *please, no.*

RUTH SAW HER COMING, Ellen wadded so tightly inside herself she looked no more substantial than the dandelions stirred up from the pasture floor by the trampling feet of Georgia's country folk going home to milk the cows—or just coming in from their evening chores to recapture a piece of their childhood.

She waited with her bonnet tied under her chin, ready for the news that floated along behind Ellen like a new silk scarf.

"You got a job." Her niece was even with her now, trying to learn how to breathe deep again.

"Did you see a vision?"

"No, but I seen a spunky pregnant woman who wouldn't take no for an answer head out of here to find work."

"You're looking at the new circus teacher."

When Ellen sank onto the grass under the tree, Ruth noticed how her feet were swollen and her arms looked like toothpicks.

"Ain't never been a better one." She reached into a sack and handed over Ellen's supper. "Here. I bought you two hot dogs and a pile of french fries. And I aim to see you eat ever last bite."

Between bites, Ellen told her about the tent where she'd teach children and a circus backyard that felt safer than her neighborhood in Tupelo.

When she told Ruth her false name, Ruth saw stars and smelled citrus, though the sun was still painting the skies, the moon was nowhere in sight, and they weren't even hollering distance to a grapefruit.

She saw something else, too, a new trouble that circled over Ellen's head like a flock of blackbirds.

"We have to think of a name for you, Aunt Ruth. I could call you Granny."

"When Lola was a little bitty thing, she'd run toward me with arms held straight up, yelling, 'Me. Me.' The name stuck. Even after she got too old for me to pick her up, she still called me Mimi. I ain't heard it since she left."

"Until now, Mimi Star."

"Starting over at my age. Ain't that a sight?"

While Ellen finished her food, Ruth leaned her tired old bones against the trunk, as durable as the oak and twice as tenacious. She'd been through tornadoes that ripped her barn apart and hailstorms that tore up her roof. She'd bested crows in her corn, an army of tomato worms in her garden, and boll weevils in her cotton. She'd turned Jim Hall and his ravings around with her shotgun and a promise of britches full of buckshot.

And she'd do the same thing to Wayne Blair if he came around messing with Ellen. And he was coming. Make no mistake about it.

Still, she'd have plenty of time to rest up before that happened. All the signs pointed to a respite while Ellen grew strong—the way the wind picked up without rattling a single leaf, the shadow of the red-tailed hawk, and the single dragonfly that hovered just beyond her niece's shoulder, his wing turning silver in the setting sun.

13

THERE'S A CERTAIN FREEDOM that comes from having all your possessions in a car. No mortgages, no cleaning and cooking, no husband. That was the best part. Ellen's home was now a traveling circus and Wayne was clueless in Tupelo.

Still, driving into the small town of Cusseta on the outskirts of Fort Benning in search of a Laundromat and a clean bathroom, Ellen was an open target. Wayne or someone he had hired could be anywhere: in the white van parked a block down from Clean Up and Dry; in Snookie's Café across the street, sipping a cup of coffee and watching through the plate-glass windows for a wife who had run away and needed punishing.

As she and Ruth gathered their dirty clothes from the car trunk for the short trudge into the Laundromat, a poster fluttered from a nearby telephone pole. The face of a woman, blond, the word *Missing,* the details suddenly a blur.

Had Clarice seen the poster? Had she already come into town for a bite at Snookie's and was this very minute telling her husband and the Great Giovanni that the new schoolteacher was a woman named Ellen Blair whose husband was searching for her? Even worse, what if she'd already told the police?

Clutching her plastic bag over her belly, her heart threatening to beat out of her chest, Ellen raced toward the poster. But the woman had brown eyes, not blue, and she was from Decatur, Alabama.

Ellen had to lean against the post until she could compose herself. And then she searched in all directions before she joined Ruth at the coin-operated washing machine. Thankfully, they were the only two people inside the Laundromat.

"They got a good clean bathroom. I done checked it out."

"Why don't you wash up first, Aunt Ruth? I'll start the laundry."

"Holler if you need me."

"I will."

What would Ruth do? Her shotgun was in the car, and her eyesight was so bad Ellen didn't know if she could hit anything if she tried.

Across the street, a dark-haired man walked into the café, Wayne's height and build, his swagger. She ducked behind a washing machine.

The woman on the poster was believed to be kidnapped. Should Ellen have faked a kidnapping? Her own death? Maybe she should have run across the border to Mexico instead of Georgia?

Sweat rolled down her face and she got a cramp in her leg. The washing machine started bouncing with an uneven load, every knock the sound of fists hitting bone. Ellen was scared and hot and thirsty. She wanted to pee and to scream, all at the same time.

With one hand over her mouth and the other over her womb, she listened for the click of the door latch, footsteps on the linoleum floor, coins jingling into the machines, anything, anything at all that would tell her she was not alone.

"In the sweet bye and bye . . ."

Ruth. Singing in an unwavering alto as she sponge-bathed in a strange bathroom.

Ellen stood up and opened the washing machine lid to shift her load of wet clothes. If Wayne had found her, he wouldn't go into a café. He'd already have barreled into Clean Up and Dry with his fists loaded.

Besides, it was too dark to pick out faces. She had probably imagined a man who looked like her husband.

With Ruth's hymn swirling around her like a promise, Ellen did her laundry and dreamed of a day she would bare her arms to the sun and walk down any street she pleased without being followed by shadows.

AT NIGHT THE CIRCUS is a fairy tale waiting to happen. Strains of music from a band long silent weave among the constellations and fall back to earth as starlit dreams. The memories of artists on flying trapezes, dancing horses, and pink-caped elephants swirl on the night air, so that dreaming, the performers smile.

If Razz noticed anything extraordinary, he wouldn't have told you. As grounded as the well-worn boots on his feet, he was a man on a mission.

The Andalusians stirred as he passed by, and Betsy the elephant pushed her stake back into the soft Georgia clay.

"Hah. Caught you!" He walked close enough to hand her a pocketful of peanuts and pat her trunk. "Don't even think about raiding the cabbages tonight. I've got enough trouble without Cookie Two going on a rampage."

The last show was over, the last spectator long gone, the concessions closed tight, and the midway rides locked down. All over the circus backyard, blue lights glowed from Airstreams as the performers relaxed in front of their TVs.

Even Al, normally a night owl, had bid Razz good night and turned in early. "The show'll be moving tomorrow night," he said, as if Razz were getting senile as well as old and ugly. "Get a good night's sleep."

Sleep was the last thing on his mind. He'd told himself he needed to patrol the circus grounds in case the bear decided to strike. He'd even told his tiger.

"Sheikh, I'm going out to catch a thief. At least I can put a stop to that."

He gave the sideshow tents only a cursory search. Lifting one flap after another, he said, "I'm watching, and if you're in there stealing, I'm mean enough to do something about it."

He saw nothing, not even a shadow. Maybe the bear had a sixth sense. Maybe he had his ears to the ground and knew Razz would be out and about tonight. If he was smart, he'd blow the show before he got caught.

But it wasn't the sideshow or the Tilt-A-Whirl or even the Tunnel of Love that caught Razz's attention. It was the car in the meadow. An old Ford Fairlane parked all by itself over by the oak tree.

Razz could be as silent as his cats. Anybody who couldn't learn from a big cat after more than fifty years didn't deserve to be part of the show. He didn't have much he could be proud of except that one thing: he'd learned stealth, cunning, and the art of seeing the truth from lions and tigers.

He crossed the pasture without breaking so much as a twig and was at the car window in no time flat, just standing there silent as a shadow.

An old woman on the backseat curled into herself like a dried-up oak leaf, her mouth open in snores as loud as any he'd ever heard. Helpless, she looked, till you saw the shotgun propped on the floorboard beside her. Nobody would be messing with her.

Good, he thought, for no other reason he could imagine than he admired spunk.

The young woman asleep on the front seat stole his breath. The moonlight showed the scar on her forehead, arms mottled in the way fading bruises will do. But it was her left foot that almost brought Razz to tears. Bare, blue-veined, and vulnerable, it stuck out from the patchwork quilt that covered her.

"In case I have to run," Lola had said, and he was sorry he'd asked, sorry he was responsible for the shadows that crossed her face, the shiver that started in her bones and turned her skin two shades paler.

"Who did this to you and why are you here?" Still staring through the car window, Razz wasn't aware he'd spoken aloud till he heard the sound of his own whisper, caught in the summer wind like a dragonfly.

The girl stirred in her sleep, moaning, and the quilt slid to the floor. He wanted to pick it up, to cover her, to tell her there was nothing to fear.

But most of all, he wanted to get back across the pasture as fast as he could, shut the door to his trailer, and forget he'd ever been so foolish as to search for things he didn't want to see, things that felt as dangerous to him as knowing he'd loved a woman he was destined to lose.

THE SCHOOL TENT WAS blue and white striped, set up between the cook tent and the manager's trailer, close enough to smell that lunch would be something cooked with cabbage and to know that when Mark DeChello left, he was within calling distance if Ellen needed any help.

The tent looked inviting and cheerful with its child-size red and yellow chairs and a bouquet of multicolored balloons tied to the entrance. Still, Ellen was glad she had her aunt. If anybody could quell Clarice DeChello, it was Ruth Gibson.

Aunt Ruth sat in a folding chair close enough to the tent flap to catch a breeze, her knitting in her lap. The children smiled at her as they filed in, probably thinking of their own grandmothers.

One by one they took their places in a circle around Ellen, and Mark introduced her summer school students. Eight-year-old Lucy Kuzmicki in pink tights and tutu had no fear of her mother's high wire, but was scared to death of numbers.

"She'll need tutoring in math to get her up to speed for the school term at circus winter headquarters," he told Ellen.

Bobby Harvey, sporting a red clown wig and two bright red circles on his cheeks, was the son of head clown, Jocko. He loved everything about clowning and nothing about reading.

"He needs to get through the fourth-grade reader so he'll be ready for fifth grade after the circus season."

Bobby's sister, April, had on the kind of sunsuit any ordinary four-year-old would wear, but there was nothing ordinary about the little girl. She wore a silver cape over her romper, and she wanted to be just like her mother, Rose, who climbed a tower daily and took a swan dive toward a bucket of water the clowns working all three rings of the big top called their swimming pool.

"But how does she do that without getting hurt?" Ellen wished she hadn't missed that part of the show.

"She gwows wings and fwies," April piped up, and then she flapped her arms and out from the cape flew a miniature set of wings.

"April's smart as a crackerjack," Mark said. "She likes to come to school because Bobby does."

Ellen felt like a woman who had gone to the bank to cash a ten-dollar check and was handed a chunk of gold. The circus manager who gave his love so freely to innocent children would surely have enough left over to make allowances for a woman with a murky background and no proper identification. How long would Mark wait for her to finish filling out her paperwork?

As soon as the circus schedule took them through a larger town, she'd make sure Eve and Mimi Star had credentials so believable nobody would dare question them.

"That's it," Mark was saying.

"Only three?"

"You'll have more in the regular school term."

If Ellen never got a chance to help the little boy who couldn't talk, then Clarice had already won. Even without exposing Ellen's secret, she'd report to the Great Giovanni that the new teacher had failed, then Ellen and Aunt Ruth would be back in their car, searching for another safe haven.

She couldn't let that happen. Not to Aunt Ruth and not to her own baby.

"But what about Nicky?"

"Clarice doesn't think you can help him."

"I'd like to try." Ellen had not gotten this far just to be stopped by a fearsome woman with bitterness in her craw. "My degree is in special education."

She started to tell him about one of her former students, Elizabeth, who tested on the high end of the autistic scale and who looked at her feet and barely spoke in a whisper when she first came to Ellen's class.

But had she already revealed too much? Wouldn't a husband looking for a runaway wife post all the facts of her life for the world to see?

"Thank you, Eve. We'll see."

When he left the school tent, Ellen might have cried if the little girl with wings hadn't saved her.

April popped out of her chair. "Miss Stah, can I wead fust?"

"You can read?"

"She sure can," Bobby said. "But don't get her no Dick and Jane. She don't like them baby books."

"What do you like to read, April?"

"Huckabewwy Finn."

"She reads Mark Twain?"

"Just the comic books. Look at this, Miss Star." Bobby somersaulted across the tent and honked his nose at Aunt Ruth, who dropped her knitting and pretended to jump out of her skin.

"See what I can do!" Lucy made a quick pyramid of the

three chairs and then balanced on top, her tutu standing out around her like the petals of a flower.

There in the blue and white circus tent, Tupelo vanished as completely as the lost city of Atlantis, and with it Wayne Blair. Body blows and hair pullings faded until they were no bigger than a piece of straw under Ellen's feet, something she could walk all over without thinking twice. She was Eve Star, a woman reborn, laughing with circus children and learning from a four-year-old with wings.

Yesterday was a thousand years away, and tomorrow a dream made possible.

From the back of the school tent, Aunt Ruth nodded at her and smiled.

RAZZ SAW HER THE minute she came into the cook tent, the strangely disturbing girl flanked by the formidable old woman who slept with a shotgun, and three of the circus children: Jocko's kids and that cute little Kuzmicki kid who was the spitting image of her mama.

Not that he had any personal interest. But wasn't it his business to watch after the interests of the circus? If a circus owner couldn't keep tabs on newcomers, who could?

The kids liked Eve Star. That was as obvious as if Betsy was standing in front of his nose. The way they sat as close as they could, chattering nonstop, and the way she was smiling so her eyes lit up told him three things. She was good with kids, they liked her, and she liked them.

The old woman caught him staring and glared like she might be planning to gouge his eyes out. He turned his attention back to his pinto beans, but not before he'd seen Magic Michelle, who'd inherited her mother's way with birds, take her seat beside the new teacher, and Indian Joe sit down by the old woman. Joe struck up a conversation like it was going out of style and he had only five minutes to speak his mind.

"Mail call." Mark DeChello walked into the cook tent with a small packet of letters, but Razz knew none of them would be for him. Sometimes circus folk, usually performers, left behind families and schedules so that loved ones could send letters timed to arrive at the local post office where the circus was playing. It was a haphazard way to stay in touch, but mostly it worked. Sometimes not. Acts of God and the U.S. Postal Service played a hand, and some letters never found their rightful owners.

As the mail was passed around, Razz was glad to be distracted by Al.

"I could use a good prime rib." He plopped his plate down beside Razz and heaved into his chair. "What's eating you?"

"Why should anything be eating me? I'm just a dried-up old fossil with a tiger."

Al tried to turn his head far enough to look all around the cook tent, but Razz could have told him that wouldn't work. He was too fat and too old and too stiff.

"What?" Al shouted. "Where's Nicky? She's supposed to be teaching my grandson!"

"Sit down, Al, before you give yourself a heart attack."

Ignoring Razz, he stared at the new schoolteacher, his face getting redder and redder. Razz had been kidding about the heart attack, but now he wasn't so sure. Should he get up and lead Al back to his Airstream? He'd be about as easy as a herd of spitting llamas.

Fortunately, the cook tent went as quiet as if President Nixon had walked in. Razz didn't have to glance at the entrance to know what that meant. Luca was here. His arrival was the equivalent of a lightning strike. Everybody stopped what they were doing, especially the women, and gaped for a full three minutes before they could overcome the shock.

He was at the table and holding on to Al's arm before anybody was even aware of him moving. That's how fast and quiet Luca was. Razz approved. The boy was a sponge, soaking up everything the circus had to teach him. His stealth and grace, he'd learned from tigers.

His good looks he got from his mother and his grandmother. God knows, he didn't get them from Al, who looked like a bad chiseling job on a mountain.

"Grandpa, what's wrong?" Luca eased Al back into his chair and handed him a glass of iced tea. "Drink this, you'll feel better."

Al drank his tea, as obedient as Clementine, Indian Joe's most docile elephant. If anybody else had ordered him around like that, he'd have gone into a Great Giovanni rage. Most folks thought the *Great* moniker came from Al's performances as an equestrian, but circus folk knew its true origin. Though lately he was more pussycat than lion, when he took a notion nobody could shake the ground with wrath like the Great Giovanni.

Luca straddled a chair and watched while Al took another long swig of tea.

"What I want to know is, where's Nicky?"

"In town with Mother. Getting new shoes."

"I'm sure she wouldn't deliberately keep him away from his first day in school." Having developed a sudden appetite for pinto beans, Al started shoveling them in.

Razz winked at Luca. Both of them knew full well the regular school season wouldn't start for a few weeks and that in any case, Nicky was too young. They also knew when the Great Giovanni was up to something.

"I'm equally sure that when he gets back with his new shoes," Al said, "you'll take him over to the school tent and introduce him to the new teacher."

Luca glanced over at Eve's table, but if he knew she was the teacher or had any opinion at all about her, he didn't let on. Luca never let on about much of anything. He wound his way through the circus like a river. Seeing him pass by, folks never knew he was the source of the tranquillity and hope that suddenly washed over them in cooling waves.

"The children have taken to her," Luca said.

"She's going to teach Nicky to talk."

A shadow flickered over Luca's face, but he kept a smile turned to his grandfather. Razz wondered what it would be like to have grandsons who loved him like that. But the thought was only fleeting. Dwell too long on what might have been, and you'd drive yourself crazy.

"I'm sure she will, Grandpa." Luca patted his shoulder, then left to get a plate.

"That's how you do it," Al said.

"Do what?" Razz knew perfectly well what his old friend was talking about, but these days young folks took care of everything, including feeding his cats before the matinee, and he didn't have much to pass the time except shooting the breeze with Al.

"Get around Clarice. Do you think she'd sit still for me arguing with her over Nicky?"

"I've never seen Clarice back down from anything, especially not a fight with you."

"All I have to do is plant the idea in Luca's head, and she never knows she's putty in my hands."

Razz doubted that Clarice missed anything, let alone her father's manipulations, but he didn't say so. He cleaned his plate, said, "See you at the Grand Spec," and headed back to his trailer. If he hurried, he could get in a little nap before the matinee, and nobody would be the wiser.

Sheikh greeted him at the door, demanding a belly rub followed by a bucket of clean water. Finally Razz finished with the tiger and stretched out on his bed, but his mind was whirling so he couldn't sleep. What if he overslept and missed the matinee? He didn't believe in alarm clocks.

If he missed the show on account of a nap, Al would suggest getting somebody younger to train the cats and Razz would feel like an old horse too broken down for anything except a mercy killing.

And what had Indian Joe found out about the old woman? What had he been telling her?

Then there was the girl in the Ford Fairlane. He couldn't get comfortable on his bed for thinking about her crumpled up in her car, one foot uncovered and ready to run. Maybe she'd told Magic Michelle something.

"Tarnation!" He rammed his baseball cap back onto his head and stomped out of the trailer.

He found Indian Joe at the menagerie tent with his babies.

"How's it going, Joe?"

"Can't complain."

"Don't guess you've had another visit from the bear?"

"You'd a heard me cussing a mile."

"Thought so."

Betsy reached her long trunk toward Razz and stole his baseball cap. He got it back by trading a handful of peanuts.

"I saw you sitting at the new schoolteacher's table."

"Yeah. Eve Star. Pretty woman."

"I didn't notice. Who was the old woman with her?"

"Mimi. Feisty as hell. Smart, too."

"How's that?"

"She knows about animals. Said she'd been her own vet back in the olden days. Self-taught." Razz just nodded his head. The best way to find out anything from Indian Joe was just to let him talk. "She's interested in tigers. Wanted to know if she could come over and see them. I said circus family is always welcome."

"Where's she from, Joe?"

"She didn't say."

"She ask anything else?"

"Wanted to know who made the circus costumes. Said she sewed. I told her it was Needles."

Coco "Needles" Hart wasn't called Needles because of her sewing ability. Her tongue could turn back a shark.

"The sewing tent sounds like a good place for this old lady. I don't want her coming around the cats and getting hurt. Or any of the animals, for that matter. The horses could trample an old lady to death. And then we'd have a scandal on our hands."

"I didn't think of that, Razz. Next time I see her, I'll tell her she can't come unless you're here."

"I don't have time to baby-sit. Tell her to stay away from the menagerie tent. And keep me out of it."

He stomped off, kicking up hay and dust. If he didn't get hold of himself before the matinee, the cats would pick up on his agitation and take it personally. Cats took everything personally. Show turmoil and they'd rip off a chunk of your hide just to get your attention.

From the direction of the big top, he heard the band warming up.

Now look what the old lady had done. If he didn't hurry he wouldn't even make the Grand Spec.

14

THE SOUND OF MUSIC from the circus matinee drifted into the school tent, and tranquillity washed over Ellen in cooling waves. The woman she'd been drifted away bit by bit, leaving behind a circus teacher filling herself up with joy. Still, the joy was tempered by the sobering thought that Giovanni had looked like a thundercloud when she'd marched into the cook tent without his great-grandson. If the child didn't show up, she'd lose her job.

Pushing the disturbing thought out of her mind, she handed Bobby the fourth-grade reader.

"Let's start with page one, Bobby," she told him, but he had other things on his mind.

Fidgeting like a worm in hot ashes, he grinned up at her.

"Bet you don't know what the circus parade is called."

"I'm afraid not."

"It's the Grand Spec, short for Spectacular."

"He's talking so he won't have to read," Lucy said, and then to show what a good student she was, she ducked her head toward her math book.

April *flew* around the tent on unfurled wings, and in her chair by the opening, Aunt Ruth dozed.

From the big top, the brass band played on, and in the distance an elephant added its trumpet call. Though the setting was unlike any school Ellen had ever seen, she felt the same sense of belonging she always got when she stepped into a classroom filled with twenty-five wooden desks and a view of the playground beyond the window.

Her view through the tent flap was Magic Michelle and her birds, of spangled girls riding elephants heading toward the big top, Indian Joe in top hat running alongside.

She loved that she knew their names, that she and Aunt Ruth had already made friends at the circus. She loved the little girl twirling on wings and the one who hated math, the little boy who struggled to read and the innocence, wonder, and fierce truth they brought into the classroom.

With Bobby finally reading the first story, his finger following the lines, Ellen settled into her chair to make a list of supplies she'd request of Mark.

Suddenly a large shadow blocked the tent opening. Wayne! She ducked her head for the blow and looked sideways toward the intruder. Backlit by the sun, he was tall and well built and faceless. But he was also wearing blue leggings, a gold shirt, and the kind of soft shoes Wayne Blair wouldn't be caught dead in.

He made his way toward her, his movements as fluid and silent as they'd been when he'd somersaulted across the backs of galloping horses. His face, now unshadowed, had the kind of remarkable male beauty that made you want to close your eyes and say a prayer.

"I'm Luca, and this is Nicky."

She hadn't even noticed the little boy. Or if she had, it was only as an extension of his father's shadow.

Father and son stood in front of her, solemn and respectful. But there was something else about them, too, something broken, as if tragedy had latched on and wouldn't let go.

"Hello, Nicky." She smiled but didn't reach toward him. Children who are special, no matter what the cause, need respect and patience. And a child like Nicky, one with nightmares hidden in his eyes, had to be approached with the same caution you'd give a wild canary on the wing. "I'm so glad you came."

Luca squatted beside his son and spoke as softly as wind ruffling the heads of daffodils. There was something so soothing in his voice that Ellen found herself dreaming of moonlight picnics and star-washed creeks and fireflies that sent their language of light across Aunt Ruth's mountain meadows.

Nicky nodded and ran to April, who took his hand so he could fly.

"Now I will tell you about my son." Then Luca, still half kneeling in front of Ellen, told her of the little boy who stopped talking because he'd seen his mother die.

Ellen wasn't aware of crying until she tasted tears. "Please understand that I'm only a teacher who has studied special education. I don't know if I can help Nicky. But I'll try."

"That's all anybody can do." He went quiet, studying her in a way that made her wonder what he was seeing. The scar on her forehead that makeup couldn't quite hide? Her zigzag hairstyle that no woman in her right mind would pay for at the beauty salon? If anyone else had looked at her that intensely, she'd have been uncomfortable, perhaps even afraid. But Luca was a river, deep and cool and soothing. She sat quietly, returning his scrutiny, even wondering what it would be like to dip a toe into the water.

Finally he stood, a blue and gold figure who would have looked at home in Italy among Michelangelo's beautiful statues.

She thought of him, fearless, jumping through a ring of fire.

"I saw your performance. It really was wonderful."

"Sometime if you'd like I'll show you the horses."

"I'm afraid I'm not very brave."

"Perhaps you are braver than you think." He studied her face again in a way that left no doubt he saw beyond her facade, saw her soul, shivering.

"I'll return for Nicky after the matinee. He's very obedient, and he's at home with the other circus children."

After Luca had gone, Ellen watched Nicky racing around the tent with April. She'd studied selective mutism. It had many causes and no identifiable cures. Certainly, the trauma of watching horses trample your mother would be enough to make a terrified child retreat into silence.

And yet, he showed nothing of his thoughts except pleasure in the moment. Like Ellen, he masked his terror with a smile. Watching either of them, you'd never know that deep inside dwelt monsters too horrible to face, dark creatures with claws and sharp teeth just waiting to catch you unaware.

Ellen wanted to fold the little boy into her arms and not let go. Instead, she looked through the tent flap at the sun dappling the coats of twelve white horses and whispered, "Please, God."

Then she left her chair. Somewhere she recalled reading

that play therapy had been used to break the barrier of silence.

"Nicky, will you let me fly, too?" He studied her awhile,
and finally nested his hand in hers, fragile and trusting as a
baby bird. "April will be the wings and I'll be the words. Let's
fly high. Fly high."

Not content to be merely the wings, April parroted, "Fwy
high," while Nicky giggled. "Say it, Nicky. Say fwy high."

Abruptly he sat down and studied his red sneakers that
looked new.

"That's okay, Nicky." Ellen squatted beside him. "You
don't have to talk, but we need you to be the wing man."

"Can Bobby and Wucy fwy, too?" From the front of the
tent, Aunt Ruth snorted and jerked awake. "Can she play,
too?" April ran over to Ruth. "What's your name?"

"Mimi, and I can fly with the best of 'em. I might even get
me a pair of wings."

"You talk funny," Lucy said, and Bobby said, "Does not.
She's just a grandmother, silly," then grabbed Ruth's hand and
led her into the midst of flying circus children.

Seeing the pleasure that bloomed across her aunt's face
made up for the harrowing race across three states, meals on
the run, and nights in the so-called Fairlane Hotel.

They trotted around the school tent flapping their joined
hands, four children and two adults, safe in a world apart until
a shadow fell over them.

Clarice DeChello stood in the tent flap, blocking the sun.

"Mimi, stay here with the children," she told Aunt Ruth,
and then hurried to intercept the woman who had become her
enemy.

Imperious and forbidding, Clarice didn't even bother with the niceties of *hello.*

"I've come about my grandson."

"He's with the other schoolchildren."

"I know."

Would Clarice try to snatch him away?

"Luca brought him to me."

"My son lets his soft heart rule his head, but I don't suffer the same misfortune." Clarice had only two inches on Ellen, but when she drew herself up, she seemed at least six inches taller. "If any harm comes to him, in or out of this school tent, I will hold you personally responsible. Is that clear, *Miss Star?*"

She practically spat Ellen's name. Did she know something? Had she already put her formidable mind to finding out who *Eve Star* really was?

"Mrs. DeChello, I can promise you I won't let Nicky get hurt."

"I'm not talking about skinned knees, *Miss Star.*"

With that parting shot, Clarice marched off. Ellen turned to join the children, but suddenly she had lost her taste for flying.

LATER THAT AFTERNOON AS the spectators poured out of the big top, Ruth sought the breeze coming through the flap of the school tent. She sank into her chair with the relief of a woman getting too old to fly. She began to nod off, and when she jerked upright she thought she might have dozed a little, but she couldn't be sure.

It was the scent of citrus that drew Ruth's attention to the man entering the school tent. Sorrow drifted behind him, attached to the roots of his black hair, his blue jeans, and his white shirt, visible to Ruth as a trail of smoke. But there was something else, too, a sense of light trapped inside like a soul straining toward joy.

Nicky raced to the man who looked ordinary in his street clothes unless you knew how to see his heart. The man swung the little boy onto his shoulders.

"Mimi," Ellen said, "this is Luca, Nicky's dad."

Horses flashed by and Ruth heard the screams, saw the blood, the past stitched to this man as tightly as the soles on his boots.

She put her hand over his and looked into his eyes. "Everything will be all right."

"Thank you."

He left with Nicky, and the other three children hugged her niece before scampering along behind him. When April turned in the tent's opening and called, "Bye, Miss Stah. I wuv you best," Ruth saw her own future, surrounded by children.

Whether it was a vision or just the longings of an old woman, she couldn't tell. And she didn't much care. The aged needed all the dreams they could get. She was going to cling to hers, and she'd dare anybody to tell her any different.

"Knock, knock. Is the circus teacher in?" Magic Michelle trotted into the school tent, looking as ordinary as Josie without her doves and her pink spangles. "I came to invite you both for tea and cookies."

Ruth was hoping for sweet tea served with ice in a Mason jar, but it turned out Michelle loved her tea hot, served from a porcelain teapot that had belonged to her mother, Magic Melinda, and served with cream.

Michelle looked about Josie's age, or a little older. Ruth studied the trailer. You could learn a lot about a woman by her surroundings. Michelle had crocheted doilies on the arms of all her chairs, every last one of them pink. She kept pink plastic flowers in a white plastic vase on the end table, and beside it was a group of framed pictures. A woman who looked just like her and a little girl, probably Michelle and her mother, Magic Melinda, the woman Lola had mentioned in her letters. Michelle in pigtails with the doves. Magic Melinda in pink spangles and a slender woman in white leather.

Lola. Ruth got so excited she nearly spilled her tea.

"Growin' up in the circus, I bet you met lotsa famous folks."

"The Wallendas were with us for one season."

Ruth wondered if Lola had seen the aerialists. She hoped so. She wouldn't mind seeing that old man herself. Karl Wallenda. She'd sit down and ask him what it took for a man of almost seventy to still be sky-walking between tall buildings. Courage was obvious, but it had to be something more, some life lesson she'd like to learn. If you didn't learn what Mother Nature and human nature were trying to teach you, you might as well just curl up and die.

"That must a been a sight."

"It was, but I didn't think of them as famous. For circus kids, the extraordinary is normal. Even somebody as extraordinary as Lola Hall."

Magic Michelle passed around a porcelain plate of sugar

cookies, but Ruth didn't take any. She was too busy trying to breathe.

"You knew her?" Ellen's color was high, but other than that she didn't look any different.

"I was just a little kid." She picked up the photograph and handed it to Ellen. "This is her with my mama. I remember that white leather jumpsuit she wore, and all those tigers. I'd never seen anybody let a tiger stand on his hind legs and put his paws on their shoulders. And I've never seen it since."

"What's so special about that?" Ruth took the photo Ellen handed her, her heart beating so fast it's a wonder she could talk.

"That's the way a tiger brings down his prey."

"I wish I coulda seen it."

"It was amazing. Even Razz won't let his tigers do that."

"Razz?" The room whirled. If Ruth blacked out with visions now, she might as well just die and go on to heaven. Or hell. Whichever would have her.

"Razz Hogan. The tiger trainer and one of Eve's bosses."

He was in love with me, you know.

Lola stepped from the frame of the picture in her white leather jumpsuit and stood by Michelle's white plastic flowers as pretty as you please.

At first, he tried so hard to cover his feelings it was downright comical. He shadowed my every move. When I started training tigers, it was weeks before he'd let me in the cage by myself—and that was just with Rajah and Sheikh, who were still nothing but big pussycats.

Finally, though, he saw I had a way with tigers, and found two more overgrown cubs for me to work with. Seems like tigers and I spoke the same language. They didn't go about broadcasting what they were feeling, and neither did I.

The other reason the tigers and I got along so well is what I learned from Razz. Over at Ringling, Clyde Beatty subdued his cats with whip and chair, but Razz's whip was just for show. Reward, that's the thing that worked.

Sheikh and Rajah already knew to expect me to scratch them behind the ears and talk baby talk, not to mention hand out the raw meat. Anybody who watches animals knows a leader rules the pack. Sheikh was the animal leader, but he allowed me to be the human leader.

As my menagerie of tigers grew, it didn't take the others long to catch on to the pecking order.

Like any family, my tigers and I had our share of upsets. One day, Rajah took umbrage about being the last in line for the circle of sixteen. It was too late to explain to him that the wheel tiger, the one on the end who knows when to turn, was as important as the leader.

We settled our differences with a little scuffle. That tiger outweighed me by hundreds of pounds, but I wasn't about to give him the upper hand. I socked him in the nose as hard as I could and yelled, "Seat!" He finally skulked off, but not before he sideswiped me with claws that tore through my leather jacket and filled my sleeve with blood.

That shook me up a little, but I knew I had won. If Rajah had meant to kill me, he'd have done it in two seconds flat, one to take me down, another to disembowel me.

He was just teaching me a little lesson, that's all. A tiger demands respect. By giving him orders first and explaining later, I brought the battle scar on myself.

See, that's why a smart trainer wears leather. Sequins and feathers were just for show in publicity posters. In a ring with sixteen cats, you want something that's not easy for claws to tear.

That day Rajah ripped into me, I thought Razz was going to pull me from the cat ring and not let me back in. But I played to his soft side, and when the wound healed, I was back in the ring, doing what I knew best.

I wasn't very good at being a mayor's wife and I might have been just as bad at being Josie's mother. But I was good with tigers. And good for Razz, too.

Be patient with him, Ruth. He's like a tiger. He'll keep his true feelings bottled up until something triggers the release.

Slowly Lola dissolved back into the photograph, and Ruth waited for her head to stop spinning.

"Aunt Ruth, are you okay?" Ellen squeezed her hand and held on a minute.

"I'm fine." Ruth set the picture down and picked up her tea-cup, but she had as much talent for subtlety as the old jackass in her barn. The best she could hope for was that Magic Michelle thought her shaking hands were due to the palsy of age.

Michelle was putting the photo back on her table when somebody knocked on her door. The sharp rap was followed by the appearance of a rooster-legged man with a face like a pinched prune.

"Speak of the devil . . . Razz, have you met Mimi?"

"I don't have time for socializing." He glared at Ruth like she'd been the one handing out good looks when he was born and had deliberately passed him by. "I stopped by to ask you to make sure Eve follows you when the circus leaves. No sense in losing another teacher."

He stomped off without another word.

"Razz's not much on manners," Michelle said.

"If you ask me, he ain't got none."

"You're right, Mimi. But he has a good heart." Michelle turned to Ellen. "The big top will come down after the last show. Most of the circus will leave here around midnight, but performers usually sleep and catch up in the morning. Where's your trailer parked, hon?"

"I'm not in a trailer. Yet. I'll find you in the morning and follow in my car."

"Listen, the cook tent will be gone. You and Mimi come over here around six and I'll fix breakfast."

"I'll pay you."

"I don't want your money, kid. But I'll think of something."

Michelle hugged Ellen and even Ruth, prickly as she was. That woman's heart was so big, the drumbeat of it followed Ruth after they left the trailer and all the way across the circus backyard.

Still, as good as it was to have a friend who obviously felt motherly toward Ellen and could made tea cakes might nigh as good as hers, Ruth couldn't say she was sorry to leave. In the circus backyard, she got back her wind and her wits both.

That Razz was going to be a cagey one. But Ruth had never seen anything, man nor beast, that she couldn't outsmart, outlast, and outfight if she tried.

"Aunt Ruth, I was thinking that if I had a hand puppet, I could use it with Nicky. Let the puppet talk for him until he's comfortable enough to talk for himself."

"I can make one."

"Can you make an elephant?"

"Give me enough skeins of yarn, and I can knit a slipcover for the Empire State Building."

15

WHEN THE CIRCUS FOLDED, the magic vanished from the pasture in Cusseta like fireflies trapped in a colored jar. With the props and lumber and riggings gone from the big top, the quarter poles and cable holding the bail ring loosened, the red and white striped canvas floated to the grass with a sigh as audible as a woman tucking in her last rambunctious child and getting ready for bed.

In the light of a moon and stars so close they looked like you could reach up and touch them, roustabouts unlaced and folded the canvas, while Indian Joe walked Betsy around the perimeter where she snatched stakes out of the earth with the ease of a child removing candles from a birthday cake.

Soon the lot would be vacant again. Except for the trampled grass, you'd never know it had been the source of such wonder the entire town smiled in their dreams.

Though Razz didn't have to oversee the dismantling of the big top, he was always there. Let Al sleep. Sandusky used to, as well. It was Razz who was vigilant, Razz who knew that if you didn't keep a close watch, everything you loved could vanish. A car could go over a ravine, and with it your life. You could leave a blue-eyed woman asleep in a train car, dreaming of a future free of fists and filled with children, and return to find everything had been snatched away.

In the shadowed pasture behind him was a Fairlane with a mean old woman and a fragile girl. He didn't turn to look. Didn't trust himself to look.

"Damned old fool." Not knowing whether he was talking about himself or Mimi, he strode toward the circus backyard where Magic Michelle's TV was still going.

She came to the door with her hair in curlers and a white dove on each shoulder.

"What brings you here this time of night, Razz?"

"Tell the girl and that old woman to park that Fairlane in the circus backyard. I don't want to wake up and find them murdered in their car."

"I think that's a bit drastic, but the girl does need to be here where I can keep an eye on her. She's pregnant."

"How do you know?"

"A woman sees these things. The way she—"

"I don't want to know."

He stomped off, the lightning bolts that suddenly appeared behind his eyes a sure sign he was developing a migraine. If he didn't relax, the headache would turn full-blown and vicious and he'd have to drop out of tomorrow's show. It would be suicide to nurse a blinding headache and get into the cage with tigers.

Still, all he could think of was the girl being with child. He and Lola had planned to have two, a boy and girl to go with Josie. If she hadn't contracted TB. If she hadn't died. So many ifs.

He went back to watch the spool truck eat up the canvas, but he was careful to stand where he couldn't see the car.

WHEN SOMEONE TAPPED ON the window of the Fairlane, Ellen covered her head with her blanket, thinking Wayne had found her and was going to grab her out of the car.

"Miss Star." A man's voice called to her, but it was not a familiar voice.

Was it the cops? A security guard hired by Clarice DeChello to throw her out? Sent by Giovanni to ask why Nicky couldn't yet talk?

"Miss Star, I didn't mean to startle you." Another small tap. "I didn't mean to scare you."

She peered out from under her blanket, and Jocko the clown stood in the faint light of dawn, studying her through the window with the same intensity Luca had used on his first day in the school tent.

One of the scariest things about leaving behind the life you'd always known and becoming someone entirely different was deciding whom to trust.

"Just a minute," she said. Ellen peeled herself out of the blanket, ran a hand through her sticking-up hair, and stepped from the car.

Jocko Harvey was a tall man, in his element cavorting with clowns but ill at ease in front of her.

"I didn't mean to keep you standing out here, Mr. Harvey."

"Call me Jocko, Miss Star."

"Call me Eve."

Jocko shifted his big feet and Eve fell into silence. But it was not the silence of terror she'd experienced with Clarice De-Chello; it was the comfortable stillness of two people trying each other out for friendship.

"You can follow me and Rose in the caravan to Lumpkin. It's forty miles or so. I don't want you to get lost."

"That's kind of you, but Michelle has already offered."

"She's a good woman. Like her mama." Jocko stuffed his hands into his pockets, and a sudden squawk like a duck made Ellen jump. "Sorry," he said. "Words fail me, but clown tricks never do."

"I see where Bobby gets his sense of humor."

"I'm more like my son than you'd imagine." The way he said it, each word weighted, stole Ellen's breath. "I wonder, Miss . . . Eve. Can you teach me to read?"

The poignancy of his request brought Ellen to the brink of tears. As she stood there, batting them back, the duck in Jocko's pocket squawked again, and he turned to leave.

"Wait. Please, wait. It will be my pleasure to teach you."

"Bobby and April don't know," he said.

"I'll never tell."

"Can you come to the clown tent after school?"

"I'll be glad to."

Jocko got so quiet Ellen thought he'd changed his mind. The duck squawked twice more. "All right then. I'll wait for you after the matinee. And thank you, Miss . . . Eve."

He tucked his head, grinning, then walked back through the dawn while Ellen watched him with the gratitude of a beggar who had come to the circus expecting a crumb only to find an entire banquet laid out before her.

Ruth was still asleep when Ellen climbed back into the car.

She waited till the sun was up, then shook her aunt awake to start another day at the circus.

Michelle, waiting for them at her trailer, had cooked a big breakfast that left even Aunt Ruth speechless.

"Road days, I eat like one of the DeChello horses." Michelle's laughter rang like bells while white doves flew around her head.

By the time they were done eating and Ellen had pulled her Ford Fairlane into the caravan behind Michelle's trailer, she was beginning to feel as much a part of the circus as she imagined her grandmother had when she started training to step into center ring with tigers.

Ellen didn't plan to step into center ring, or any ring for that matter, and she was going to stay as far away from the tigers as she could get. But still, as she drove south across Georgia and Aunt Ruth pulled out her knitting needles to start the yarn elephant, Ellen felt as successful as Noah floating in the ark he'd built to withstand the flood.

Aunt Ruth was making the elephant from bits of yarn she found in her knitting basket. Blue and yellow, purple and green, it would be rainbow colored and exactly what Ellen wanted for Nicky.

Ellen followed close enough to Michelle's trailer not to get lost, alternately admiring the elephant, watching the road, and scanning fence posts for missing posters. There was nothing she could do if she saw her picture, but at least she'd be warned.

By the time she rolled into the circus backyard in another green pasture on the outskirts of Lumpkin, the big top was up and Mark DeChello was directing roustabouts as they erected the school tent. In the distance, Luca and Nicky galloped in a circle atop one of the twelve dancing horses.

Mark saw her watching them. "Nicky's never shown fear of the horses," he said. "Even after the accident."

"That's a good thing." If he ever stopped being afraid of his bad memories, he might talk again.

Behind her a balloon popped, and Ellen jerked, suddenly back in her kitchen, Wayne's fists smashing into her face while birthday candles blazed on his cake. Would she ever stop being afraid?

"Miss Stah!" April pranced up, followed by Bobby and Lucy. "Come see the Andawusions."

Mark laughed. "Go ahead. It will be another hour before the school tent is ready."

"Go on," Ruth told her. "Take a look at them horses. I'm gonna find a shade tree so I can knit in peace. I'll join you later."

Lucy caught Ellen's other hand, and they dragged her across the pasture where the galloping horses looked as powerful as elephants, and twice as dangerous.

"Don't be nerbous," April said. "Are you nerbous?"

"A little."

"Horses ain't gonna hurt you," Bobby said. "All you gotta do is be nice."

"Miss Star is always nice." Lucy stuck out her tongue at Bobby and steered Ellen to the shade of a Georgia pine.

Luca said something that was more music than words, his voice flowing across her like a river, and eleven white horses began to march while he and Nicky galloped toward her on the twelfth. April clamored for a ride, and he helped her up behind Nicky.

"How about you, Eve? Would you like to ride?"

"Not today."

He saw her fear, acknowledged it with a nod, then led the horse off at a pace that wouldn't have scared a kitten.

"Wait," she called, and without a word he turned back and helped her onto the horse.

Atop the big white stallion, she thought of women who scaled cliffs and swam rivers. She thought of women who flew planes and piloted boats and navigated their own homes free of flying fists. Something inside her unfurled, a small kernel of hope.

Today she was a woman with an ever-growing circus family—Michelle who served her tea; the children who called her Miss Star; Indian Joe who sought her and Aunt Ruth out in the cook tent; Jocko who would be waiting for her in the clown tent to teach him the magic of words; and now Luca who trusted her with his son and taught her the language of horses. Today she was a woman brave enough to ride a huge circus horse. Underneath the tree, Lucy and Bobby applauded.

IN SPITE OF THE headache that threatened to fell him, Razz saw the schoolteacher on the horse. How could he help it? She and the children were laughing and having so much fun, even the roustabouts noticed. Instead of going around with their usual sourpuss looks, they smiled while they worked, and some of them even whistled.

Razz stomped off to find Michelle. She was in her trailer feeding the six birds she said would die of a broken heart if they stayed in the menagerie tent with her others.

"What's wrong with you, Razz?"

"Why should anything be wrong with me?"

"Your eyes are all bloodshot and your head's tilted sideways. Have you got another migraine?"

"If I have it's from that old woman and the teacher. I don't like them sleeping in the car."

"I don't, either, Razz. But it's not my fault."

"Ask her to stay with you."

"I already did."

"When?"

"This morning at breakfast. I told her and Mimi if they could stand the bird feathers to move in with me."

"What'd she say?"

"'No, thank you.' She's an independent little cuss."

So was somebody else he knew.

"I won't take your charity." Lola snapped the whip better than he did, her a little slip of a woman who had just barely learned how to make leather sing, and him the seasoned big-cat trainer.

"You're not getting into the ring with lions and tigers."

"If you won't teach me, I'll go over to Ringling. I'll bet they'd love to have a woman in the cat cage."

He gave in. How could he not? Nobody could resist Lola.

They started with Sheikh and Rajah, three hundred pounds and growing—and putty in Lola's hands. Next he'd found her two more half-grown tigers, young enough to be teachable and too young to be feeling their oats.

The first time one had scratched her, he thought he'd die. He'd dressed her wound and made her stay out of the cat cage till it healed. Let a tiger smell weakness, and he takes gleeful advantage.

It wasn't long before he learned Lola didn't have any weakness, not a jot. He'd been in the cage and she'd been watching on the sidelines when Congo took off half his scalp.

Roaring into the cage like a fury, Lola grabbed his whip and backed off a five-hundred-pound lion with a taste for blood while Al and the cage man got Razz out.

After that, there was no question that Lola could do whatever she set her mind to.

Razz beat back his memories.

"We'll just see about that." He stomped off to see Al about the show, but Michelle didn't comment. She was like her mama, steady and reliable through and through. The circus could use more like her.

THOUGH SHE HAD HER knitting needles and yarn, Ruth didn't go looking for an oak tree. She guessed she ought to feel guilty about her little white lie, but she didn't. Maybe she'd live to be a hundred and maybe not. Before she died, she had things to find out.

As she made her way across the circus lot, Clarice DeChello stepped out of the manager's trailer and stared at Ruth like she had cow shit on her shoes, but Ruth didn't mind. She saw Clarice's heart as clear as she could see the menagerie tents in the distance. It was puckered on the edges where sorrow and fear had worn it down, but at the center, it still beat with a mother's love.

"Howdy." Ruth waved at her, smiling, and then kept on walking. She wasn't one to stop and fix things the universe would take care of in its own time.

Straw crunched under her shoes, and the familiar smell of

animals announced she'd finally reached her destination. The line of elephants swayed over their water buckets, some dipping inside to take a drink and others spraying their backs. They reminded Ruth of oversize children playing under a water hose.

Suddenly a soft gray trunk reached toward the yarn in her hand.

"Better step back, Mimi," Joe called. "Betsy loves to play tricks." He barreled forward, took her arm, and led her away from the menagerie tent.

"Wait. I was comin' to set a spell with you."

"I don't have time to socialize, Mimi. There's too much going on with the menagerie today."

"You got a sick animal in there? I know a right smart of stuff about 'em."

"The boss likes me and Big Glen to take care of the animals."

He turned red in the face and hemmed and hawed. Ruth didn't need a vision to tell her when somebody was telling the truth and when they were making up the story as they went along.

"What's wrong with you, Joe?"

"Me? Nothing."

"Then how come you actin' like I got the plague and you can't get rid of me fast enough?"

"Aw, Mimi." He scratched under his cap. "I can't let you come in the menagerie tent. That's all. You might get hurt."

"All right." She could pretend, too. "How about if we set on this bale of hay out here?"

"Maybe that'll be all right." He propped his foot on one

bale and Ruth sat on another. "What you got there, Mimi?"

"Elephant. I'm makin' it for Nicky." She stuffed the yarn into her apron pocket. "I ain't gonna beat about the bush, Joe. I consider you my friend."

"Same here, Mimi."

"There was a famous tiger-training lady here a long time ago. You ever hear anything about Lola Hall?"

"That was before my time, but yeah, I heard about her. She's a circus legend. They say there was no tiger trainer before or since who can equal her, even that hotshot over at Ringling."

A mist appeared in front of Ruth, and she peered at it, expecting Lola to float by. But it turned out to be nothing more than spray Betsy had aimed in their direction.

"What do they say about her?"

"When she was in the center ring, they say her hair glowed like a halo. Some even say you could see faint outlines of wings in the glow."

"Guardian angels watching over her."

"I don't know that I ever heard anybody say that, Mimi, but yeah, I guess it might be true."

There was no guessing for Ruth. How many times had she gotten down on her bony old knees and asked for heavenly intervention for her sister? Before today, she'd figured God wouldn't pay any attention to a tough old bird like her.

"Anything else you know about that legend?"

"Only some stuff I heard the women say, stuff I don't put much stock in."

"What women?"

"Jocko's wife, for one. I think Needles Hart was talking about it, too." He pulled a handful of peanuts from his pocket.

"I've got to get going, Mimi. My babies get impatient if they don't get their treats."

"Thanks, Joe. I won't say a word about bein' here." Ruth was so full of gratitude she'd bet anybody watching her trot toward the school tent would see an old woman whose head was touching the clouds.

LULLED BY THE SOUND of Aunt Ruth's knitting needles and the stumbling voice of Bobby as he read aloud, Ellen could almost believe that all her days would be like this, her baby's first flutterings in her womb, the sound of circus music outside her door, and Nicky cuddled into her lap, Luca's child who was now wedged as close to her heart as her own.

Something fierce rose up in her, a mother's determination to open up the silent world for this child of her heart and hear him speak in the same beautiful river of words as his father.

Still holding Nicky, she leaned down to pat Bobby on the head.

"That's great, Bobby. You're making wonderful progress." Would Jocko be as quick to learn as his son? Ellen could hardly wait to find out. "I want you and Lucy and April to play at the fun table now."

She settled the three children in a corner of the tent where she'd arranged picture books, coloring books, and crafts, then she led Nicky to a quiet corner where they sat cross-legged on one of Aunt Ruth's handmade quilts.

"We're sitting in Mimi's flower garden, Nicky." She ran her hands over the patchwork of pink and yellow flowers, their green stems and leaves covered in the tiny cross-stitches her aunt had made. "Feel how pretty they are."

He sat without moving, staring at her with solemn regard. Still, she continued her quiet exploration of the quilt design.

"If these flowers could talk, what do you suppose they would say?"

He made no attempt to answer her, but reached toward a red flower. For a heartbreaking moment, his hand hovered there, and then he snatched it away and shrank back into his silent world.

"I think the flowers would sing, Nicky." Trying to imitate Luca's soothing tone when he talked to the horses, Ellen began to sing. Though her voice was nothing like the flowing river of his, it was passable. And the song was as familiar to her as her own hands: "Deep and Wide." How many times had she sung that while her students joined in?

Deep and wide. Deep and wide. There's a fountain flowing, deep and wide.

There was a quiet tenderness in the song that made her baby stir. Even Nicky leaned forward, as if his hearing had vanished along with his voice, and he was desperately trying to catch the words.

"We can even make the fountain with our hands, Nicky." As she sang, she caught his little hands and moved them in a flowing motion. Slowly the other children gathered around, moving their hands and singing along.

Nicky's face bloomed with wonder, and when Ellen let go

of his hands, he continued to flutter them in wondrous imitation of waters flowing through a river.

Heady with her progress, Ellen glanced toward Michelle, who had just entered through the tent flap.

"Hey, Eve." Michelle was dressed in a pink spangled costume. "Big Al wants all the children for the Grand Spec this afternoon. Don't ask me why."

Bobby, Lucy, and April raced out of the tent whooping.

"Where should I take Nicky?"

"Don't worry, kid, I'll see that he gets where he's supposed to be. Are you coming to the show?"

"I think Mimi and I will just rest awhile."

"No sense staying in a hot tent. Use my trailer."

Ellen didn't want to be a bother, but there was Aunt Ruth, who could probably use some respite from the heat.

"Thank you."

"Door's open. Make yourself at home."

WITH THE TV GOING and the teapot waiting on the stove, Michelle's trailer felt like home. Ellen made tea while Aunt Ruth sat on the sofa and ran her hands over the photo of Magic Melinda and Lola.

"She looks happy. Don't you think she looks happy, Ellen?"

"I think my grandmother must have been very content here. I am. The circus is beginning to feel like home, except better." She placed Ruth's cup on the coffee table and sat down with her own. On the TV screen, Phil Donahue strolled onto the set in front of a live studio audience. "Do you want to watch something else, Aunt Ruth?"

"Leave him on. He ain't smart as Paul Harvey, but he'll do to pass the time."

Leaning back with her cup of tea, Ellen thought about her small stash of money and wondered how much more she'd need before she'd feel comfortable buying a trailer. Just a small one. Ruth deserved four walls, and so did her baby. She'd have to get one before winter, no matter what.

"Today we have two special guests." Phil Donahue's toothy grin filled the screen, as if his guests were something to smile about.

As the TV audience applauded, Ellen wondered how she'd ever find a place that sold fake IDs and how she could get pre-natal care in a traveling circus. She worried about Nicky, about whether he'd ever trust her enough to talk, and if she could keep her job, regardless.

"With us today," Phil said, "are Josie Hall Westmoreland and Wayne Blair." Ellen turned to stone, cold, nerveless, and unmoving. "They're here to talk about a wife and daughter missing for almost a week."

Wayne leaned forward, his face filled with concern. "I want my wife back. I won't rest until she's home where she belongs." He draped his arm around Josie. "And neither will her mother."

"I'd like to shoot him," Ruth said, while the TV Josie twisted a lace-edged handkerchief and dabbed at tears. Ellen tried to breathe.

"This thing is driving us crazy," Josie said. "We don't know if somebody kidnapped her. We don't know if she's dead or alive. All we know is that we love her and we miss her and we want her back."

Did her mother miss her? Did she wonder why Ellen had

run? Did she remember her daughter's long-ago plea for help and regret her bad advice?

Still, she missed Josie, missed the endless chatter, the barbecues in the backyard, the Sunday dinners around the dining room table. She even missed the gold shag carpet in the living room.

Ellen put her hands over the growing lump where her baby lay snug in the womb, trusting its mother would never let her down. From the TV screen, Phil Donahue seemed to be looking right at her.

"This grieving husband and mother have offered a twenty-five-thousand-dollar reward for any tips that will lead to the return of Ellen Blair."

A picture flashed across the screen, Ellen standing on the beach smiling, her hair blowing in the wind and her head-to-toe bruises covered with a caftan.

"We'll stop at nothing." Wayne glared at the camera as if it were Ellen and he intended to take off her head. Then, probably thinking better of it, he composed his face and posture into grief. "We think her great-aunt, Ruth Gibson, might be with her."

A grainy picture of Ruth flashed onto the screen, taken the last Christmas Josie had allowed her to attend the family's celebration in Tupelo. Her hair was mostly brown and her face only partially lined.

"Ain't nobody gonna know me from that."

Ellen agreed, but she didn't trust herself to speak. If she opened her mouth she might start screaming and never stop.

Phil Donahue's mouth was moving, but Ellen couldn't hear anything except the screams she was holding inside. The pictures were flashed side by side with her home phone number in bold black letters underneath.

The man who had sold her the Ford Fairlane would see the show and call to collect his reward. The boy in Walgreens who advised her to get a dog would suddenly remember and seize his opportunity to strike it rich. Even worse, Clarice DeChello would race to tell the Great Giovanni, who would drive her from the circus.

"Somebody will tell." She clapped her hand over her mouth. Give voice to fear, and it can turn around and claw you to pieces.

"Now, you listen to me." Ruth rubbed Ellen's cold hands. "Ain't nobody gonna get you while I got breath and a shotgun."

A laugh bubbled up and Ellen's fear almost gave way to hysteria. "I should have known Wayne wouldn't settle for a local TV station."

"How'd that jackass get on national TV?"

"He has investment clients in Chicago. For all I know, Phil Donahue is one of them."

And she was sleeping in a car, in plain view of anyone who passed by, as vulnerable as a newborn bluebird, an easy target for wagging tongues and dark dreams that will rip you to pieces if you're not careful. If you don't keep a close watch every waking minute. If you don't forget to look over your shoulder. If you don't forget to wear sensible shoes so you'll be ready to run.

A feather from one of Magic Michelle's doves drifted through the living room and settled on the coffee table beside Ellen's tea, a white question mark. She reached for it, but her aunt stayed her hand.

"Don't. I gotta see."

Ruth's eyes turned misty and she seemed to be shrinking inside her calico dress, the outlines of her growing so faint she threatened to disappear altogether. Ellen blinked, desperate to hold on to sanity before her own fear caused her to lose everything she loved.

"Wayne ain't close. He's flittin' around the country with no more idea of where he's gonna land than a feather."

Ellen lifted her teacup and breathed.

RAZZ'S BLINDS WERE CLOSED against the sun, which would pierce his eyes and make his headache worse. He had a cold cloth on his forehead, warm socks on his feet, and the TV turned down low. He'd have turned it off altogether except lately he couldn't stand silence, couldn't bear the thought that he might die alone without even the company of some fool on TV urging him to use Preparation H.

When Phil Donahue announced Wayne Blair and Josie Hall Westmoreland, Razz got up so fast the bath cloth flew across the room and he nearly broke his fool neck slipping on the floor in sock feet.

He searched Josie's face for her mother, but didn't find a single thing of Lola except the blue eyes. Still, if things had turned out differently, she would have been his daughter. She'd have lived all over the country in train cars and a canvas big top. She'd have loved balloons and cotton candy and tigers.

The stern woman on the screen didn't look like she'd ever had anything to do with the circus, let alone been born to one of the greatest circus stars of all time.

A picture of the girl flashed across the screen, her hair exactly like Lola's, her lips turned up in the same wistful smile he'd seen when he first pulled Lola out of the wisteria. Ellen Blair had chopped off her hair and dyed it a torturous red. Ellen Blair was using heavy makeup to cover gashes and sleeping in an old car. But there was no mistaking Lola's granddaughter.

"I want my wife back," Wayne Blair told Phil Donahue. "I won't rest till she's home where she belongs."

Razz shook his fist at the man on the TV screen. "I'll bet you won't, you lowlife piece of shit."

He could spot insincerity and bad intentions a mile away. Even through the blur of a migraine and a weak TV signal, he saw that Wayne's concern was as false as the scales on Slither Jones, who passed himself off on the midway as the Snakeman.

Razz's head was hurting so bad he thought it would explode. Let it. If Wayne Blair showed his face around the circus, he'd take his leather whip to him. And if that didn't work, he'd take Indian Joe's bull hook.

He put on his shoes and left the trailer, his teeth set against the jarring pain in his head.

He found the arrow man in the menagerie tent feeding the surly llama. Just about everybody did double duty in a circus.

Edna saw Razz coming and aimed a wad of spit. In spite of his head, Razz sidestepped.

"She nearly got you that time." Big Glen Newcomb was the only one who would have pointed that out and then laughed about it. He was a jovial soul, large as a freight train and black as patent leather if you cared to notice, which nobody in the circus did. He did his job in the menagerie tent, then left in the midnight hours ahead of the circus to post eight-by-five-inch signs to mark the route to the next site. The signs were printed with a red G fashioned with little arrow-shaped caps to signify the Great Giovanni Bros./Hogan & Sandusky Circus. Arrows pointed up meant *go straight ahead*. Pointed down meant *slow down and get ready for a change*. Sideways meant *turn*. A host of arrows meant *You're Here!*

A good arrow man kept the show from getting lost, an easy thing to do on backcountry roads. A good arrow man could find just the right fence post and telephone pole for the signs, then sense when somebody had come along to rip them off, and go back to put up more.

Glen was one of the best. And he knew how to keep his mouth shut.

"I've got a job for you, Glen."

"Anything you say."

"When you leave to put up arrows, you might find posters about a missing woman named Ellen Blair. Pretty thing. Blond hair. Tear every one of them down and bring them to me."

"You got it. Anything else?"

"If you see a brown-haired man about six feet tall messing around the circus backyard, asking questions that are nobody's business, drag him out of there and ask questions later."

"Nobody will get past Big Glen."

16

IN THE MIDDLE OF the night, while Ellen tossed with night-mares in her Ford and Ruth dreamed of filling Wayne's britches with buckshot, Razz waited with a cold rag on his head for the arrow man to bring posters of a missing blond-haired woman. When none were reported, he removed the compress, took an aspirin, and waited for dawn to take the circus to Preston.

It rained for both shows. The animals were surly, the crowds were small, and nobody could wait to get out of Preston. Rains followed them to Plains, the light truck got mired in the mud, and even pot roast served in the cook tent couldn't lift the mood.

The only person happy about the rain was Ruth. She sat in Magic Michelle's trailer for two days knitting and hoping it was raining on her corn crop in Arkansas.

By the time the circus arrived in Americus, Georgia, the sun was shining, the mood had lifted, and the multicolored elephant puppet was finished.

After another restless night in the Fairlane followed by a quick bath in Michelle's trailer, Ellen left Ruth and the bird trainer having coffee and stepped outside. The air was so fresh she could almost taste the dew. It was the kind of golden morning that wiped out fear and sent nightmares back into the dark corners of the mind.

The circus was beginning to feel like a real home to Ellen. Her spirits lifted when Indian Joe headed her way.

"Good morning, Eve." He doffed the cap that obviously was used for more than keeping the sun out of his eyes. Here was a man who valued time spent with his *babies* more than time spent with a hairbrush.

"How are you, Joe? Are you off to see about your elephants?"

He laughed. "Better start calling them bulls unless you want Jocko's little boy to correct you."

"More than likely, it would be April. Bobby's a perfect little gentleman."

"You bring that out in everybody." Joe tipped his cap again. "Tell Mimi I said hello."

Joe was whistling when he left. It was such a perfect sound for the morning, Ellen decided on the spot she'd teach her baby to whistle.

She'd just turned to go back into the trailer when Jocko's wife, Rose, saw her.

"The children talk of nothing but their pretty new teacher." Rose took hold of Ellen's hand, but Jocko just smiled, a man sharing a secret with the woman who was rapidly moving him through a first reader.

"Bobby and April are delightful." Ellen included both of them in her smile. Had Jocko told his wife about his reading sessions? He'd never said and she hadn't thought to ask. "Especially April."

"She's a live wire, like her dad." When Rose punched Jocko in the ribs, it sounded like the crack of a ball against a wooden bat. She giggled. "That's my Jocko, always with a trick in his pocket."

"So I've heard," Ellen said, and Jocko's grin widened.

"If you haven't eaten yet," Rose said, "come to the cook tent with us."

"Thanks, but I'm delivering this to Nicky." Ellen held up the rainbow-colored yarn puppet. "Mimi made it."

Rose heaped extravagant praise on the yarn elephant and Mimi, too.

"Have fun, then, Eve. Ready, Jocko? I'm starving."

"Eve." Jocko's voice rumbled on bass notes like a bassoon. "One of these days I'll show you how I camouflage my movie star looks as a silly buffoon."

"Movie star looks, my foot." Rose poked her husband again, and the bat cracked against the ball again. "Come on before you tell a fib so big you can't get out of it."

Rose trotted off, dragging him along, but Jocko looked back over his shoulder. "I'll teach you the tricks of clown makeup, Eve. *Soon.*"

He knows something. The truth rang through Ellen as clear as the music of the morning, hammers against metal and thundering horses' hooves mixed with animal calls from the menagerie.

Suddenly it seemed ridiculous to Eve that she'd ever thought she could escape the long reach of Wayne Blair. Her arms were now bare of both bruises and long sleeves, but she still had to use makeup to cover the scars on her forehead. She glanced in every direction before heading toward the edge of the pasture where Luca and Nicky galloped on a white horse.

Ellen shaded her eyes to get a better view. How natural they seemed, how happy, father and son, their laughter floating behind them like a yellow kite. Would Wayne have loved their child, or would he have seen it as a threat to his position, a nuisance who had to be dealt with?

Luca saw her and dismounted, then swung Nicky from the horse. The little boy ran toward her with his arms wide open. She squatted to catch him, then shifted his weight to her left arm and slipped her right hand into the puppet she was carrying.

Using her best elephant voice, she said, "Good morning, Nicky. My name is Rainbow and I'm your new friend." The little boy giggled. "Can I play with you?"

When he nodded, Ellen slipped the puppet onto the little boy's hand, then moved the mouth while Rainbow said, "Good morning, Luca."

Luca solemnly shook the elephant's trunk. "Welcome to the circus, Rainbow. I hope you like horses, because I know a little boy who will take you for a ride."

Nicky nodded, and Ellen manipulated the puppet to say, "Oh, yes!"

Luca took his son. "First, I want to show Rainbow a new trick. You, too, Eve." Luca whistled and the white stallion trotted to his side. "This is Aladdin, and he loves to have his muzzle stroked."

Nicky was first to reach toward the horse, giggling as he used the puppet's trunk.

Though Ellen had ridden the horse once, it was Luca who had helped her up. Huge and powerful, the Andalusian could rear up and come crashing down on her skull. One blow from his hooves could break her like a melon.

She stepped back. "I'm not very good with animals." Except that summer day in her childhood when she'd played with a tiger. So very long ago the memory had no more substance than a faded watercolor. "I've never even had a dog."

She'd asked for one when she was seven, but Josie had said, "They shed," and that was the end of the discussion.

Luca studied her with eyes that held a river of heartbreak. But beyond, deep in the place where memories and dreams still waited, you could see something else, a single spark that refused to die.

"Don't be afraid, Eve. Staying on when he gallops is the hard part. Saying hello is easy."

She anchored herself to that single, glowing spark and held on. Simply held on.

"If Nicky can do it, so can I." When she reached out and touched a velvety soft muzzle, she felt something inside her sigh, let go, stand up, and shout *yes.* "Hello, Aladdin. I'm Eve, and I think you're spectacular."

Luca slipped a carrot from his pocket to hers. "This is what I want you to do." He leaned over and whispered in her ear, his voice as soft as the wings of hummingbirds. When Luca straightened up, he said, "Be commanding. Take charge."

"Aladdin, kneel!" she said. To her astonishment the huge horse went down on his forelegs, and stayed there waiting. She climbed onto his back unassisted while Nicky applauded.

"Now, give him the second command and the reward."

"Aladdin, up!" Horse and rider rose, and Ellen felt as if she were sprouting wings. If a woman could grow wings, she could fly over disaster and heartbreak and fear. She could soar beyond the reach of a raging husband, a tracking dog who chased lost souls to hell, and a famous TV host who offered a reward for wayward wives.

"Brava, Eve," Luca said, his praise sweeter than strawberry ice cream on a summer day. He settled Nicky onto the horse, then vaulted up behind her, and they galloped off.

If you glanced up and saw them, you'd see a blur of color in their wake and mistake it for flowers in the meadow. But if you were Ruth, glancing out the window with one hand wrapped around a coffee cup, you'd see how the sunrise and the heart's dreams and the passing of time had braided themselves together into a pink plume of hope.

ONE THING WAS CERTAIN about the circus season: when the town was big enough, you'd see Jimmy Johnson strolling onto the lot, his shoes spit polished to a shine, his red bow tie in place, and a big smile on his face. Jimmy had lots to smile about. He'd made a fortune selling trucks and cars and mobile homes to show people.

Americus was big enough, and Jimmy was just the man Razz had been waiting for. With only a residual twinge from his migraine, he hurried across the lot to the cook tent, where Jimmy had already bummed breakfast and was now handing out yellow plastic ballpoint pens. "Ride with Jimmy" was printed in red across the barrel, and nearly everybody in the cook tent already had one sticking out of his pocket.

"Razz! You old son of a gun! How're the big cats!" Jimmy spoke in exclamation points, a tribute to his lean days as a sideshow barker.

"I've got a proposition for you."

"Are you in need of a new trailer? I've got just the thing! Brand new, shiny as a copper penny! A couch big enough for that pet tiger!"

Heads turned. Razz didn't like his business blared about, especially his current business.

"Finish your breakfast, Jimmy, then come and find me in the menagerie tent."

The animals couldn't talk, and even if Big Glen was about, he'd keep his mouth shut.

Razz headed in the direction of his big cats. If he was the kind of man who believed in the kind intervention of a higher being, he'd thank God for two things: no posters along the roadside for the missing Ellen Blair and a fortune amassed through a lifetime of stinginess.

BY THE TIME THE matinee was over, the new trailer was parked between Magic Michelle's Airstream and the Ford Fairlane, sleek and low, easy to pull, two beds and a living room big enough for a baby crib, a kitchenette and a bath, and a small table where a pregnant woman could put her feet up and sit down with a cup of tea.

Michelle stood in her doorway gaping at the trailer.

"I want you to give it to Eve," Razz said. "Don't tell her where it came from."

"What do you want me to tell her? The fairies brought it?"

"Tell her any damned thing you want. Just don't involve me." He wheeled around and headed off.

"Razz Hogan, don't you dare stomp off! You didn't intimidate my mama and you don't intimidate me."

That's the reason he liked Magic Michelle, and always counted on her. She wouldn't back down from the devil.

"Spit it out, Michelle."

"I want us to come up with a plan. And you might as well drop that scowl."

"Tell her it comes with the job."

"She won't buy that unless Mark says it."

"I don't want Mark knowing, either."

"Then you'd better think of something fast because she'll be out of that school tent and heading this way for tea in about fifteen minutes."

"I appreciate you taking care of her."

"I'm not doing it for you."

When Michelle smiled, the transformation from bordering-on-homely to outright beauty was so sudden you'd be taken aback unless you were Razz, and had seen it a million times, first in her mother and now in her. "I got it."

"What?"

"Never mind. You told me to handle it, and I will." She wiggled her fingers. "Bye, Razz. You're an old softy."

"Don't tell."

"I wouldn't dream of it."

He was on his way to find Al when Jocko caught up with him in front of the marquee, probably to talk about the clown act. Jocko was one of the most inventive clowns on the circuit, and even Ringling had been heard to say so. He was always coming up with some new twist that would send the audience into hysterics. That bit he'd thought of last year with one of the Giovanni Andalusians would go down in circus history. Pretending to be drunk and blundering all around the horse,

Jocko had lost his hat, his pants, and his coat. The sight of Big Jocko running around in pink long johns had the audience howling. But when he'd vaulted over the horse and tumbled over his pile of clothes, then stood up redressed in the whole shebang, the audience went wild.

"How're you doing, Jocko?" It would be a relief to finally hear something besides trouble. When Jocko pulled out a red bandana and honked his nose, it sounded like a freight train whistle. "That gets me every time. I needed the laugh."

"Are you worried about the teacher, Razz?"

You can feel bad news coming in your bones. Razz's felt heavy as Betsy.

"Should I be?"

"I saw her husband on Phil Donahue. If that man ever finds her, there'll be trouble."

"Did you tell anybody else, Jocko?"

"Nobody. Not even Al."

There was no need to ask if Jocko wanted to collect the reward. He'd come close to killing a man just like Wayne Blair. His sister's husband. Somewhere up in Iowa, if Razz remembered correctly. As far as he was concerned, one less abuser would be nobody's loss, but losing Jocko to the circus world would be a tragedy.

"Good. Al's got enough worry with his health and the little boy."

"What do you want me to do, Razz?"

"Keep your eyes peeled, and if Eve's husband shows up, try not to kill him."

* * *

RUTH WASN'T A BIT surprised to discover that the new trailer belonged to Ellen. She'd seen it last night in her dreams, clear as water, the two of them traveling down the back roads with a movable house, four walls with a roof and a little kitchen where she could fry bacon and eggs the way she liked them. Cookie Two never blotted the grease.

"The circus people took up a collection for it," Michelle was saying, but Ruth could see the lie hanging over her head like a gray cloud. Why, she didn't know. And it didn't much matter. Ellen would no longer have to sleep in a car where anybody who took a notion could see her and drag her out.

It wouldn't be long now. Wayne was coming as surely as the storm she'd sensed in the atmosphere since they'd left Plains. She wished she knew when, but that was the trouble with visions. Sometimes the universe just wanted you to figure things out for yourself. All she knew was that Ellen was growing stronger every day, and that was a very good thing.

"I'll have to thank everybody." Ellen was holding on to her new door keys, tears rolling all the way down to her chin.

"I wouldn't say anything, Eve. Circus folks are a private lot. Public displays embarrass us, even when it's simple as a thank-you."

"But, Michelle, how can I thank all of you?"

"You already have. By being kind to the circus children."

"That's easy."

"Not as easy as you think. The last circus teacher was a barracuda. Bobby had his fill and turned Edna loose in the school tent. That fool llama spit all over the place."

"I'll make sure not to get on Bobby's bad side."

A flock of birds black as the souls in hell passed over, and a single feather floated to the ground at Ellen's feet. Bad news was coming.

Ruth put her arm around Ellen. "Why don't we christen our new home?" *Lord,* she'd almost said *Ellen,* and wouldn't that be a mess? "Michelle, you'll have to bring the tea and the teapot."

"I'll bring some sheets, too. You'll need them tonight."

The trailer smelled like new upholstery and possibility. It had brass lamps and gold shag carpet and a blue plastic vase filled with yellow daisies you couldn't tell from the real thing unless you looked close. Their new home was as fine as anything Ruth had seen.

While Michelle and Ellen made tea in the little kitchen, she sat on the blue plaid Early American sofa and searched her surroundings for dark spirits and bad omens. If they were there, they might as well not try to hide from Ruth. She could spot trouble so small it would fit between the cracks of the kitchen tiles.

She searched every nook and cranny, even getting off the couch to poke around the corners of the tiny bathroom. But all she saw was sunlight pouring through the windows.

17

THE CIRCUS PERFORMERS DROVE through the early morning mists, congratulating themselves on their successful show in Americus.

Even Ellen, following Michelle and pulling her new trailer behind her car, felt such a growing sense of freedom she almost forgot to look along the roads for missing posters bearing her name. Seeing none, she breathed a sigh of relief. As the miles clicked off, she planned how she would use the elephant puppet with Nicky.

But Ruth, watching out the passenger side of the window, saw disaster barreling toward the circus with the intent of a wild dog gone mad. It was not a flock of blackbirds that held warnings for Ellen, though Indian Joe had told her that Clarice was threatening to take Nicky to a specialist in Atlanta and tell her daddy to get another teacher.

Instead, Ruth saw blackness hovering over the horizon waiting to swallow them all. Though she squinted her eyes into the distance and concentrated until her head hurt, Ruth couldn't make out what was coming, nor when and why.

She sank back into her seat, relieved she didn't have to race about issuing warnings to folks who might or might not believe her. Just as she was settling into something resembling normal, that damned phantom tiger went streaking past her window.

She was so tired she didn't even want to know. Still, when she looked again, she saw her sister floating along beside the car, her hair in long waves and the fringe of her pink silk robe flying out behind her.

You have to know that I fell in love with Razz. I think it was about the time Congo took off half his scalp and I thought I'd lose him.

It was a miracle for both of us, a love so unexpected, so tender, it made me sit at the window of our car while the train hurtled through the night and dream of how Razz would confront Jim and I'd be free. I imagined a circus wedding, and then the two of us driving up the mountain, husband and wife, to get Josie. We'd let Magic Melinda teach her about the birds and the clowns teach her how to laugh.

There never had been much laughter in the Hall household. Maybe it was those early, joyless years that made me keep looking over my shoulder for disaster, even when I was lying in bed safe with Razz at my side. Maybe I was some kind of magnet for trouble, so that when we stopped in that little Texas town where a few people came into the big top coughing with every breath, I was the one who caught what they had. When the doctor said TB, Razz and I both cried. We knew then: life never does turn out the way you wish it would.

Ruth wanted to hear more, but Lola and the tiger had both vanished and in their place was nothing but deep woods, whizzing by the window so fast they made her head spin.

STANDING IN THE LOT in Plains, waiting for the arrival of the performers, Razz watched the canvas men and Indian Joe with the bulls work to get the circus tent up. Though he'd seen the same thing too many times to count, he never tired of the sight. The big top held so many memories it was almost as if Razz himself were woven into the red and white striped canvas.

"Razz." He turned to see the arrow man striding toward him, his hands full of papers. Razz hurried to meet him. "Is this what you're looking for, boss?"

Missing: Ellen Blair, 5'8", blond hair, blue eyes.

Beloved wife of Wayne Blair, Tupelo, Mississippi.

$25,000 reward for information leading to her whereabouts.

All contact numbers were listed underneath a photograph of Ellen, with the advice that whoever found her could also contact the local police.

"That's it. Keep up the good work."

He hoped Glen didn't see how his hands shook when he took the posters. He hoped nobody noticed when he left. Giovanni often slept through the raising of the big top, but it was unheard of for Razz.

When he stepped into his Airstream, Sheikh shook the trailer with his roar. You can't fool a tiger. He can read moods as easily as he can sense danger.

"My thoughts exactly." Razz hurried by his tiger without even stopping to scratch behind his ears. He spread the posters on his Formica tabletop, six of them. And how many more? How many roadsides, cities, and parks would be covered with the girl's image? He'd need the bird's-eye view of one of Magic Michelle's doves to find them all.

As he sharpened his butcher knife to cut the posters into little pieces, he figured the best he could do was keep them off the roads and keep his eyes out for Wayne Blair.

He still blamed himself for Lola's death. Maybe if he'd been more vigilant, she wouldn't have gotten TB. Maybe if he'd been more sensitive, more generous, she'd have been so happy her body would have refused to succumb to a deadly disease.

His memories threatened to undo him.

"Tell me we can always be this happy, Razz."

It's so early the sun is not even up. Lola's standing on the beach in Galveston, our favorite getaway place and the one we always come back to. The wind blows her hair and her skirt, and waves lap her ankles while the tigers romp in the water like children. Overhead, a seagull tries to call up the morning.

I catch her hand, my heart so full I don't trust myself to speak.

"Tell me you won't let him find me and destroy everything." *She studies me awhile, then squats beside Rajah, who rolls over in the waves so Lola can rub his belly.*

She's strong now, her bruises only a memory, her sleep undisturbed by nightmares, her cat act one of the most famous in the circus. This is what scares me most. With her fame has come publicity. Any man who'd once had Lola would never let her go. Any man looking for her would track the posters, the newspaper stories, straight to the Great Giovanni Bros./Hogan & Sandusky circus.

"Tell me, Razz. Say it so I can believe it . . ."

He glanced up from the rubble of missing posters on his table to the red and gold image of Lola on his wall.

"I won't let any harm come to your granddaughter, Lola. I swear to you."

Razz raked the scraps into a garbage bag and carried it to one of the fifty-gallon drums where the circus trash would be burned.

He was on his way back to the big top when the performers' trailers started filing into the circus backyard. When the Ford Fairlane with the circus teacher's new trailer pulled in, Razz reached for his handkerchief to mop his eyes.

"What's wrong?" Al said.

As big as he was, how could Al have sneaked up on Razz like that?

"Bug in my eye."

"Well, get it out. I'm ready for breakfast and I don't like to eat by myself."

Neither did Razz. As he headed toward the cook tent, he remembered breakfasts with Lola, always a celebration, and remembering, he yearned.

ELLEN WOULD ALWAYS REMEMBER Plains. It was there she had her first breakfast in her new trailer home. Michelle had brought over the fixings, and at the insistence of both Ellen and Ruth had stayed to eat homemade biscuits she declared the best she'd ever had.

"If I ate like this every day, I'd get fat," Michelle said.

"You ought to taste 'em with some of my muscadine jelly," Ruth said.

Ellen held her breath, waiting to see if Michelle would use Ruth's slip as a chance to ask questions about their past.

But she only said, "That sounds delicious," then stood up and said she had to get going. The door popped shut behind her.

"You can quit worryin' about Michelle." Aunt Ruth stood up to gather the dishes. "I seen her intentions clear as day when she come through the door this mornin'. That woman's pure gold through and through. And quit worrying about Clarice, too. I seen her heart. It ain't as bad as you think."

"Are you sure about that?" Though Clarice had not confronted her again, she never failed to turn such a malevolent stare Ellen's way that she felt pierced.

"Positive. Now skedaddle so you can beat them children to the school tent."

Though Ellen arrived fifteen minutes before her usual time, the children were already there, standing in a bright-faced row facing the school tent opening. Luca's child slid his hand into hers as if that's exactly where it belonged, and somehow she believed it did.

"We got a 'prize!" April yelled.

"Not a prize, silly," Bobby corrected her. "A surprise."

Lucy caught her hand. "Come with us."

"My, this is certainly mysterious." Ellen was laughing as the children led her across the yard to the huge red and white striped tent in the center of the circus grounds.

They stepped through the canvas opening, and Ellen felt the kind of awe she did on Sunday morning when she entered church.

Before the show, the big top has the look and feel of a cathedral, the silence so big it sings with its own melody. In the hush, dust motes dance around the ceiling and the trapeze swings as if phantom artists are doing their tricks. The bleachers are empty, the bandstand quiet, the high wire beckons with a mystery all its own. Even the net underneath can't diminish its dangerous beauty.

Standing in the center of the big top underneath the high wire, surrounded by her pupils—Nicky clutching her with one

hand and Rainbow with the other, Bobby in full clown regalia, April wearing a blue sunsuit with her wings, and Lucy in
a pink tutu bouncing on the balls of her feet—Ellen felt her
baby's kick. Though she didn't have Ruth's gift of foretelling,
she took the moment as a sign that her baby belonged under
the big top, that she'd made the right choice in running to the
circus.

"It's quite wonderful." Ellen meant every word. She'd never
seen the big top empty of animals and performers, peanuts and
cotton candy, an audience and a brass band. Tranquillity stole
through her, unexpected and amazing. "Now, what is this surprise?"

"It won't be a 'prize if we tell." April flung out her wings
and raced around the center ring. "Come on, Nicky. You and
Wainbow can fwy, too." The little girl, precocious beyond her
years, leaned over to manipulate the puppet. "Okay," she said
in a squeaky voice.

Did Ellen imagine it, or did Nicky actually move his
mouth?

A noise near the circus back door glued her feet to the
freshly spread hay underneath. Frantic, she glanced around the
empty big top. There was no place to hide, no place where
she'd be safe from a husband determined to drag her home.
But not before he punished her. Not before she felt bone
against bone, fists tear into skin, blood drip from cuts that
would require stitches. Not before she remembered the awful
shame and helplessness of being beat up, body and soul.

"Please," she whispered.

"Surprise!" Bobby yelled, and Magic Michelle strolled
through the back door followed by Aunt Ruth, Jocko and Rose

Harvey, the Kuzmickis, Linda without her ocelot, Luca without his horses, and Needles Hart from the sewing tent.

Then, to Ellen's astonishment, one of the circus owners came into the big top, the man Ellen had first thought to be one of the workers. Why was Razz there? Had he come to fire her?

He might as well have been a phantom for all she'd seen of him since joining the circus. Why had her grandmother named him as her best friend? And what had happened while Lola was with him?

With him cloaked in a shroud of mystery and her cloaked in a secret identity, she might never know.

"Miz Stah," April grabbed her hand. "We gone give you a baf."

"Not a bath, silly," her brother corrected her. "A shower."

Josie had excelled at giving showers complete with petit fours and mints, linens and roses on the table, a Simon and Garfunkel record playing softly in the background. The gifts were wrapped in white embossed paper and tied with ribbon, stacked on a table beside the honoree, who sat in a velvet chair.

Ellen perched on a folding wooden chair Jocko snatched from Giovanni's roped-off section while her circus family piled housewarming gifts at her feet—a pot without a lid Linda said she no longer needed; two cups Rose and Jocko said they'd never miss plus a box of tea and half a bag of sugar; assorted cutlery, a skillet, and an unopened four-pack of toilet paper from the Kuzmickis.

When Michelle put a porcelain teapot into the pile, Ellen

said, "I can't possibly accept your mother's teapot, Michelle. It's your treasure."

"You and Mimi are the best friends I've ever had at the circus. That's the real treasure. Besides, I've been meaning to replace that pot for a long time and get one that's not breakable."

Michelle waved her arms and yelled, "Come on, everybody. Let's show some circus spirit." She started singing, "For she's a jolly good teacher," and everybody joined in. Everybody except Razz, who stood with his cap bill pulled low and his face telling nothing.

Afterward, the circus children did a special show for the teacher, and she saw how it was possible for even an eight-year-old to walk the high wire without fear, knowing that if she fell, the net would be there to catch her.

When the show ended, Michelle called, "The party's over," then she rounded up Jocko and Rose, Linda, and the Kuzmickis to follow Mimi back to the trailer with the gifts. Razz slipped through the tent flap behind them.

Luca watched from afar, waiting for Nicky, Ellen supposed. And why wouldn't he? The child clearly adored him, and at four, he was too young to spend all day with his teacher.

"I wanted to get something to show my appreciation for what you're doing for my son." Luca handed her a folded piece of paper.

At the top it said *IOU*. Underneath Luca had written, *A helping hand . . . Anytime you need help with a job that is too big and too heavy, find me. And if you just need to escape, I'll teach you the secrets of the Andalusians.*

Ellen looked up to say thank you, but Luca had vanished like smoke, and in his place, dust motes danced in the early morning sun.

THAT EVENING LYING IN her new bed, Ellen felt gratitude so big the trailer wouldn't contain it. She slid into pedal pushers and a T-shirt, noting that soon she'd have to buy pants with a bigger waistband and tops large enough to accommodate the child growing in her womb.

Tiptoeing so she wouldn't wake Ruth, she slipped outside. The big top was gone, the midway empty, the trailers scattered across the pasture dark, the performers inside sleeping. A sliver of moon and a scattering of stars wove in and out of clouds that scudded across the sky. In the distance, on the far side of the pasture, a lone figure stood in the midst of twelve galloping white horses.

Luca was a beacon, guiding her from the safe haven of her trailer into the night where anything might ambush her—dark memories, a husband with a soul black as a coal train, her own fear. Still, Ellen walked on, the horses ever in her sight, the man in their midst her goal.

"Eve. You came." Luca separated himself from the horses. "I'm glad."

"I couldn't sleep. I didn't expect to see you and the horses."

"Occasionally, I let Nicky go ahead with his grandfather and I stay behind so the Andalusians can have the run of the lot."

It was amazing to see them running free. A fence around the pasture kept them safe and the man beside her kept them coming back, not by anything he said or did, but simply by

standing there. The white horses flashed by, occasionally slow-
ing their gait and coming so close Luca could have touched
them.

In a movement so fluid she barely noticed, he stepped into
the path of a galloping stallion and held out his hand. The
horse came to a standstill, then lowered his muzzle for a pet-
ting before flying off again into the night.

"How do you do that?"

"It's a matter of trust. Do you want me to show you?"

"Yes."

When he moved behind her and reached around, the memories that trembled through her were so dark they threatened
to block out the moon.

"I won't hurt you, Eve."

"How did you know?"

"When I first brought Nicky to you I saw the bruises."

"I don't want to turn into the kind of woman who is afraid
of her own shadow."

"Then hand your fear to me." He took her right hand. "For
five minutes, just let it all go."

"I'll try." Ellen pictured peaceful meadows and cool
breezes, ice cream on a summer day, the blue swing set she'd
had as a child, and the big-eared, shaggy-coated golden dog
she'd someday get for her child. She melted, flesh and bone,
her arm becoming Luca's as he reached out once more, a gesture of trust so powerful it brought a galloping stallion to a
standstill.

"Aladdin, kneel," he said, and when the huge horse did his
bidding, the two of them slid onto his back as easily as mount-
ing a bicycle.

"Thank you," she said.

The wind took her gratitude and lifted it toward the night sky where the slice of moon came out from hiding behind a dark cloud. There were no sounds expect the pounding of horses hooves and the steady breathing of Luca, who felt like a solid wall of safety. Ellen leaned into that wall, pressed so close she could feel his accelerated heartbeat.

And when it was over, when the horse came to a stop without Ellen even being aware of the command, when Luca guided her to her trailer with the carefulness of a man tending a set of rare and fine china, she stood on tiptoe and kissed his cheek.

"It was magical," she said.

"Which part?" Merriment twinkled from his eyes, so unexpected from this solemn man she felt as if she'd seen into the soul of a star.

"All of it."

Leaving him standing in the moonlight, she went quietly into her trailer so she wouldn't wake Aunt Ruth. And for the first time since she'd left Wayne, Ellen slept that night with both feet under the covers.

NOTHING ABOUT THE LOT on the outskirts of town gave any indication that Albany, Georgia, would be anything except an ordinary stop on the circus circuit. Luca found more than the usual number of rocks that might cause the stallions to stumble, but that was easily fixed with a good raking. Al came down with an upset stomach, which his wife said was another sign he ought to retire, but he blamed the cabbage soup and wouldn't hear of a future without the big top. Edna got loose and created a ruckus with Michelle's doves, but after the feathers settled, nobody was hurt and the mean-tempered llama was led back to the menagerie tent.

Only Ruth saw trouble, dark as smoke, snaking across the midway, curling around the big top and weaving its way through the circus backyard. Sitting at their new kitchen table with its gold Formica top, eggs and bacon and coffee they'd borrowed from Michelle in front of her, she glanced out the window again, hoping the signs had changed. But disaster was so close now it swirled in the air.

"I have a list as long as my leg." Ellen stuffed her list into her purse. "Mark said it would be all right if I don't get back till late. The children will be glad for a summer-school break. You sure I have everything you want, Aunt Ruth?"

"If it ain't on the list, I don't need it." The wind picked up speed, trouble howling at the door. It would be on them soon. The problem was, Ruth couldn't see how soon. "Maybe you oughtn't go."

"We won't get another two-day stop for a while, Aunt Ruth. Nor be this close to a big city. This is my best chance to get the things we need."

"You be careful. Take an umbrella."

Ellen got an umbrella and for good measure tied a scarf around her head. Still, when she left, Ruth's throat closed up and she couldn't swallow her eggs.

She sat there counting to ten until she could finish breakfast. If there was one thing she hated, it was waste.

She cleaned her plate and washed the dishes. Then she took a bath in their fine little bathroom, thinking that circus life was making her soft. Back on her mountain, she'd have been dressed for hours, a bucket of peas already picked and ready to shell on her back porch.

She fastened her calico dress then put on her bonnet and set out across the circus backyard, every step she took full of purpose.

EVEN WITH THE SUN shining Ellen knew better than to ignore Aunt Ruth's warnings. When Ruth said to take an umbrella, you could count on rain. She just hoped it held off until she got back.

She found the shopping center just across the Flint River,

the parking lot filled with cars, a large Wal-Mart in its center. She could get everything she needed there, including maternity tops and groceries. Still, the sight of it brought back that awful day when she'd left Ruth's mountain full of expectation and ended up in a hospital with hope beat out of her, her body held together with a surgeon's stitches.

Suddenly the parking lot looked as wide and treacherous as a rain-swollen river. The wind picked up speed, and the sun ducked behind a cloud. If she were Ruth, she'd read the signs, but she was just an ordinary woman with only a fading scar on her forehead to tell what she'd left behind and why.

Still, she searched for a parking place close to the door, and for a crazy moment even considered parking in a hand-icapped slot and praying she didn't get a ticket. After circling around three times hoping somebody with a car close to the door would leave, she parked the Fairlane by a light pole on the far west side. When she got out, she stood with her back against the door, checking in every direction so she'd be ready to hop behind the wheel and run if she saw anything suspi-cious.

She saw a housewife with two preschool-age children two aisles over, and an old woman using a cane almost at the door. Nothing alarming. Nothing to keep her from enjoying the tri-umph of bare arms and the delicious sense that she had friends at the circus, real friends who cared enough to share their be-longings and a special friend who took her fear so she could ride on a white stallion in the moonlight.

Thinking of the ride, of how Luca had held on to her elbow as he escorted her back to her trailer, she was smiling when she entered the store. When the clerk at the door said, "Good morning, welcome to Wal-Mart," she even said, "Good morning," right back, and meant every word of it.

In the women's clothing section, she smiled back at the clerk, and in the grocery section she didn't have a single urge to throw pork chops at the butcher.

Tupelo seemed far away and Wayne a lifetime ago.

WHEN SHE CAME OUT of the store, her cart loaded with the things she needed and the things she'd bought to surprise Aunt Ruth, cookies and potato chips and two six-packs of Baby Ruths, the junk food she loved but pretended she didn't, the sky had turned ugly and the first fat drops of rain had started to fall. Ellen opened her umbrella, and the wind tried to tug it away. After a brief tussle she won. With her head down against the rain that started pounding the pavement in earnest, she struggled across the parking lot.

She might never have seen the poster if the wind hadn't ripped it off and thrown it at her feet. It landed faceup, just behind her open car trunk. *Missing: Ellen Blair.* Her picture. Her phone number. The big reward a carrot dangled in front of the greedy.

She stared at the poster while the wind snatched her umbrella and sailed it toward the street. Drenched and trembling, she saw posters flying off every light pole, her image landing on windshields, floating into the paths of shoppers hurrying toward their cars.

Who had put them there? When? She was positive the posters hadn't been there when she'd arrived. Had Wayne come while she was buying a pink maternity top? Was he lurking behind the black van one aisle over, toying with her? Was he hiding behind the garbage can, daring her to try to escape? Was that black-haired man hurrying in her direction her husband bent on revenge? Was he in disguise, the large old man bent over a walker, oblivious to the rain, moving fast in spite of his age?

Panicked, Ellen considered jumping into her car and leaving her purchases behind. Ruth would understand why they didn't have new dish towels, a cast-iron skillet for corn bread.

The white horses thundered through her memory, and Luca, holding on to Ellen's fear.

She loaded her bags into the trunk, her hands shaking, her mouth set in lines Josie called her stubborn Gibson look. "You're just like Ruth," she'd say. "When you make up your mind to act like that, nobody can talk sense into you."

Still, when she got back into her car, she drove as fast as she could without slipping off the road in the beating rain.

RAZZ SAW HER COMING, moving faster than any old woman had a right. Lola used to talk about trying to keep up with her on that mountain in Arkansas. He might have admired her grit if he didn't have his own reasons for not talking to Ruth Gibson.

Still, there was nobody but him to confront the old woman. Glen was outside helping Indian Joe with the elephants. The wind was kicking up like the devil, and the last thing a circus wanted in the middle of a storm was a bunch of elephants running loose.

The old woman was building steam, moving in with the steely purpose of a locomotive.

"You can't come in here," he bellowed, but that didn't stop her.

"Watch me," she said, sassier than wildcats in a sack.

"You trying to get yourself killed?" He was so mad he could feel his face blazing. "These animals are dangerous."

"So's that storm a-comin'."

He stopped her just inside the tent. They were toe to toe now, Razz and Lola's sister who didn't look a thing like her. Nor act like her, either.

"Any fool can see a storm's on the way." In fact, he and Al had already canceled the matinee and the evening show, too. The rain that suddenly started pounding the menagerie tent told him they'd been right. This was no ordinary rain; it was a tropical storm, the kind of natural disaster that could spawn floods and tragedies too horrible to contemplate.

"Get out of my way. I've got to make sure the cat cages are secure."

"It's gone take more than locks to beat this storm. I seen it clear and I come to warn you."

Lola had told him about her sister's visions, how eerie it was when her predictions came true.

"Old lady, I want you to go back to your trailer and batten down the hatches so you and Eve will be safe."

"She ain't here."

Razz had cats to tend, circus tents to secure, concessions to shut down, a midway to empty, performers to take care of. But all he could think of was Lola's granddaughter off somewhere in the path of a raging storm.

"We announced in the cook tent we were canceling the shows, for everybody to stick close. How come you let her leave?"

"We didn't hear no announcement, and Ellen's got a mind of her own."

The old lady didn't notice her slip of the tongue, but Razz did. The next thing he knew, everybody at the circus would know the girl's true identity. Though there was no more tight-lipped, loyal group than the circus family, he couldn't guarantee that some newbie wouldn't turn her in for the reward.

"When did she leave?"

"Early this morning, right after breakfast."

"Tarnation, woman!" The howling wind echoed his outrage. "Why didn't you tell me sooner? I'd have sent somebody to bring her back."

"It ain't her I'm worried about." He'd like to know why the devil not, but the old woman was getting so wild eyed Razz wondered if he ought to tackle her and tie her up, call the authorities to take her to a looney bin. "Disaster's a-headin' this way. I seen it clear and true."

The trumpet call of an elephant rent the air, and Betsy went thundering past, followed by Indian Joe. Suddenly the menagerie tent tore loose of its moorings and sailed off, and the alarm cry of animals almost drowned out the groaning of metal. Through the driving rain and howling wind, Razz saw the Tilt-A-Whirl lean sideways and crash to the lot. Midway personnel scattered, their screams picked up by the wind and turned into an awful sound he'd hear in his dreams. In the distance the big top collapsed into a heap of red and white.

Tigers and lions screamed, their outcry overpowered by the roar from the direction of the circus backyard.

"Sheikh!" Razz tore off toward his Airstream, the old lady's scream of "Stop!" hardly even registering.

He never saw the flying skillet from the cook tent that landed upside his head, never knew when Ruth Gibson grabbed him under the arms and dragged him through the swirling water and mud, past Andalusians pawing the air, past the rubble that was once a cotton candy stand, past Betsy raging around the school tent chased by Indian Joe, past Luca carrying a fallen Giovanni. He never saw the effort it took her to heave him up the steps of the new trailer he'd bought in secret, nor the way she had to sit at the kitchen table and rest before she could get him out of his wet shoes and rolled onto his back on the couch.

"You ain't gonna die," she said, but he never heard.

WINDS BATTERED ELLEN'S CAR at an alarming speed, and rain beat against her windshield in sheets that made visibility almost impossible. She slowed to a crawl, and finally a complete halt, caught in a snarl of traffic trying to cross the bridge over the Flint River. Her car swayed, buffeted by winds so strong she feared she'd soon be airborne.

She thought of Aunt Ruth, safe in their new trailer at the circus, she hoped, and of her baby, safe for now in her womb. She wrapped her arms around herself and tried to see her surroundings. The river came to her in brief snatches, the water whipped into muddy waves and rising in anger against the indignity of trees, cowsheds, and even cows flung into its midst.

The car swayed and threatened to overturn. If she could just get out. Ellen pushed against the door, but the wind pushed back. Trapped by a brutal wall of gray, she tried to calm herself by thinking of all the words she knew that started with *X*. X-ray. Xylophone. Xenophobe. Xed out. Or was that exed out?

Was Ellen going to be wiped out, washed off the map before Wayne could find her and do it with his fists?

She'd escaped once. She could do it again. Trying to shut out the howling storm, she thought of escape plans. She was a strong swimmer. If the river rose over the bridge, she could swim to shore—if she could get out of her car. If she got trapped inside, the car would float. For a while. She would rise to the top and breathe the pocket of air trapped there. Until it ran out.

A strange and eerie calm came over her. The curtain of rain parted, and outside her window she could see the river, higher by several feet than earlier, but still under the bridge, still too far away to wash her off the bridge.

Ahead of her, a man emerged from his car. Ellen could do the same thing. Open the door and talk to the man, find out if he knew something she didn't. She had her hand on the door handle when a howling giant bore down on her again, winds at velocities she'd never seen, and rain fierce as tigers.

The second wall of the storm.

Where had she heard that? From Aunt Ruth, who had lived through every kind of natural disaster? Her mother, who for all her pretended shallowness knew about the planets and how many men had walked on the moon and the significance of a total eclipse? Or had Ellen read it?

In front of her, the man was swept off the bridge, flailing his arms, swimming in midair. Or was he trying to fly?

Was April safe, her fake wings tucked around her? Bobby and Lucy? Nicky and Luca and the horses? Ellen wished she'd never left the circus, never decided that a skillet and a new maternity top were more important than staying behind with her students.

The second wall passed, the silence that billowed over the

bridge the kind of quiet that follows tragedies. Ellen sat in her car, momentarily paralyzed by fear and indecision. All across the bridge, people were pouring from their cars, some racing to the railings to look at the river, some bent double crying, others shading their eyes to see what lay ahead.

Ellen got out, but all she could see was a wall of cars and humanity. She clambered onto her hood, and from there clawed her way to the top of her car. Crouched on all fours, she could see for miles it seemed, and everywhere she looked there was water. The road ahead and the road behind were flooded.

There was nothing left to do but wait. And hope.

RAZZ CAME TO WITH a headache as fierce as any migraine he'd ever had. He found the lump on his head, and blinked to clear the fog. The first thing he saw was a vase of yellow flowers. The second, Ruth Gibson.

"You got hit on the head with a flying skillet and I drug you here, if that's what you're wondering. And don't look so sourpuss. I could have left you out there for that elephant to tromp."

"How long have I been out?"

"Through the storm. It ain't no more than a heavy rain now."

"I've got to go. I've got things to see about." He tried to sit up and fell back like an axed tree.

"You ain't goin' nowhere yet." The woman who called herself Mimi wet a cold cloth and pressed it on his head. "While you waitin' to git your legs back, you might as well tell me about Lola."

"Lola?"

"You kept callin' her name."

It was a graceful way to pretend they didn't share a bit of history that was burning them both up inside, her with questions and him with answers he'd never tell.

"She was famous at this circus. A long time ago."

"I wish I coulda seen her in the circus. What was she like?"

The longing in her voice reached out and unlatched the gate to Razz's walled-up past. What she knew of her sister's life at the circus would have come from the letters Lola had written, letters she'd kept deliberately vague in case Jim Hall got his hands on them.

He wondered what it would have been like for Ruth, loving a sister and not being able to see her, to hear her, to know how she was. Ruth Gibson was not asking him to describe a tiger act; she was asking about Lola's well-being. Didn't he owe her that? How many other old women would have so much grit they'd drag a crotchety old tiger trainer through a storm to safety?

"The rest of the performers loved Lola and so did the circus fans. When she took her bows, they'd toss flowers to her, sometimes whole bouquets of roses. They'd bring candy and notes and home-baked cookies. In all the years I've been in the big top, I've never seen a performer receive that kind of adoration."

"Ain't that something?"

"She was very happy here. I can still see her with her head back, laughing."

Considering his debt paid, Razz held on to his head and lifted himself off the couch, taking it in stages this time so he wouldn't topple.

"Did Eve make it back?" he asked.

"Not yet. But she will. I seen it clear."

"Where is she?" If the old woman noticed he'd validated her visions, she had enough class not to say so. At least she shared one trait with her sister.

"I don't know. All I can see is water, and Eve above it, high and dry."

It was time to go. Past time, before he revealed more than he meant to. He put on his shoes and reached for his cap, still damp and lying on the coffee table.

"Thank you," he said, and she nodded. There was no need for more. He knew and she knew. Razz had rescued her sister, and now she had rescued him. Full circle.

He stepped out of the trailer onto soggy ground, still trying to come to grips with the amount of water that had washed over it. Razz stood a minute taking in the damage— one midway ride and a concession stand gone; the menagerie tent already being dragged out of the mud and erected by six roustabouts; the big top down. That was an immediate problem. It would have to be spread so any rips and tears in the canvas could be repaired, the damage underneath assessed.

They were lucky the circus lot was outside the city and on high ground. A tropical storm of that strength would flood low-lying areas, especially those close to the river.

"Razz!" Mark DeChello strode toward him. "I've been looking all over for you."

"I hit my fool head, and I've been out awhile."

"Are you okay?"

"I'm all right. Where's Al?"

"In his trailer. He had a sinking spell in the middle of the storm, and Luca carried him there."

"His heart?"

"His stomach. Indigestion."

"Anybody hurt?"

"Just a few bumps and scratches."

"The animals?"

"All safe and accounted for."

If Razz had been a praying man, he'd have thanked God. For now, he and Mark left to find the light truck and see about getting the generator running again. The good thing about living in a traveling circus was that you didn't have to depend on the whims of nature and the electric company. Albany would probably be without power for days, but the Great Giovanni Bros./Hogan & Sandusky Circus would have it by the end of the day.

CLOUDS STILL COVERED THE moon but the rains had stopped. Inside his Airstream with a cold compress on his head and his aching legs propped up, Razz watched the news coverage of the tropical storm that had ravaged Albany, Georgia.

Aerial views from a helicopter showed streets flooded, cars and houses washed away, people stranded on rooftops, treetops, and the bridge over the Flint River. As the camera panned over the collapsed big top and the fallen Tilt-A-Twirl, an off-camera voice described the havoc wreaked by the storm on the Great Giovanni Bros./Hogan & Sandusky Circus.

"Rescue teams are working around the clock." The camera panned to the reporter, a young woman in yellow rain gear, her slicker blowing in the wind, and then zoomed in to the bridge over the Flint River. "But for the two hundred people stranded here, waiting to be airlifted from the raging river below, there is some unexpected relief."

Framed in the lens was a slender woman, her hair sticking up in red spikes, a white bag in her hand.

"For hours now, the woman you see has been passing out food and kindness on this bridge. The more than two dozen people already rescued here call her the Angel on the Bridge."

A close-up of the angel's face showed Eve. The cold compress slid from Razz's hand, and he shook his fist at the reporter. "Busybody." Now look what she had done.

"In times like this, it's ordinary people who become heroes," she said.

If Razz had seen Eve on TV, how many more people had? Friends and family in Tupelo, her husband, sitting in his armchair discovering that his wife was trapped on a bridge in Albany, Georgia?

Leaving the TV commentator blathering on about heroes, Razz grabbed his cap and headed for Eve's trailer. It was past ten, and most of the performers were already in bed, exhausted from battling the storm. A few windows still glowed blue with lights from TV screens—Magic Michelle, a night owl; Mark, who never missed the news; and Al, an insomniac, probably from years of traveling the back roads after midnight. Whether he was sleeping in front of his TV or watching his circus teacher on the bridge, Razz didn't know. He'd find out tomorrow at breakfast.

Razz arrived at Eve's trailer out of breath, then stood in the dark outside the door calling himself an old fool. Ruth Gibson was going to find him standing there and get the wrong idea. She'd think he had a personal interest in her and her niece. The next thing he knew, she'd be expecting him to talk, and before you could say *here comes the band,* she'd be expecting him to act normal.

He'd already turned to leave when the door swung open.

"Don't just stand there. Come on in."

"How'd you know I was out here?"

"I seen you in my dreams."

He couldn't tell if Ruth Gibson was kidding or not. "Did you see the news?" he asked.

"You didn't come over here in the dark to ask me about the news."

"Eve's safe."

"I done told you that."

"Then I guess you don't want to hear the rest of what I've got to say."

"Don't git yourself in a wad. Come on in."

He might as well. He didn't have anything else to do. Perching on the edge of the couch, he took his cap off. At least he still had that much social grace.

"How you like your coffee?"

"I don't want coffee."

"Suit yourself. I'll just make a pot anyhow. I won't be able to rest easy till Eve's home safe."

"I saw her on the news coverage. She's fine. They're calling her the Angel on the Bridge."

"I ain't surprised. I just wish somebody else could a been the angel and got their face plastered all over the TV."

If he started that conversation, before you knew it she'd

find out just what lengths he'd go to in order to protect Lola's granddaughter.

"She'll be off the bridge soon. The rescue crews will work nearly around the clock."

"Don't guess we'll be leavin' for a while."

"No. The roads are closed and we've got damage to repair."

"Is that all you seen on TV?"

"There were lots of aerial shots of the flooded city."

"I ain't talking about the city. I'm talking about Eve."

"What Eve does or has done is not my business. All I'm interested in is that she's a good circus teacher."

Ruth Gibson didn't strike him as the kind of woman who would back down from anything, and that included a line of questioning that would lead back to a past he'd buried nearly fifty years ago. He rammed his hat back on and hurried out.

From behind the closed door, he heard her footsteps on the linoleum. She was probably pouring herself a cup of coffee. Then she started singing an old hymn that made it impossible to tell whether the music was inside him or floating around the circus backyard. Razz remembered "Little Church in the Wildwood" from the long-ago days when he'd had a wife, a child, and a belief that had compelled him to worship on Sunday.

He stood in the night filled with the music of an old mountain woman, the lullaby of circus animals and memories he couldn't stop if he got down on his knees and begged . . .

The little church is near the beach in Galveston, close enough to see the water and far enough back to be almost hidden in a grove of pines.

"This is where we'll be married," Lola says, and standing there holding on to her hand like I'd invented courting, I believe her vision for

the future. I believe her husband will give her a divorce and we can get married and have children the way we've planned.

"I'll go back to Tupelo and present him with the papers."

"I'll go with you." I'm not about to let her face Jim Hall alone, no matter how many tigers she has trained.

"I knew you would. He won't have any choice but to set me free."

"No choice at all."

"We'll go as soon as the circus season ends . . ."

Lola had never seen the end of the circus season.

Razz tried to shake himself loose, but as he hurried to his trailer the past haunted him like a blues song that would rip your heart out if you'd let it.

20

THERE'S A SOUND A swollen river makes, a barely contained fury not unlike an abusive husband before he grabs you by the throat and tries to drown you in the bathtub. It's the kind of sound you remember long after you've filled your lungs with air and discovered you're alive. It's the kind you can't forget even after you've been airlifted off a bridge and are sitting on the back end of an emergency vehicle with a blanket wrapped around your shoulders, counting each breath and discovering that you've survived.

Chaos surrounded Ellen. Red beacons from the fire trucks and ambulances illuminated survivors wrapped in blankets and Red Cross jackets. Volunteers swarmed around them, occasionally calling to each other in the dark, "Over here. Stretcher."

A young woman with a Red Cross logo on her jacket handed Ellen a Styrofoam cup filled with hot coffee, and another asked her if she needed anything.

A hiding place, is what she thought. "Nothing, thank you," is what she said.

TV reporters were everywhere, dragging their cameramen and their microphones along like sacred gods.

"Over here!" one of them shouted. "It's the Angel on the Bridge!"

Ellen glanced around to locate the angel, and suddenly found herself trapped in a glare of lights. Frantic now, she searched her surroundings, but there was no place to run, no place to hide.

Talking into her microphone about candy and cookies and the kindness of strangers, the woman in yellow rain slicker and boots stalked Ellen with the single-mindedness of a husband who needs an outlet for his rage.

"Tell us your name." The TV reporter thrust the microphone at Ellen, who sat paralyzed on the back of a truck, numb with the image of Wayne sitting on their Early American sofa with a beer in one hand, the other balled into a fist. His rage would be so huge the living room wouldn't contain it. He'd stomp to the backyard, and then race back, remembering that his wayward wife was still on TV and he didn't want to miss a thing.

Or maybe he'd already seen her on TV. Maybe he'd already called in detectives and trackers with wild-eyed dogs. Maybe he was already barreling toward Georgia, daring the Flint River to recede back into its banks before he could grab his wife and drag her back to Tupelo.

But not before he meted out an abandoned husband's justice.

Ellen held her hand in front of her face.

"You're a hero. Tell us who you are."

"No, please." Ellen shielded her face with her hand.

"Eyewitnesses claim they saw you come in with the circus. Is that true?"

She ducked behind her blanket, curling herself into a ball no bigger than a dandelion puff.

The woman talked on while Ellen breathed in damp wool and panic. She would suffocate. The wet blanket would do what the Flint River could not, and Wayne would carry her body home and bury her in a pink casket. He'd sit in the front pew at church, sobbing, while all the neighbors said what a good husband he was.

Ellen balled her hands into fists. Not while she had breath in her body.

With the blanket still shielding her face, with only a peep-hole to see, she stood up and walked straight to a uniformed policeman.

"I'm feeling sick and I don't want to be on TV."

He moved between her and the TV reporter, a human shield the size of a linebacker.

"The lady wants to be left alone."

"Thank you," she said, and then fled beyond the glare and into the night.

HE'S COMING. RUN. RUN.

Ellen's right foot hit the floor and she shoved back the covers to bring the other foot down. Poised for flight, she found herself staring at the paneling that covered the bedroom walls of her new trailer, Aunt Ruth in the bed beside her, the moon glinting through the high window and off the metal of the shot-gun barrel, propped against the wall.

Relief set off a chain reaction, and Ellen had to wrap her arms around herself to stop the shivering before she could walk into her little kitchenette to get a drink of water. With the tap water in one of the new plastic glasses she'd bought at Wal-Mart, she walked to the window and peered through the curtain.

The circus backyard looked the same in Bainbridge as it had in Camilla, and before that Newton. Her Ford Fairlane was parked beside her trailer, and next door, Magic Michelle's windows were dark. Nobody lurked in the shadows; no animals from the menagerie tent lifted cries of alarm. There was not even a sign of Razz, who had taken to staying behind when the circus pulled up stakes after the last show so he could patrol the backyard while the performers who'd remained slept.

He'd never admit it, even if she asked. But she wouldn't. He'd didn't pry into Ellen's business, and she didn't pry into his. He was a loner, a taciturn, curmudgeonly old man who kept to himself except for the occasional company of the Great Giovanni and the more constant company of his cats. Ellen respected that. As much as she'd love to hear what he had to say about her grandmother, she had more pressing things on her mind.

Why hadn't Wayne come after her?

They'd been stranded in Albany for three days, and back on their circuit for another three—more than enough time for Wayne to have caught up with them and tried to drag her home.

Where was he? Was he at the circus even now, hiding out with someone on the midway to whom he'd paid obscene amounts of money, playing some horrible cat-and-mouse game? Did he hope to drive her crazy and then haul her off as docile as the doves that perched on Magic Michelle's shoulder?

Still holding on to her tepid water, Ellen stood at her window searching the moonlit yard for movement in the shadows.

Suddenly she saw it, something moving with the stealth of an animal of prey. Or a human who planned a sneak attack.

Ellen ducked back and stood with her hand over a heart beating much too fast. Something was out there, just beyond her trailer. She'd risk one more look. If it was Wayne, at least she'd have time to wake Ruth and hand her the shotgun.

And then what? Ellen had never imagined beyond her aunt holding off her husband with a weapon. Neither of them had a bent for violence, a taste for blood. Maybe having the gun pointed at his chest would stop him long enough for their screams to bring help.

She parted the curtains again, and almost screamed. The tiger in the moonlight looked twice as big as he did in the cage during Razz's big cat act, and ten times more magnificent. Running free, darting in and out of shadows, the tiger looked as if he were chasing the moon.

At first Ellen didn't see Razz, but when he stepped into a path of stars hanging so low they looked as if you could reach up and touch them, the tiger charged. When he was even with the old tiger trainer, the big cat reared onto his hind legs, put his forepaws on Razz's shoulders, and licked his face. They looked as if they were dancing, man and beast, turned silver by the light of the moon and wearing a crown of stars.

Razz's pet tiger Sheikh was legend. Bobby had told her endless stories about the two of them, with April chiming in that *Wazz wasn't 'fwaid of nothin'*.

How would it feel not to be afraid?

Until the tropical storm, Ellen had just begun to understand. She'd just begun to hope.

With one last longing glance at the man and the tiger in the moonlight, Ellen went back to bed and pulled the covers over herself, all except her right foot.

SHE LEFT THE TRAILER early, even before Aunt Ruth was up. Except for Luca at the edge of the pasture with his horses, Linda walking her ocelot, and the smell of fried bologna announcing that Cookie Two was making breakfast, nothing stirred.

The only hope Ellen had that the man she wanted to see would be out and about was what April had told her.

"Daddy's insane and back," she'd confided. "That means he don't neber sleep."

She found Jocko in the clown tent, sitting in a lawn chair with a third-grade reader.

"It's so wonderful to see you reading," she said.

"I read out here so I won't wake Rose and children. I'm an insomniac."

"April told me." He offered his chair and unfolded another for himself.

"I've been expecting you. And not just for a lesson."

She sat for a while, letting that sink in. Finally, she said, "I worry about shopping in cities filled with strangers and greed." Looking into her eyes without wavering, he nodded, and that simple gesture told Ellen everything she needed to know: Jocko was not only a good friend, he was a man who cared enough to be a silent protector.

"You have a beautiful nose. Distinguishable. Follow me."

He led her to the makeup table and in one deft movement turned what appeared to be a blob of wax into a hawkish nose that looked so real Ellen hardly recognized herself. "When I saw the Angel on the Bridge, she had red hair." He fitted a brown pageboy wig over her head. "But the circus teacher has brown."

"How long have you known about me?"

"Awhile." Jocko pulled out her chair. "My real name is Harvey, but nobody except Rose even remembers it now."

"Thank you."

"You're welcome, Eve."

He pulled her nose off and stuck it into her pocket. She removed the wig and tucked it under her arm, then stood on tiptoe to kiss his cheek. Her kiss made a sound like Fourth of July firecrackers.

"How do you do that?"

"A clown never reveals secrets."

WHEN THE GREAT GIOVANNI Bros./Hogan & Sandusky Circus crossed into Florida in the wee hours of the morning, Al remarked that it looked like rain and Razz worried about the circus' bottom line. As they waited for the matinee, the performers glanced at the sky and hurried inside their trailers to secure loose items in case of another tropical storm, while Indian Joe, who fancied himself an amateur weather prognosticator, went in search of a bigger stake for Betsy. The elephant just winked and waited for her chance to sashay into the cook tent after lunch, when Cookie Two would so busy cleaning he wouldn't notice a two-ton elephant snatching a little snack of cabbage.

Ruth glanced out the window at the cloud and nodded. It was so heavy with the dreams and plans of the circus family it's a wonder it didn't fall out of the sky and burst wide open. She poured herself a cup of tea, sat down in her new movable home, and smiled.

IN THE SCHOOL TENT, Bobby and Lucy folded their books and raced each other to lunch, with April flying along behind yelling, "Wait for me," while Ellen stayed behind with Luca's child.

Though Nicky loved Ellen as she loved him, with arms and heart wide open, he still showed no signs of wanting to talk. How much longer before Clarice snatched Nicky out of her care and made good her threat to take him to a specialist in Atlanta? How much longer before Giovanni lost patience with the teacher who couldn't teach his great-grandson to talk?

As Ellen bent over the little boy holding on to his yarn puppet, she wondered what it would be like if the child in her womb were born without speech. She'd move heaven and earth. She'd breathe fire in the direction of anyone who tried to get between her and a cure. And she certainly wouldn't hesitate to fire somebody whose feeble attempts to help yielded nothing.

Clarice and Giovanni would be exactly right if they sent her packing for her failure with Nicky.

Bending toward Luca's silent little boy, she breathed a silent prayer, a plea for a miracle for Nicky's grandmother and great-grandfather, and thanksgiving for Nicky's father, who gave everything and asked nothing in return.

"Rainbow, what do you like for lunch?"

Nicky didn't say a thing, but he watched every move as she slipped her hand over his to manipulate the puppet's mouth, and in her best elephant voice said, "Candy. I want candy."

Nicky's laughter was as uninhibited as it was rewarding. Though he played and laughed with the other children, this was the first time Ellen failed to hear that little note of sadness.

"Candy? Did you say candy?" She pretended shock. "How about soup, Rainbow? Soup's good for you."

Nicky's face lit up as he leaned close to see what Rainbow would say next.

"Candy." Ellen moved the puppet's mouth. "I want lots and lots of candy." She rubbed the elephant's tummy with his trunk. "Yum. M&M's."

When Nicky rubbed his own tummy, Ellen pretended not to see. Instead she reached into her purse for a bag of M&Ms.

"Is this what you want, Rainbow?"

"Yes. I want candy. I want candy." She made the puppet jump up and down and speak in a singsong voice. Nicky started jumping, too, excitement sparkling in his eyes.

"You be a very good little elephant, Rainbow. After lunch, I'll give you an M&M."

"Nicky, too?" she asked in her elephant voice, and then answered in her own. "Of course. Nicky, too."

A smile bloomed across the little boy's face. The reserve he'd had when he first started coming to the school tent was gone, and in its place was the natural, open expression of an ordinary four-year-old.

Praying that she wasn't pushing the little boy too fast, she was getting ready to ask if he wanted an M&M when a large shadow crossed the tent opening, not Luca but the Great Giovanni himself.

Ellen pushed down her sharp disappointment, then silently chided herself for selfishly thinking of her own desire instead of a great-grandfather's need.

In the split second before he strode into the tent, Nicky's mouth formed one word. *Papa.* Silent as the moon, and just as splendid.

"Look at my fine boy." Giovanni squatted beside his great-grandson. "Are you ready for lunch, Nicky?"

As the child stared at the circus legend, his beloved flesh and blood, Ellen thought of dreams so fragile you cup them safe in the palms of your hand, afraid that if you open too wide, they'll turn blue as morning mists and evaporate into the sky. She thought of hearts that can be broken with one look, one word, one event that can never be reversed, no matter how hard you pray. And she thought of hope, a single silver trickle that you might turn into a shining river if only you knew how.

Suddenly Nicky lifted his arms. "Up, Papa," he said, his voice as fresh as a spring shower. "Rainbow wants to ride."

The Great Giovanni, who was never without words, stood there speechless while tears streamed down his cheeks.

"Papa!" Like any four-year-old who doesn't receive instant gratification, Nicky tugged on Giovanni's pants leg. "Up!"

"Did you say up?" Giovanni swiped at his eyes. "Why, I'll lift you high as the sky!" He swooped down and swung his great-grandson onto his shoulders while Nicky's laughter filled the circus school tent.

"Eve, I can never thank you enough."

"You gave me a fresh start. I'm so glad I could give you something in return."

"It's more than something in return. You gave me back my great-grandson . . . Are you ready, Nicky? You're the famous equestrian and Papa's the horse."

"Dance, Papa."

"Looks like it's showtime, Eve. Stop by Mark's office to-morrow. You deserve a raise for this." He winked at her. "And for putting up with Clarice."

"She's just a protective grandmother."

"When she's not being an overprotective daughter."

Humming the Blue Danube Waltz, the Great Giovanni began to dance, and as he did his clumsy waltz toward the tent flap, Nicky waved his hand that held the puppet, his smile as wide as the sky.

Imagining Luca's pleasure in his son's miraculous recovery, Ellen smiled as she hurried along to her trailer to fetch Aunt Ruth for lunch. If she could make Nicky talk, anything was possible, even that a husband who had offered a reward on Phil Donahue had finally given up in disgust. At this very minute, Wayne could be telling his friends how worthless she'd been as a wife and how lucky he was to be rid of her. He was glad she was gone, he'd say. It saved him the trouble of sending her packing.

RAZZ FINISHED CUTTING UP the latest batch of missing posters. They'd increased since the tropical storm in Albany. Every night the arrow man came back with more posters plastered with Ellen Blair's face.

If you looked on the dark side, and Razz usually did, that meant Wayne was still desperate to get his wife back, and he'd stop at nothing to get her. The only good thing about this whole fiasco was that he hadn't made his move in spite of the Angel on the Bridge story. What was stopping him?

Razz didn't have time to dwell on the motives of a crazy fool. He stuffed the poster pieces into a garbage bag for disposal after dark, and hurried to the cook tent, already late for lunch. He hated that. Not that he was a stickler for punctuality except when it came to the show. He just didn't like the idea of making an entrance and everybody watching. The big top was one thing, but the circus family was another. They'd band together against the outside world in a heartbeat, but inside, they liked to swap stories, most of them exaggerated beyond anything that resembled the truth. Still, he reckoned that was just human nature.

He could smell lunch long before he got to the tent. Shrimp. Fresh oranges. A sure sign they were in Florida. That ought to lift a few spirits. Since the storm, it seemed even the animals were having a hard time keeping their minds on the show.

Up ahead, he saw Mark, his arms full of mail. Razz hurried to catch up.

"Looks like you've got a load today, Mark."

"You can always count on circus mail waiting in Tallahassee." Mark rifled through the letters. "I've got one that I think was sent to the wrong place, though."

The name Ellen Blair leaped off the envelope and Razz nearly tripped over his own feet. He snatched it up, then tried to act casual as he stuffed it into his pocket.

"It's probably for Ringling. He's over at Fort Walton Beach, and they're the only other show in Florida right now."

"Probably. It wouldn't be the first time folks got their circuses mixed up."

"Any more of these come, just give them to me. I'll tend to it."

"There's no need for you to bother, Razz. That's part of my job."

Razz clapped him on the shoulder, tried to act jovial. "It's not a problem. I've been meaning to get in touch with Ringling anyhow. They've got a lion cub over there I'd like to buy, and if I can do them a favor, they might take more kindly to my offer."

"Good luck with that."

Finally they were at the cook tent, and Razz was off the hook. He hoped. While Mark stood in the opening saying,

"Mail call," he tried to decide what he'd say to Al about buying a lion cub Ringling might or might not have with money the Great Giovanni Bros./Hogan & Sandusky definitely didn't have.

Now look what he'd done. All because he'd let himself get softhearted over a girl who was nothing but a pack of trouble. She and the old woman were sitting at their usual table with Magic Michelle and Indian Joe. Luca was there, too, leaning over Eve like he thought she'd hung the moon. Nicky was wedged between Luca and Al.

Al never ate anywhere except at the owner's table. What in the heck was going on? Make one little mistake, and the whole world turned crazy. He should never have let a woman with blue eyes and her mouth shaped like a heart become part of the circus family. If he'd argued against Eve hard enough, Al would have caved in. Maybe.

Razz rammed his hand into his pocket, hoping the letter had magically vanished, but it was still there, rolled up in a pack of lies he was now going to have to tell his best friend.

By the time Razz sat down at the table, his appetite for shrimp and fresh oranges was completely gone. He glared at Ruth Gibson as if it was all her fault.

ELLEN WAS ALWAYS GLAD for a two-day stretch without travel. As with most of the larger cities, Tallahassee would be four shows instead of two.

One of the signs of her advancing pregnancy was how tired she got behind the wheel of a car. Soon there would be other signs, and she'd have to decide whether to simply show up in her pink maternity top or to give some advance warning.

At least she could now drive into any city she pleased to get supplies, unrecognizable in her new nose and pageboy wig.

Holding her cup of tea, she settled into the sofa while Aunt Ruth fiddled with the TV to find her favorite show, *The Waltons.*

"That John and Olivia know how to handle children," Ruth said, as if the TV characters were personal friends and she planned on sitting down to dinner with them to share parenting tips. "The way you got that little boy to talk, I'd say you're might nigh as good as the Waltons."

"Maybe even better, Aunt Ruth."

Nicky had been a regular little chatterbox at lunch. From what she'd read about his condition, that was true to pattern. The victim would start talking as suddenly as he had stopped.

During lunch, Giovanni had heaped praise on her, but it was Luca she thought of most, the way he caught her hand when he thanked her for helping Nicky, the way he held on, the way he looked straight into her eyes as if he were seeing her soul.

It saddened her to think that his mother was so bitter toward her. She wondered if Clarice would ever thaw, if she'd show up in the school tent to say thank you. Even if she didn't mention Eve's role in Nicky's recovery, perhaps she'd unbend a little, wave as she passed or even say hello.

Ruth settled into her rocking chair and pulled out a skein of yellow yarn while Ellen sipped tea. It felt so ordinary, so safe, that if Ellen didn't think about the past, she might believe that nobody wanted them badly enough to put a price on their heads and nobody was looking.

"What are you knitting, Aunt Ruth?"

"Bootees."

"Boy or girl?"

"I ain't tellin'. Why you think I'm usin' yeller?"

"What do you think I ought to do about letting our friends know I'm expecting a baby?"

"Nothin'. Just let nature take its course." Aunt Ruth's needles clicked. "I like the part where the Waltons all call they good nights to each other."

"When the baby gets old enough to talk, we'll do that, Aunt Ruth."

"Won't that be fine?"

With Aunt Ruth's knitting needles clicking and the easy conversation of the Waltons flowing around her, Ellen found herself planning for the future instead of being afraid of the past. Soon she'd put on her wig and ugly nose and shop for a tiny blanket and a little rattle with bells inside so her baby would always have music when she wanted it.

"I think I'll name her Mary."

"I still ain't sayin' nothing."

The knock caught them both by surprise. Michelle was the only one who visited, and rarely at night. And when she came over, she always called out, "Yoo-hoo!"

The knock sounded again, more persistent this time, and Ellen felt herself shrinking.

"Who's there?" Ruth called.

"It's me. Razz."

"Well, why didn't you say so instead of knocking the door

down?" Ruth got up to open the door. "Don't just stand there. Come on in."

"No. I just brought this." He thrust a letter into Ruth's hands.

Ruth stood so long looking at the letter, Ellen wondered if she'd had a transient stroke.

"I don't know anybody by this name," she said.

"I don't, either. But I thought you might want it."

Razz rammed his baseball cap lower and stalked off. Ruth drifted back to the chair as if she'd lost both legs and was being carried along by the long white envelope in her hand.

Stroke is what Ellen was thinking. She pictured hospitals and forms and a paper trail that would lead Wayne straight to her.

"Aunt Ruth. What is it?"

"This." She placed the letter on the coffee table, while Olivia Walton called out, *Good night, John-Boy.* In the string of good nights that followed, Ellen picked up the envelope bearing her name. The return address said only Tupelo, Mississippi. There was nothing to tell her who had sent it except the handwriting, slanting letters with loops and swirls, Josie's idea of the way a real lady should write.

"It's from Mother."

Ellen shrank back against the sofa as if lights from a TV camera had followed her all the way from Albany to a circus lot in the Panhandle where children chased fireflies under the moon and crickets sang outside the door.

"Ain't you gonna read it? It might tell us somethin' useful, though that'd be a first for Josie."

Ellen slit the envelope and pulled out the letter. Written on Josie's pink monogrammed paper, it was three pages long.

She read aloud so Aunt Ruth could know.

Dear Ellen, I guess you know you've driven us all crazy. Sim refuses to allow your name spoken in this house, and if he knew about this letter, there's no telling what he'd do. Have a conniption fit, for one. Not give me that pink sapphire ring I've been wanting for my birthday, for another.

Aunt Ruth snorted. "Josie never did know how to get to the point."

That's another thing, Ellen. Did you ever think how it would hurt me for you to be gone on my birthday? For me to have to find out where you were by seeing you and that sleazy circus on the TV? Whoever did your cut and color could use some lessons. It took all your beauty away. I wouldn't even have known you except for seeing with a mother's heart.

"A mother's heart, my fanny. Josie ain't even got one."

Ellen hoped Aunt Ruth was wrong. She still believed that somewhere behind the social posturing and the attempt to be seen as perfect, Josie harbored a mother's love. Still, she couldn't blame Ruth for thinking otherwise after Josie had abandoned her on her mountain like a cast-off toy.

I had to put two and two together. I don't know why I didn't figure it out sooner. What did you mean running off like that? It's bound to be that crazy old woman's fault. It's just

like Ruth Gibson to drag you off to the same fleabag circus
where my own mama made an ass of herself. If it hadn't been
for my daddy's family, I don't know what would have become
of me.

"Josie must a got her stinger from the Hall side of the family. She ain't nothing like Lola."

"You're not crazy, Aunt Ruth, and it was mean of Mama to say so. I should have skipped over that part."

"Don't skip nothin'. Bein called names don't hurt me. I got plenty a faults, but bein' stuck on myself ain't one of 'em. Keep on readin'."

You don't know what it cost me to find out how to get in
touch with you. Sneaking around so Sim wouldn't know.
Biting my tongue so I wouldn't blurt it out to Wayne.

Hands trembling, Ellen laid the letter in her lap. A different hair color would never fool her husband. Even a wig and a different nose wouldn't be enough. He'd know her by the shape of her neck, her mouth, her eyes. Why hadn't she thought of that before?

"He doesn't know, Aunt Ruth. If we leave tonight, maybe we can go to a place he'll never find."

"They ain't no such place."

"I know. But maybe we can postpone being discovered long enough for me to have the baby."

"Ellen, you listen to me. One of these days you gotta decide if you want to spend the rest of your life runnin'."

She wasn't even aware of crying until she saw the words blur on the page. Ellen wiped her hands across her eyes and continued to read.

> *Your husband was at a convention in Cancún when that*
> *Angel on the Bridge story hit the airwaves. He sure didn't see*
> *it, or he'd have already been in Albany bringing you home.*
> *It was just the stroke of luck I needed so I'd have time to talk*
> *some sense into you. After I got over being relieved you hadn't*
> *been carried off by hoodlums and murdered, and then spit-*
> *stomping mad that you'd run off to the circus just like your*
> *flighty grandmother, I seized the opportunity to help you.*

"Ain't you a little late for that, Josie?"

Ellen didn't blame Ruth for talking back, even if it was only to a letter. She felt the same way herself. Where was Josie's urge for compassion when Ellen had first reported her husband's abuse?

> *Poor Wayne's worried himself sick over you, and when*
> *he's not worrying he's working his poor fingers to the bone*
> *trying to make a good living for you and the baby. Not to*
> *mention that he's spent a fortune on detectives and search*
> *hounds and flyers and I don't know what all. If you'd come*
> *on back instead of waiting for somebody to come and beg you*
> *on bended knees, it would be better for everybody concerned.*
> *Plus you'd save Wayne a $25,000 reward. You're trying*
> *everybody's patience, and wearing me down to my last nerve.*
> *A lot of women in Tupelo would give their eyeteeth to have a*
> *good husband like Wayne.*

"If he's a good husband, I'm a jackass."

"Here's the last paragraph, Aunt Ruth."

Call me and tell me you're going to use the good sense you were born with and come on home to make things right with your husband. Hugs and kisses, Mother.

From the direction of the menagerie tent, Betsy trumpeted. She could have been singing to the moon or complaining about her supper. But the shivers that went through Ellen told her the old circus elephant was sounding a warning.

"How soon before he finds us, Aunt Ruth?"

"You got time."

"For what?"

"To decide what you're going to do."

Ellen's anxiety wouldn't let her sit still. "I'm going for a walk."

Somewhere in the distance, twelve Andalusians thundered across the circus lot, their white coats as pure as a newborn before living makes its dark marks. Ellen opened the door and started in the direction of the horses.

RUTH WAITED UNTIL ELLEN was out of sight, then grabbed her bonnet and set out on her mission. She didn't have to inquire as to the whereabouts of Razz's trailer. He was parked on the edge of the circus backyard, close enough to be part of the circus family, but set far enough away so there could be no doubt that he liked his privacy.

If that wasn't enough to tip Ruth off, the tiger was. It was not sound or sight that guided her toward the tiger, but a phantom in white. The ordinary passerby might have mistaken Lola for a patch of moonlight, but Ruth had a seer's instincts and a dreamer's heart. She smiled as she followed her sister to the tiger trainer who had saved her life.

She knocked and said, "It's Mimi."

"There's a tiger in here. You can't come in."

"I ain't scared of no tiger."

"He could eat a skinny old woman like you in one meal."

"I'm so ornery, he'd spit me out. Let me in. We need to talk."

"We've said all we need to say. Go back to your trailer."

"I ain't leavin' till I've had my say."

There was no sound from inside the trailer, a clear indication the man didn't want to talk, but Ruth waited anyhow. Any man who thought a tough old woman taught by a mountain would back off after one attempt was sadly mistaken. She'd outlasted snowstorms and tornadoes and bore worms stealing her whole crop. She didn't aim to let a man with a tiger stop her.

It came as no surprise when Razz cracked open his door and stepped outside. What did surprise her was the poster on his wall. She'd had only a glimpse, but that was enough. The man who wanted folks to believe he had no heart kept a life-size poster of her sister.

"Well," he said. "What do you want?"

"Josie knows where we are." There was no use denying he didn't know who she was talking about. His face told its own story. "I don't know if she'll tell that sorry son-in-law, but if he gets his hands on Eve again, he'll kill her."

"Nobody is going to kill anybody in my circus."

"Good." Ruth didn't have to ask what he meant to do. His intent shone around him bright as the moon that made a path back to her trailer. Razz Hogan would do anything in his power to protect Lola's granddaughter.

Ruth nodded her good-bye, and he went back into his trailer without a single word. Let him, the old sourpuss. Soon enough he'd have plenty to say.

As she passed the marquee where the children romped, Ruth saw April separate herself and race in her direction. When the child caught her hand, she felt like she'd lopped ten years off her age. It made her wonder how come she'd sat on that mountain like a stubborn old fool and let Josie deprive her of the time she might have spent with Ellen. It made her mad at herself for missing too much.

"Mimi, I got a birfday."

"You do? When?"

"The day after yestermowwo."

"That's a good time for a birthday. I'll make you a present. What do you want?"

"A wainbow heffalump like Nicky."

"I can do that. Or I can make a tiger."

"Oh, a tigah! He'll be the bestest. *You* the bestest."

"You are, too, little silver-winged birthday bird."

April raced off, giggling, and Ruth hurried on, led by a vision. But this time it was not her sister in the mists, it was the smell of citrus and the shapes and colors of golden tigers and white horses.

LUCA STOOD WITH HIS back to Ellen, facing the horses, the moon turning him silver. His voice was no more than the whisper of the wind, and his hands were fluid as water, sending silent signals to the Andalusians. Without the music of the band, their dance took on a mystery found only under the stars. They were an endless river of white, flowing through the night as Ellen watched, breathless.

The hateful letter from Josie faded; the awful things it represented became no more than an oak leaf that suddenly turned loose from the tree and floated toward her feet.

I am here, she thought. *I am Eve, and I am here.*

"Eve?" When Luca turned, his smile was a beautiful thing to see. "I'm glad you came."

She thought of the way he'd entrusted Nicky to her without reservation. She remembered the way he'd shared the secrets of the horses with her, his patience and kindness. Lies cannot stand in the face of such trust.

"My name is not Eve."

He was tranquil as the night, the horses behind him still flowing in a pale river.

"I know."

"And I'm pregnant."

"A small miracle." He put his hand over her abdomen, his fingers spread as if he were cradling her baby. "This child will know nothing but love."

She felt the hot pressure of tears and knew she was going to cry. But in a night where truth seemed the most important thing, she didn't try to hold them back.

If there was ever a kinder man on this earth, Ellen had no idea where he'd be.

"I don't know why I thought you'd be upset, Luca. Worry has been a part of my life for so long, I don't know how to let it go."

"Just cry." He cradled her head. "Give your worry to me."

Suddenly the floodgates opened and she sobbed such a river of remorse it drenched the front of his shirt. She cried for Aunt Ruth who'd left her home and Josie who couldn't see the truth; she wept for her waste of a marriage and the years of abuse. When she was empty of everything except gratitude and hope, she lifted her head and looked at the man who had ridden a white stallion into her life, a fairy-tale hero who spoke the language of horses and the language of love.

"I'm done with tears now. I'm starting over."

Smiling, he put his hand on her cheek and tenderly traced the tear tracks. "The circus lets you become anyone you want to be. And so do I."

"Somehow I knew you'd say that."

"Who do you want to be?"

"Eve," she said, and when he wrapped his arms around her, she held on, simply held on.

"Thank you, Luca."

"Thank *you*, Eve. You gave my son his speech, and you gave me *you*."

She might have stood in the circle of his arms for minutes or hours. Time didn't matter. Only that she was Eve and that someday she might be like Jocko, with Aunt Ruth the only person who remembered her old name.

BAD NEWS HAS A stench that clings to it and pollutes everything around it. The first thing Ruth smelled when she woke up was the tang of brimstone. It didn't take her long to come awake enough to know the source. Josie's letter lay open on the table between Ellen's and Ruth's beds, meanness dripping from every page.

She'd half a notion to rip it to shreds, but it wasn't hers to destroy. Easing her feet to the floor so she wouldn't wake Ellen, she studied the walls, the floor, the ceiling, even the covers over her niece, looking for omens, a cricket in the corner, a dark shadow that didn't belong, a foretelling dream so bad it left a trail of soot in the air.

The only thing she saw that ought not to be there was a beetle that had made its way through the cracks and was crawling across the floor trying to find its way home. Ruth bent over and cupped it in her palms, then carried it to the door and set it free.

"Go on home, ladybug. Ain't nothin' here for you except a peck of trouble."

She dressed with the efficiency of a woman who'd made a practice of getting up with the sunrise and working every blessed minute till sundown. Then she went into the kitchen to put on the coffee so she could have a cup with the morning news.

She was glad they didn't have to travel today. She liked everything about the circus, even the traveling, which allowed her to see places and sights she'd never dreamed of. But what she liked best were the mornings, when she could ease into her day and then reel it out slow, like a kite that knew it took patience to wait for the wind. Today she'd get started on knitting April's tiger.

She turned on the news with the volume down low, then tried to decide whether to make breakfast in the trailer or just go down to the cook tent, as they usually did. Her coffee was ready, so she poured a cup and sat on the sofa. She had plenty of time to decide.

On the TV screen, Richard Nixon stood at a podium behind a presidential seal, trying to look earnest. Ruth could have told him it was a losing battle. No matter how hard he tried, he could never look as trustworthy as Walter Cronkite.

Ruth caught the word *resignation* and turned up the volume. Ellen walked through the door just in time to hear the president of the United States resign.

They looked at each other, flabbergasted. When they'd joined the circus, they'd entered into a world of fantasy filled with dancing horses and tigers that jumped through hoops of fire. Spangled costumes were more prevalent than bell-bottoms and miniskirts, and the most common hairstyle was either a clown's wig or the tight buns of the aerialists. The world beyond the big top faded and in its place was a Grand Spectacular under spotlights.

"The world went on without us," Ellen said, expressing exactly what Ruth had been thinking.

They were like that, the two of them, one able to pick a thought out of the other's head and give it voice. She wondered if her niece knew she had a gift. Someday she might tell her. But not now, not while that hateful letter was on Ellen's mind.

"Wayne made a donation to Nixon's campaign."

"That don't surprise me none."

Ellen poured herself a cup of coffee then sat on the sofa with her marital past hanging around her like a dirty shawl. Ruth wished she had the power to snatch it off and burn it, but it was no more hers to deal with than the letter was.

"I don't know what to do about the letter, Aunt Ruth."

When Ruth lifted her cup, she caught a glimpse of Josie swirling around in the dark coffee, a confused woman trying to find her footing.

"Josie don't know for sure you're here."

"That's what I think, too. But sooner or later, she'll go to Wayne with her news, whether or not she's certain. And there's always the chance that somebody else recognized me and will tell him. Maybe if I call her, I might be able to talk Mother into keeping my whereabouts a secret."

Ruth thought there was about as much chance of that as pigs flying.

"I wouldn't count on Josie's good nature as far as I could throw Indian Joe's elephant."

"I just don't know what to do."

"The end justifies the means, is what I say. Call her up and tell a lie."

"Like the one you had Ray Boy tell about you dying?"

"Well, I am gonna die. Someday."

When Ellen started laughing, Ruth got her tickle box turned over. Before she knew it, she was laughing so hard she had tears rolling down her face, which explained why the knock at the door caught her by surprise. One of her best gifts was in knowing when somebody was coming. But the Great Giovanni's daughter standing at her door was enough to make her wonder if she might be losing some of her powers.

Clarice was a handsome woman, the kind who aged well. She had a firm chin that said she'd brook nonsense from no man, and deep eyes that showed both her intelligence and her compassion, a trait she tried hard to keep under wraps. Ruth saw it all. Someday she'd sit down under a shade tree and tell Clarice it was all right to let go and show a vulnerable side, that she didn't have to be strong for everybody.

But today was not the time. Clarice was standing there in an embroidered shawl with her shoes wet from dew, just standing there looking from Ellen to Ruth, waiting to have her say. Ruth aimed to let her do it her way.

"I came to say I was wrong about you, Eve, and Daddy and my son were right."

Ruth felt Ellen's relief, saw it in the way the shawl of her past started to fade. But she held herself still. It was her niece's place to decide whether she would forgive this woman.

"Thank you, Mrs. DeChello. That means the world to me."

"I thought it might." When Clarice smiled she was truly beautiful. No wonder her son, Luca, looked like one of the film stars Ruth had once seen when she broke down and let Ray Boy carry her to the movies. "Please, won't you call me Clarice?"

"I'd like that, Clarice. Won't you come in for coffee?"

"Some other time, perhaps. Mark says I'm stubborn, and I guess I am. It will take me a while to start thinking of you as a friend." She shaded her eyes against the sun and swiveled around at the sound of horses' hooves before turning back to Ellen. "You've been good for both my son and my grandson."

"They've been good for me."

When Clarice left, Ruth caught a whiff of orange blossoms, a scent she instantly recognized in spite of the fact she'd never been near an orange grove.

"I like that woman," she said. "She says what she means and means what she says."

"Luca said she used to be a great equestrian."

"I reckon it come natural."

Mist covered her glasses, and for an instant she could see it all—the Great Giovanni leaving the big top, standing on a white horse just as Lola stepped into a cage of tigers.

When the mists cleared, Ruth was filled with such urgency to know what had happened with Lola and Jim Hall that she could taste her longing. It tasted like lemon drops with just enough sugar to avoid being tart.

"I've made up my mind, Aunt Ruth."

"About what?"

"I'm going to call Mother."

"I'll go with you."

"I'm not calling while we're in Tallahassee. In a city this big, there's too much chance someone saw me on TV and will recognize me. I'll wait till we're in a small town."

23

IT WAS WELL PAST midseason for the traveling circus, and the Great Giovanni Bros./Hogan & Sandusky Circus had fallen into a rhythm as predictable as the brass section of the band. Each segment of the circus had a part to play, performed exactly on cue—roustabouts, canvas men, props managers, midway bosses, menagerie men, and performers. Even the animals had settled into a routine with only an occasional uprising, mostly from Edna, who enjoyed private spitting walkabouts when she could get loose, and Betsy, who enjoyed stealing hats as well as cabbages.

They left Tallahassee on schedule, and the big top was already up in Madison when Ellen pulled her trailer into the circus backyard. It was one of those blue cloudless days that made you think of running barefoot through cool sprinklers, the kind of day that dared trouble to come calling.

"Does this look like a tiger to you?" Sun slanted across the passenger side of the Ford Fairlane where Aunt Ruth sat with a skein of pink yarn in her lap and an unfinished crochet piece of pink and yellow and turquoise in her hands.

"It looks like Sheikh, except rainbow colored. April's going to love it."

"Reckon it's *the day after yestermorro* yet?"

"We can ask Rose and Jocko at breakfast."

Ellen hopped out to unhook her trailer from the hitch. When she'd first gotten the mobile home, Big Glen, the menagerie/arrow man, had always been around to help her with it, but she'd insisted on learning, and now she could perform the task as efficiently as he had.

If Wayne could see her now, he'd be furious. He'd spent every waking minute trying to keep her dependent and subservient. She realized that now, remembering all the car trips where he'd said she was too nervous to drive; the trips they'd made to Sears where he'd told her to let him do all the talking because he didn't want her to bother her pretty head about appliances; even the trips to the garden center where he'd been the one to select holly bushes and nix forsythia because he said the yard was a man's territory.

She finished unhooking the trailer then stood up and put her hands in the small of her back. A breeze caught her new pink maternity top and wrapped it close. There was no disguising her growing belly. She was glad she'd told Luca. Before the drive this morning, she'd gone over to tell Michelle.

I've been knowing ever since you set foot in the circus backyard, Michelle had said, and when Ellen had asked how, she said, *The way you carried yourself, like you had precious cargo onboard and would fight Razz's meanest cat to keep it safe.*

Now, thinking that that's exactly what she would do, Ellen was turning to tell Aunt Ruth the trailer was unhitched when she spotted the car. Black and white. "Madison Police Department" printed on the side. Frozen, she watched two men in uniform get out and head in the direction of the big top.

Both Razz and the Great Giovanni were there, one with his baseball cap rammed low and the other with his white mane blowing in the wind.

Please, please, please.

Ellen shook off her paralysis and jerked open the car door.

"Aunt Ruth. Cops!"

Ruth scrambled out of the car with her crochet and raced after her into the trailer. Ellen slammed and locked the door, then leaned against it, willing her legs to hold her up.

"It's Wayne. He sent them to get me."

"Maybe. Maybe not."

"Can you tell?"

Ruth put her arm around Ellen and led her to the couch. "Baby, if I could call up the future as easy as I can a good herdin' dog, I'd be rich, and purty, to boot."

"How's that, Aunt Ruth?"

"I'd get me a face-lift." Ruth chafed Ellen's cold hands. "Now, you listen to me. We safe in here. Ain't no cops I ever seen can look through walls."

"What if they come knocking on doors?"

"We'll act like we deaf."

"They can get court orders or something."

"Ain't no use borrowin' trouble, Ellen. Them cops has to get through Razz first, and I don't think that man's got a mind to let anybody else run his business."

"Neither does Giovanni. Until you learn what an old softy he is, he can scare you to death."

"Now, that's a winner talkin'."

Still, there was no use taking chances. Both of them agreed. Ruth started breakfast while Ellen put on the disguise Jocko had given her. In spite of the sunshine, which both of them enjoyed, they kept the blinds closed. If any of the circus family came to inquire why they weren't at the cook tent or why Ellen wasn't in the school tent, Ruth would say she was sick and couldn't come out.

As she sat at the kitchen table in her brown wig and her ugly wax nose, she swallowed tiny bites of egg and fear, in spite of the fact that the smell of eggs made her sick and the fear landed in the pit of her stomach where it grew as big as one of Indian Joe's bulls. Trying to hold down nausea, she thought about the cops outside her trailer. Did Wayne want them to drag her home or toss her in jail on some trumped-up charge? Maybe stealing his car?

But what if they weren't looking for her? What if they'd come searching for Jocko? Bobby and April would be devastated, and Rose would be left alone to cope.

She jumped up from the table and headed toward the door, peeling off her disguise as she went.

"Ellen! Where you goin'?"

"To save a friend."

Without waiting for a reply, she burst through the door. If the cops found her, a woman whose face was on posters all over the South, maybe they'd forget about Jocko.

Filled with courage and purpose, Ellen hurried along. Someday when she could stand in the circus backyard with the sun on her arms and her child splashing in a blow-up child's pool, she'd have reason to be proud of herself. The wind would catch their laughter and toss it skyward. People from miles around would hear the happy sound, and hearing it, they would smile.

EXCITEMENT SWIRLED AROUND THE cook tent as thick and pink as cotton candy. Tomorrow was April's birthday, and everybody from Magic Michelle to Indian Joe was having a say in the surprise party.

"We can bring her in riding Betsy," Joe said, and Rose agreed that her daughter would love being on the elephant, as long as she was up there, too.

Cookie Two wanted to talk about the cake, and Linda thought it would look good in polka dots.

"Sort of like my ocelot."

"Whoever heard of a brown cake?" Cookie snorted.

"Make it rainbow colored," Clarice suggested. "Like Nicky's elephant. April loves my grandson's elephant."

Since Nicky started talking, Clarice, who usually stayed out of the general hubbub of circus life, had started entering it. Razz thought that was a good sign that she liked Eve, and he was as proud as if Eve were his own granddaughter. If he weren't careful he'd start believing she was. He might even suggest that April's birthday have a touch of gold to match his tiger's eyes.

When Big Glen appeared in the opening of the cook tent, Razz's good mood vanished. It wasn't so much the *come here quick* motion he made as the look on Glen's face that sent Razz loping out of the cook tent, leaving behind a perfectly good breakfast, half eaten, and a puzzled Giovanni saying, "What's your hurry? We haven't even had our coffee."

"Can't wait. We've been having some trouble with Jezebel. I'd better check this out."

One of these days, he'd explain all his lies to his old friend. But not now, not while Glen had ahold of his arm, dragging him toward the marquee where a black-and-white police car was parked. A short, sandy-haired uniformed officer leaned on its hood with his beefy arms crossed and his face set in lines that said he was not too happy with his reception at the circus.

"He's looking for the teacher," Big Glen said.

"What'd you tell him?"

"That I know everybody in this circus, and she ain't here."

"Good. Now I want you to find Jocko and Indian Joe. Tell them I need a huge distraction."

Big Glen tipped his baseball cap and vanished like smoke.

Razz tilted his own cap so the scars where his scalp had been stitched back on would show. It couldn't hurt to let the cop know he was tough enough to survive a lion and wasn't scared of the law.

"I'm Razz Hogan. The owner." He nodded toward the banner of the big top that clearly had his name in the circus title, then checked the officer's badge. "What can I do for you, Sergeant Haley?"

"I'm here to see you about this girl." He wasn't the least bit surprised when the cop pulled out a missing flyer with a picture of Lola's great-niece. "The husband got a tip she was traveling with this circus."

"Let me see." Razz studied the flyer long enough to keep the cop in the heat till sweat beaded his face. Ellen smiled back at him, her face lovely and her eyes just as dead as Lola's when she'd first said to Razz, *Save me.* "We have people coming and going all the time. But I don't recall ever seeing this woman."

"She's got her hair red, now. And short. Are you sure about that?"

"I make it my business to know everybody on my payroll, and their families, too. If there was a good-looking redhead traveling with the circus, I'd know it."

"All the same, I'm going to take a look around."

Suddenly Betsy rolled up like a giant storm. The cop's hat sailed upward and landed between her flapping ears.

"Sorry about that." Indian Joe looked suitably apologetic. "Betsy, let us have that hat."

She plopped it on Joe then snatched Razz's cap and set it on the cop.

Sergeant Haley threw his hands in front of his face. "Get that elephant out of here!"

"She won't hurt you, but she seems to have taken a liking to your car."

Razz grabbed his cap off the officer's head while Betsy's trunk reached over the cop's shoulders to examine the blue light on top of his car. Years of working with big cats had taught Razz how to bury his emotions so deep not even a tiger could sense he was about to burst out laughing.

"Joe," he said, "move this elephant back before she takes a notion to drive."

Joe was making a big to-do of trying to budge Betsy, when Jocko, in full clown costume, yelled, "Hey, Razz. I need to talk to you."

As Jocko honked his bulbous clown nose, the freight train sound caused Betsy to let out a trumpet that could be heard clear to the state line. That her trunk was close to the cop's ear was no accident. Sergeant Haley jumped so high he might have been auditioning for the high-wire act.

Razz couldn't have been more satisfied with Joe's and Jocko's performances if he'd thought up the whole thing. It came as no surprise to him when the cop decided the best way to deal with an inquisitive elephant was to hide in the safety of his car then glare back through the window as if they had hidden the teacher in the pachyderm's trunk.

It also came as no surprise to him that Ellen was sprinting their way, the same look on her face he'd seen on Lola when she got into the cat cage and kept Congo from ripping off the rest of his scalp.

Razz shook his head at her, *no,* then motioned for her to stop. She came to a halt by the cotton candy stand, then stood there uncertainly. But she was only watching now, thank God, and not wading right into the path of the cop, who still sat there with his motor idling.

At a signal from Indian Joe, Betsy put her trunk to the car window and gave one last trumpet. The cop tore out of the circus so fast he forgot his flyer. With a big elephant smile, Betsy stuck her trunk into Joe's pocket and came out with the peanuts she'd earned.

"That one won't be back. Thanks to my girl." Indian Joe patted Betsy's trunk and gave her another reward of peanuts.

"The opera ain't over till the fat lady sings," Jocko said. "I'm keeping my eyes open and my fists ready."

"What fat lady?" Indian Joe wanted to know. "What'd the law want?"

Razz couldn't be everywhere at once. In the end, he hadn't

been able to save Lola, but now Fate was giving him a chance to save her granddaughter. Remembering Wayne Blair from his appearance on *Donahue,* Razz felt the beginnings of a migraine headache.

"Spread the word through the backyard," he said. "Somebody's out to harm our teacher. Describe the skunk down to that self-satisfied grin on his face—six feet, dark hair, handsome if you like the sleazy type."

"If he crosses my path, I'll take the bull hook to him. Eve's a nice woman, and that Mimi is one of my best friends." Indian Joe tapped Betsy on the trunk and they set off toward the menagerie tent. "That's my good baby."

Jocko stayed behind with Razz.

"I'll have Rose alert the women not to let Eve out of their sight."

"Eve's proud. Tell them to act natural."

"There's no such thing as natural in this bunch. What are you going to do, Razz?"

"Tell Al."

It was just a small lie. He was going to tell Al, but first he had something more important to do. As soon as Jocko was out of sight, Razz strolled over to the cotton candy stand, where Eve had remained. Acting like he bought cotton candy every day of his life, he paid for a cone and handed it to Lola's granddaughter, then put his hand on her elbow.

"Walk with me, Eve." He took her elbow, then rounded the corner of the stand to the circus backyard, empty now except for performers who were scattered about the lot, practicing their acts. "That cop won't be back."

"Judging by what I saw, he's across the state line by now."

Eve giggled and then got serious. "Was he after me or Jocko?"

"You came out here thinking you'd save Jocko?"

"He's my friend."

"The day Jocko can't take care of himself is the day he'll be carried out feetfirst in a clown car. Now go on back and tell that old battle-ax you stay with that she can quit peering into teacups."

Eve laughed again, the sound so like Lola's laughter he had to wipe his eyes and mutter, "Damned allergies."

"You're an old softy, just like the Great Giovanni."

"Don't tell Al, and if you tell the tigers, I'll be missing the other half of my scalp."

"I wouldn't dream of it." The young woman who had turned herself into Eve took off his baseball cap, planted a kiss on the jagged old scar, then left him standing there not knowing whether to turn red and blustery or to break down and cry.

In the end, he did neither. He wheeled off toward the cook tent to find his old friend. Al was still there nursing a cup of coffee. The canvas men were long gone, the ringing of hammers against metal testament to their dedication to raising the big top, as were all the performers, who were now scattered about the lot, some practicing their acts, others merely enjoying the sun.

Razz got a cup of coffee from the kitchen and sat down beside Al.

"So, Razz, how was that bogus business in the menagerie tent?"

"Am I that easy to read?"

"You can fool everybody here except me. Are you ready to tell me what's going on, or do you plan to go on being the Lone Ranger like you did with Lola?"

"How'd you know this was about Lola?"

"I've still got eyes. I knew the minute I saw that girl there was something about her."

"Eve is Lola's granddaughter."

"She looks a lot like her."

"She's like Lola in more ways than one, Al."

"If you tell me that girl wants to train tigers, I'll have my doctor check you for hardening of the arteries."

"Didn't you see the bruises?"

"I didn't want to see. Besides, she's safe here, just like Lola."

Razz's dark secret made the bile rise in his throat. He'd never told Al, and never would. But the idea of carrying his secret to his grave suddenly felt like Betsy sitting on his chest.

"Razz? Are you all right?" Al slapped him on the back.

"Coffee went down wrong, that's all." He took another sip. "Eve's husband is looking for her. The cops were here this morning."

"She's such a sweet young woman. Why would anybody ever lay a hand on her?" Al teared up and didn't try to hide it. "I was my usual fearsome self when she came looking for work, did my best to run her off, but she cornered me and wouldn't take no for an answer. That girl's got guts."

"If her husband gets his hands on her again, guts won't help, Al. She'll be dead."

"Not in my circus, she won't." Al had many sides, the gruff curmudgeon, the marshmallow-hearted grandfather, but when he stood up from the table, he was the Great Giovanni, formidable in both size and temperament. "Let's go find Luca."

24

CHANGE ROSE UP FROM the chicken salad as Ruth stirred, evident in the way the egg yolks glowed gold and in the scent that wafted toward the ceiling of their mobile home, like lemons mixed with daffodils, yellow for hope.

She eased back the curtain, watching for her niece, but Ellen was still out there somewhere on the circus grounds. Were the cops still there, too?

Ruth looked into her bowl, hoping for some answers and a clear revelation, but the vision had vanished, and there was nothing to see except chicken and eggs and sweet pickles chopped up and stirred with plenty of mayonnaise.

She might as well make some fresh biscuits and see where that led her. But no matter how she poked and prodded, no matter how closely she looked, the dough was just dough. It was a great relief to her when Ellen strolled back into the trailer.

"The cop is gone, Aunt Ruth."

"Just one?"

"Yes."

"I hope he don't come back and spoil April's birthday party."

"The way he hightailed it out of here after Betsy got through with him, I'd say he's halfway to Canada by now."

As Ruth popped the biscuits in the oven, the scent of daffodils and lemons drifted upward once more, the revelation clear now. Change was not only a-coming, it was already here.

The knock on the door didn't surprise Ruth one bit, nor Magic Michelle calling, "Mimi, Eve, are you in there?"

"Just a minute." Ruth peered out the window, though the scent of lemons and daffodils overpowering the smell of baking biscuits told her clear as rain that Magic Michelle was standing out there by herself.

She opened the door and there was their friend standing in the sunshine with a bird perched on her shoulder.

"Come on in and set a spell. Do you have time for tea?"

"I have nothing but time today. I'm under the weather, and Razz thought it would be a good idea to cancel my bird act for the matinee."

Michelle's false story hovered over her head like a small white scarf, its intent somehow mixed up with Razz and his tigers. Mixed signals always gave Ruth a touch of vertigo. She set the teacups down so she wouldn't drop them, then sank into a chair while Michelle studied Ellen.

"You look a mite peaked yourself," she said. "Why don't you rest today?"

"I need to get to the school tent."

"Don't you worry about it, Eve. Everybody deserves a day off once in a while."

"I don't want Razz and the Great Giovanni to think I'm not doing my job."

"After what you did for Nicky, Al thinks you walk on

water. And Razz thinks you're working too hard. He told me to make sure you put your feet up for the rest of the day. Rose and I are going to start helping you out a little more."

"When I get so big I can't see my feet, I might take you up on that offer."

Ellen put her hand over her womb in a way that reminded Ruth of the redbird who used to swoop down out of the crepe myrtle tree to defend her young.

"Michelle, them biscuits is 'bout ready. Stay for lunch."

"Wild horses couldn't drag me away." Michelle shifted, and her bird flew from her shoulder to perch on top of her head.

If you'd have told Ruth before she started this journey that she'd be sipping tea at the circus with a woman who had a bird on her head, she'd have laughed in your face. It was remarkable the way Fate could pick you up and set you down so that the life you'd lived before was so distant it seemed like a dream.

Ruth thought about Ray Boy, back on the mountain in Arkansas, hoeing the garden and gathering the corn. Right about now, he'd be trying to decide whether to let the cornfield lie fallow a year or rotate the crops to replenish the soil.

Maybe when Ellen called Josie, Ruth would call Ray Boy, let him know that she was living in the midst of a place that created magic every day, that she was surrounded by so many unusual and glorious happenings that her own visions were beginning to lose their Technicolor edges and fade into the watercolor images of a woman simply remembering.

She took her biscuits out of the oven, served them up on three plates heaping with chicken salad and plenty of butter and strawberry jam, and poured three glasses of lemonade.

The Ellen who sat down to eat was not the scared girl who had arrived on the mountain determined to leave Wayne. The look on her face showed the kind of grit it must have taken for her grandmother to climb into the center ring with sixteen tigers. Though the circumstances hadn't changed—the same sorry husband was after her and the same misguided mother was wondering why her daughter didn't come to her senses—there was an air about Ellen that made it impossible to look at her without seeing a woman who would no longer be a victim.

"I have something to tell you, Michelle."

"You don't have to tell me anything, Eve."

"Yes, I do. I don't want to keep secrets from you anymore."

She lifted her tea, as graceful as Lola and just as beautiful, just as vulnerable, then told about the husband who beat her black and blue, her first attempt at escape, and finally the journey that had brought her to the circus.

"I've suspected this from the beginning," Michelle said. "And I have a little confession of my own. I'm not here accidentally."

"I seen that the minute you come in the door," Ruth said.

To her credit, Michelle didn't ask how. Ruth guessed a woman accustomed to seeing magic every day in the circus is more accepting of the supernatural than ordinary folk. And wasn't that a blessing? All her life she'd been viewed as different. It pleased her that at last she blended right in, as if she belonged.

"I'm here to help watch after you, honey," Michelle told her. "But remember this. You haven't done anything wrong.

The cops can't just drag you off and hand you over to that human scum."

"You're right, of course. Why didn't I think of that?"

"Because you were too busy trying to survive." Michelle snapped her fingers, and her bird flew off his perch atop her head to make graceful circles around the ceiling.

"Oh my God." Suddenly Ellen began to laugh. "I don't have to wear that silly disguise anymore."

"No, you can just be you," Michelle said. "So, what shall I call you?"

"Call me Eve."

"And you can call me Mimi," Ruth told her. "Now, let's finish off these biscuits."

As they ate, Michelle's bird flew around their trailer, his white wings lighting up every corner.

WITH A COLD BISCUIT in one hand and the other over her abdomen, Ellen felt her baby move. How such a small thing could make her feel so powerful was beyond her imagining. The conviction that had been growing since Michelle arrived took seed and began to sprout.

"I need to wash clothes and call my mother."

"I'll go with you," Michelle said. "My own laundry's piled higher than my head."

"Let me get my shotgun," said Aunt Ruth.

Michelle's full-blown laughter was contagious, and as Ellen joined in, her baby kicked again.

The three of them gathered their laundry, Michelle stowed her bird in her trailer, and they piled into Ellen's Ford Fairlane with Ellen driving, Michelle in the back, and Aunt Ruth riding shotgun.

"I hope you don't shoot the top out of the car, Mimi," Michelle said.

"It ain't loaded."

"It's just for show?"

"Heck no. In my day, I could shoot a dime out of the air. I can still hit what I'm aiming at if it's big enough. And I got the shells in my pocket."

"Remind me never to get on your bad side."

The Madison Laundromat sat back from the side of the road in a big gravel parking lot empty except for a yellow Volkswagen and Ellen's car.

"Looks like they'll be plenty a machines open," Ruth said.

"Thank goodness." Michelle hefted her laundry basket out of the backseat. "I don't have the patience I used to."

Ellen checked the area carefully before she got out of the car. To the left of the Laundromat, a used-car lot looked as forlorn as its sagging banners proclaiming "Honest John's." A log cabin restaurant on the right was doing a lively business, its parking lot filled and a line of patrons snaking out the door and spilling onto the rockers lining the front porch.

She saw two men Wayne's size and build and regretted her decision to leave behind the brown wig and the ugly nose. The cops were one thing: Wayne's henchmen were another. While Ruth and Michelle trotted back and forth with laundry baskets, Ellen sat watching the men, looking for any sign that one of them was Wayne.

She hated the fear that rose up so suddenly, no matter what kind of brave-sounding resolutions she'd made.

Nervous sweat made her hair stick to her scalp, and when she finally got out of the car, she felt like one of Michelle's birds caught in the rain.

When Ellen entered the small concrete block building, the bell over the door tinkled and a worn-looking woman in a loose gray sweat suit looked up from one of the dryers then quickly looked away, her attitude clear in every line of her face and body. If she recognized the Angel on the Bridge or Ellen's face from one of the posters, she would have no part in it. She was there to wash clothes and mind her own business. She wouldn't be saying hello and chatting about the weather, and she certainly didn't want anybody to speak to her.

Ellen walked on by, not saying a word. Before her flight to freedom, if you'd told her that she'd become the kind of woman who went out of her way to avoid conversations with strangers, she'd have said you were crazy. As she piled her whites into the washing machine, she wondered if it would always be that way. Or would time bring her back piece by piece?

She slipped her quarters into the machine, then found the pay phone hung on the wall down a hallway at the far end of the building. Backed by the distant hum of Aunt Ruth and Michelle's conversation, she dialed her mother.

Josie answered on the first ring, the sound of her voice bringing a wave of memories that almost overwhelmed Ellen—the way Josie pursed her lips when she basted the Thanksgiving turkey, the pink garden gloves she bought every year in anticipation of cutting the first bloom of roses, her outrageous pride when Ellen graduated from college.

"Hello. *Hello?*" Josie said, impatience dripping from every syllable. "Is anybody there?"

"It's me."

"Ellen? Ellen! For Pete's sake, where are you?"

"I'm safe."

"Is Ruth Gibson with you?"

"She is. And she's fine, too."

"Good grief, Ellen, I don't care if she's jumped off the side of that old mountain she lives on."

"Mother, please."

"Oh, I know you don't like me saying things about Ruth, but listen, honey, don't pay any attention to what she's telling you. Just come on home so we can be a family."

"Aunt Ruth is not the reason I left. It's Wayne."

"He's worried sick about you."

"He's not worried about me for my sake, Mother. He's upset because he has lost his personal punching bag."

"You're just upset, that's all."

"Mother, he's the reason I was in the hospital."

"It was the car wreck, honey. Pregnancy makes women imagine all kinds of crazy things."

Ellen massaged her temples. What would it take to get through to Josie?

"Mother, why won't you understand? I had to leave before he killed me. And the baby along with me."

There was no sound from Josie's end except faint music from the radio, a deep, rich voice that sounded like Nat King Cole.

Her mother would be in the kitchen where the radio sat underneath the window. Was she looking at the backyard thinking how she'd planned to put a child's swing set under the magnolia tree? Was she thinking about the Hall family Christmas with her grandchild staring big-eyed at the star on the tree?

Sweat rolled down the side of Ellen's face, and she twisted the phone cord into a knot.

"I told him about the TV story, Ellen, you on that bridge in the storm."

Was that a hitch in Josie's voice? Remorse?

"I'm not blaming you, Mother."

"I didn't know. I really didn't know."

There was the sudden sound of weeping. It would be useless to say anything. When Josie went on a crying jag, nobody could get through to her. Ellen leaned against the wall, her skin turned yellow by the naked bulb hanging on a cord, and waited her mother out.

"Mother, can you hear me?"

"Yes." There were some sniffles, and the sound of Josie searching the cabinets for the tissues she could never find. "I may be just an aging woman whose only child has left her, but I haven't gone deaf yet."

"Mother, please. Can you just this once focus on something besides yourself?"

"Why, Ellen! You've never talked to me like that."

"Maybe I should have."

"I raised you better."

"No, you raised me to keep the peace, Mother, no matter what the cost. It's high time for me to stand up for myself. And maybe you should, too."

"I don't know what you're talking about."

"Daddy walks all over you."

"Don't talk about your father like that. He's a good man."

"I didn't say he wasn't a good man, Mother. I'm just trying to get you to look at things without your rose-colored glasses."

"Is that why you called? To talk about my shortcomings?"

Ellen twisted the cord tighter. Why was it that a conversation with her mother always took the wrong turn? Taking deep breaths, she glanced down the short hallway and past the machines to the plate-glass window with its peeling black lettering.

A tall man strolled around her car then leaned down to peer in the window, shading his face with his hands.

Wayne? She almost dropped the phone, almost raced down the hall and out the door to see if he had dark hair, accusing eyes, and a cruel mouth.

Did Wayne know she'd traded cars? Would he come into the Laundromat and jerk her out by her hair before Michelle or Aunt Ruth could even move? He could slam her into the gravel and kick the life out of her and her baby with one blow.

"Mother, listen. This is important. Where is Wayne?" Josie's silence screamed along Ellen's nerves. "Mother? Is he looking for me?"

"He left yesterday morning before daylight."

"Oh my God!"

The circus would be easy to track, as easy as going to the library and finding the schedule for the Great Giovanni Bros./ Hogan & Sandusky Circus right there in the newspaper stacks.

"I only did what I thought was best, Ellen."

"Does he know what kind of car I drive?"

"Well, of course he does. He bought it for you."

Would Wayne have told Josie if he knew Ellen had traded cars? Probably not. He'd want Josie to see nothing except a son-in-law who felt betrayed by a wife who had done him wrong.

"Mother, will you please do something for me?"

"All I've done is the best I can."

Ellen pictured the way her mother stood when she felt wronged, her chin slightly lifted, her bottom lip stuck out, and one hand balled into a fist. Longing caught her unaware, a fierce need to hug her mother, to tell her everything would be all right.

"Well, what is it you want, Ellen?"

"If Wayne calls, please don't tell him you've heard from me. Or Daddy, either." In the long silence, Ellen heard the bell over the door tinkle, saw Michelle and Aunt Ruth hurrying toward the man still circling Ellen's car. "Please, Mother!"

"All right." Josie's sigh was so pronounced it would have been audible in the next room. Was Ellen's father in the next room immersed in a TV program, or was he on the golf course, seizing every advantage to be away from home? "If that's the way you want it."

Ellen said a hasty good-bye and raced down the hall. As she burst into the laundry room, the woman in the gray sweat suit never looked up. Outside, Aunt Ruth was arguing and the man was making big, angry gestures. Was it Wayne, refusing to leave? What would he do if he saw her?

Almost at the front door, Ellen veered and ducked behind a soda machine, grateful she could stand and still be hidden from the man's view. Risking a peek, she was paralyzed by the man's size, the possibility that any moment he could squeeze Aunt Ruth's neck with one of his big hands.

Something boiled up inside her strong enough to shake her like a rag doll. She exploded from her hiding place and streaked out the door with only one thought in her mind:

Wayne would not get his hands on Aunt Ruth. Not while she drew a breath.

Rage was the color of a redbird's wing. It mushroomed like a cloud, obscuring everything around her in a mist.

"Eve!" Michelle was suddenly at her side, a hand on her arm. "Are you all right?"

"Where is he?" There was no one in the parking lot except Aunt Ruth, putting a load of laundry in the car, and Michelle, staring at her as if she might vanish in a puff of smoke.

"Where is who?"

"Wayne. I saw him out here."

"It wasn't Wayne, but I suspect it was one of his spies."

"I sent him packin'." Ruth strolled up, still spitting mad. "He commenced askin' if they was a redhead owned this car, and I give him what for. Told him it was my car and he'd best be goin' before my daughter Gloria called the cops."

"Gloria?"

"If I keep hanging out with Mimi, I guess I'll have to change my name." Michelle linked arms and led Ellen back into the Laundromat. "Let's finish this laundry. I've got to get back for the evening show."

By the time they left the Laundromat, the sky was dark with clouds and the first droplets slashed the windshield. As the rain picked up speed, Ellen imagined Wayne somewhere out there, calculating how the downpour would give him an advantage, how he could turn his hat down and hide behind a shield of water. She'd never know what hit her.

She'd ditch the telltale Fairlane in a second if she had the money. But her small reserve was already depleted, and her salary was barely enough to cover living expenses, let alone buy a new car. And by the time she found a used one to trade, it could already be too late.

"It's rainin' harder," Aunt Ruth said. "Will they cancel the show, Michelle?"

"Haven't you heard the saying, Mimi? The show must go on."

And Ellen would be left in her trailer, alone except for Aunt Ruth nodding over her TV, the Ford Fairlane a dead giveaway that she was inside.

B Y THE TIME THEY returned to the circus grounds, the rains had slowed to a steady drizzle. The circus backyard might have been any neighborhood except for the glimpse of exotic creatures, sequined costumes, and the big top rising above the circle of trailers. Linda was walking her ocelot, holding the umbrella over the spotted cat rather than herself. Bobby and April splashed in puddles while Rose stood in the doorway calling for them to stay out of the mud. The roar of the Bengal tiger in Razz's trailer caused not the slightest tremble or stir. It was just another day in the life of the circus.

What had once seemed a temporary haven for her niece now seemed to Ruth like home. And wouldn't that be fine? One of these days she might invite Ray Boy for a visit. He needed to take a vacation, and wouldn't the look on his face when she introduced him to Betsy and Indian Joe be something to see?

Ruth called good-bye to Michelle, who was hurrying off to get ready for the evening show, while Ellen headed to the bedroom to put the clean sheets back on the bed.

Nothing left for Ruth to do but put on a pot of tea. A few

weeks ago she'd have called that a shiftless life, but the circus had changed her tune. She never thought she'd live to sit on the couch and put her feet up without worrying about worms in her tomatoes and blackbirds in her corn.

She was just sinking into her chair when somebody knocked on the door.

"Who is it?"

"Al Giovanni."

Ruth imagined all the reasons the Great Giovanni would come calling, but she could come up with nothing that made a lick of sense.

When she opened the door, he was standing in the mud in a tuxedo, of all things, his boots spattered with mud and the umbrella over his head wide enough to cover half of Texas.

"Good evening, Mimi."

"Well, ain't you a sight. Come on in out of the rain and have some tea."

He reminded her of her granddaddy, God rest his soul, a big man who covered the ground he walked on, the kind of man whose bluster hid a soft heart.

"I came to escort you and Eve to the evening show."

She pictured them sitting on the bleachers in a crowd of strangers, Ellen as vulnerable as a baby chicken in a garden with a hawk soaring overhead.

"That's mighty nice of you, but these old bones of mine wouldn't be too happy on them hard bleachers."

"I want you to sit in the box with me at the evening show. And I won't take no for an answer."

Ruth got a weightless feeling, as if she'd left her heavy old bones behind and become a young girl again. Finally she was going to get to live the spangled dreams that had played through her sleep for the last fifty years.

"Ain't no reason to say no. Eve needs some company besides me, and I ain't about to turn down the chance to see the circus from the owner's box. Just let me tell Eve."

"Please tell her that I'll escort both of you home after the show as a proper gentleman should."

"I can't remember the last time I had an escort. Just let me get my bonnet."

Just that fast, Ruth ended up behind red velvet ropes sitting in a chair with a red velvet cushion while sequin-covered girls on Indian Joe's elephants led the Grand Spectacular. It had taken some convincing to get Ellen to leave the trailer, but Ruth finally used the argument that if Wayne Blair was actually at the circus, it could do him good to see her sitting under the big top, pretty as you please, with none other than the Great Giovanni watching over her.

"Show 'em that you ain't easy pickings," she'd said. It worked, too. Sandwiched between Clarice and the Great Giovanni, Ellen had her chin up and a smile on her face.

Let that sorry husband of hers get a gander at that. And he would. Make no mistake about it. Wafting along behind the clown cars and the Chinese tumblers and Magic Michelle with her white birds was a wisp of evil so black it took Ruth only a minute to figure out the source. Wayne Blair was out there somewhere, hiding in the crowd, his cleverness no protection at all from a cagey old mystic who could find a thimbleful of meanness in the Atlantic Ocean.

The minute she stepped out of the trailer she'd known he was there. The air was so thick with bad intentions she could barely breathe. She guessed she shouldn't have been surprised. She and Ellen had always known he'd come. What surprised Ruth was that he'd sneaked up on her. Her dreams hadn't shown a glimmer of his arrival. There hadn't been a single sign that he was closing in, not in the song of crickets or the pattern of a spiderweb or a vision filled with darkness.

Even the man at the Laundromat had carried no whiff of Wayne Blair's presence.

She wondered if she might be losing her touch. Was it possible that she'd lost the gift that had been her blessing and her curse? Was it possible that she might go into old age free of everything except the joy of watching Ellen's baby grow?

"Ladies and gentlemen! I present a show extraordinaire, brought to you by the Great Giovanni Bros./Hogan & Sandusky Circus!" The ringmaster's voice brought Ruth back to the big top, where Michelle's doves flew in heart-shaped configurations, Jocko stood by a child's swimming pool urging Rose, in an outrageous, quivering clown wig, to jump, and aerialists twirled high above her head.

The music swelled so loud the notes floated in the air, and the smell of popcorn was so rich it tasted like butter. Ruth's glasses fogged, and suddenly there was her sister, floating high above the center ring, her golden hair glowing in the lights.

Lola spun slowly through the air, her blue eyes as clear as they'd been the day she left her baby on the mountain for Ruth to raise.

It's almost time, Ruth, she whispered. And then she was gone, leaving behind a fragrance like roses.

* * *

RUTH DREAMED ABOUT THE tiger again, only this time he was not racing along with his stripes turning to gold ribbon; he was standing in the moonlight with teeth bared. A snort jerked her awake, and she found herself in a wrinkled pile on the blue plaid couch with the TV still blaring and her mouth dry from snoring.

Where was Ellen? A minute ago, it seemed, they'd been strolling from the big top with Great Giovanni, and now there was no sign of her.

Ruth jumped up as agile and fierce as a woman who could fight bears threatening to take off her young.

"Ellen?"

"In here, Aunt Ruth." Her niece stuck her head out of the bathroom.

"Lord have mercy, I thought Wayne had done took you."

"Not unless he breaks down the door. Aunt Ruth, are you all right?"

"Fit as a fiddle."

She remembered now. She was so tuckered out when they got back from the evening show, she'd sat on the couch to rest. Had she fallen asleep the minute she sat down? She was getting soft.

To prove otherwise, she hurried to the window spry as that old jaybird that used to worry the robins around Ruth's bird feeders. The rains had stopped, and a pale moon lit the circus backyard. It came as no surprise when she saw the tiger standing at the edge of the yard. Though he was half in shadow, Razz was beside Sheikh, keeping watch over Ellen, his intent streaming out behind him like a glowing banner.

"We can rest easy now. We got a Bengal tiger for a bodyguard."

Tonight when Ruth slept in the shadow of a tiger, it would be a real one.

THE SMELL OF BAKING filtered through Ellen's nightmare. She was running through mists, running from the thing that made her heart pound. It was a relief to open her eyes and see sun pouring through the window, to hear Aunt Ruth rattling dishes in the kitchen.

Ellen dressed quickly. She wanted to get to the school tent before the children arrived so she could hang crepe paper streamers for April's birthday.

"Something smells good in here, Aunt Ruth."

"It's them cupcakes you wanted." Last night before they went to sleep, Ellen had said she wanted to have a birthday celebration just for the children in the school tent. "They ain't gonna be done for a while yet, though."

"That's okay. You can bring them when they're ready."

Ellen stepped into the circus backyard where the morning sun had laced everything with gold. Even Luca's white horses prancing in their temporary paddock had turned the color of melted butter. On a morning such as this, you could remember your childhood where you reached out to catch hope on the tip of your tongue.

Seeing nothing in every direction but her circus friends going about their usual business, Ellen stuck out her tongue, half expecting to taste the joy of a better future. The idea made her giggle, and the sound of her laughter brought an answering kick from the little girl in her womb.

It would be no other, for Ellen already imagined tucking

her in at night, saying, "Mary Star, you are special because you were born in the circus, surrounded by people who love you."

She unlaced the flap to the school tent, then stepped inside and stood breathing in the smells of textbooks and chalk mingled with the sweet grass just outside the door. Back in Tupelo, she'd loved her students, loved going into the schoolhouse with its smell of oiled wooden floors and chalk dust.

But being the circus teacher was special to her in ways her former teaching job had never been. If you'd asked her to put her finger on the cause, she might have named the circus children, and that would be true. Their unique perspective on life endlessly delighted Ellen. But if you asked her to dig a bit deeper, she might have said *peace*.

She could look out the door of her little trailer and see friends in every direction. She could ride Aladdin through the pasture in the moonlight with Luca and believe she was brave. She could sit down for tea with Ruth and Michelle and imagine that the wings of Michelle's white dove were the wings of a guardian angel.

Smiling, she hurried to the colored plastic bins along the back wall that held all the things she needed—pink crepe paper, lengths of string, multicolored balloons, colored markers, and a large section of poster board.

She spread her supplies on the art table along the back wall of the tent, then sat in a folding chair and began lettering the poster board—"Happy Birthday"—in April's favorite colors, pink and purple. She had just written the *A* for April's name in bright blue when a sound at the door made her turn.

A clown stood just inside the tent flap, his yellow wig covered with a straw hat topped by an outrageous sunflower and his bulbous nose an improbable shade of purple.

"Jocko? You've changed your costume."

"Guess again."

Panic spiraled through her. Wayne had chosen the one disguise that made him totally unrecognizable as someone who didn't belong in the circus backyard.

Run, her heart said, while her mind said, *You're trapped with no way out.*

"You've found me."

"Did you think I wouldn't?"

"No."

He still hadn't moved from the tent door. Ellen thought about spiders who weave huge webs to trap their prey, and buzzards who circled for hours before diving to tear their victims apart.

"You've caused me a great deal of trouble, Ellen. Are you ready to behave now and go home without a fuss?"

"By *fuss,* I suppose you mean another beating."

"Don't think I'll let that maternity top you're wearing stop me."

He took one step toward her, and then another, his rage hidden behind greasepaint, only his eyes showing the yellow glare of pure evil.

Forcing herself not to cringe, not to retreat, she lifted her chin.

"Leave, Wayne. I'm not going home with you. Not now. Not ever."

He stopped, but only for the time it took Ellen's heart to set up a rhythm like the wings of a trapped moth.

"I'll scream. If you take another step, I swear I'll scream so loud it will bring the entire circus to this tent."

"Go ahead. By the time they get here, you will have come to your senses like a good girl." He moved irrevocably forward. "Or you'll be dead."

There was no more room to bluff. Wayne was telling the horrible truth, and all Ellen could do was wait for his fists.

Her baby stirred, then, and the hope she'd caught on her tongue presented itself in the metal chair, clutched in her hands.

Wait, she told herself. *Be still. Don't let body language give you away.*

He came closer, his outsize clown mouth stretched into a grotesque smile. The tent opening was clear now, but Wayne stood squarely between her and safety.

Sweat poured down her face and fear made her legs so weak she wondered she was still upright. One more step and he was little more than an arm's length away.

Ellen flung the chair at his knees, so hard she heard the crack of metal on bone, so fierce she had to veer so he wouldn't fall on her as she raced toward the door.

His curses followed her outside, became fainter as she ran. Her trailer was too far away. Wayne would recover and over- take her before she could get inside and turn the lock.

There was no one she could call. The smell of frying bolo- gna from the direction of the cook tent was all the evidence she needed that performers and roustabouts alike were sitting down to breakfast.

A sound like a crying wind swept over Ellen, but she real- ized it was only the voice of her desperation. The answer came to her in a soft whinny.

"Aladdin!" She raced toward the paddocks and climbed the fence. Would the stallion remember her? Would he come?

Without Luca to control them, the twelve Andalusians looked like a pale, whirling tornado, one that could kill without thought.

"Ellen!" Wayne was behind her, pounding toward the paddock, so close she could see the sunflower bobbing on his hat.

Ellen let go and landed inside the paddock. What had Luca said?

She stood up, calling Aladdin's name, her voice no more than the peeping of a baby bird fallen from its nest. The horses galloped by, paying her no more attention than the lizard that darted under the fence.

"I'll get you for this." Wayne was close now. Any minute he'd be on the fence, grabbing her by her hair.

"Aladdin!"

To her astonishment, the big stallion separated from the others and trotted to her side.

"Kneel!" Two thousand pounds of horseflesh did her bidding, and Ellen found herself atop a stallion that would dance on command—or kill a man with one kick to the head.

"Good God!" Wayne had clambered atop the fence, but he just sat there, wonderfully, gloriously indecisive. "Get down before that horse kills you."

"What? You'd rather do it yourself?"

"Jesus, Ellen. I'm not going to hurt you. I just want to take you back home."

"My home is the circus now."

"Are you crazy? Get off that horse."

She urged the stallion closer to the fence, surprised at the surge of power she felt when Wayne leaned so far backward he nearly fell off.

"How does it feel to be afraid, Wayne?"

"I'm not afraid of you."

"But you're afraid of the stallion, aren't you? You're afraid of what I might command him to do."

Wayne teetered on the fence a heartbeat longer, and then began his backward crawl down the other side.

"Don't think I'm through with you, Ellen."

"Oh, yes, you're through, all right. I'm filing for divorce and charging you with assault and battery with intent to kill." As she edged the horse closer, she filled herself up with such sharp-edged courage she could have jumped Aladdin through a ring of fire. "Unless I decide to let this horse kill you first."

"You're bluffing."

"Why don't you climb back over that fence and find out?"

"That old mountain bat has turned you against me."

"No. You did that all by yourself, Wayne."

He started climbing the fence once more, a man sure of his own power, sure that the wife he faced was the same one who used to respond to his abuse with apologies for making him mad.

Aladdin's nostrils flared and he became restless, a trained circus stallion dancing in place to the rhythm of Wayne's rage.

Her husband paused on the top railing, uncertain now, a dawning comprehension flaring in his eyes.

"What's stopping you, Wayne? Come and get me."

In a voice like a river, Ellen gave the command she'd heard so many times from Luca, a soft, "Aladdin, up," combined with a nudge from her heels. Suddenly the great stallion reared, his sharp hooves exposed to the coward on the fence.

Wayne scrambled backward so fast he missed the bottom step and tumbled to the ground, where he crouched, as dark and forbidding as a grizzly. Memories of beatings and bruises, humiliations and nightmares pushed at Ellen, and she found herself sliding toward a role that was all too familiar: easy victim.

"I'll be back, Ellen. Don't think I'm done. The next time you won't be on that horse."

Her life spread out before her, endless years of running and fear, of cringing at shadows and jumping at sounds. But when you come to the end of your road, sometimes, suddenly, a new path appears; and though you can't see what lies beyond the trees and around the bend, you step through anyway, filled with stubborn hope.

She gave Aladdin the command, and he knelt once more. Ellen slid off his back and marched toward the fence.

"Here I am, Wayne. Come and get me now. But be warned: while I'm screaming so loud they can hear me clear to the next state, I'll kick and scratch and try to gouge your eyes. And when it's over, I'll go to the cops, even if I have to crawl."

The bravado leaked from him like air leaving a Goodyear tire punched by one small, insignificant-looking nail. She continued her advance, Sherman planning the burning of Atlanta.

"I will level charges against you that will ensure you can never lift your head in your hometown again," she said. "And when I'm finished with you, you'll be lucky they don't put you *under* the jail."

He crawled backward, all the while trying to scramble upright.

"Bitch."

The wind caught Ellen's laughter and scattered it toward

her friends and family, who were closing in—Indian Joe with his bull hook, Razz with a scarred old tiger trainer's fear of nothing, Luca with the easy grace of an equestrian accustomed to taking charge of animals many times his size. Behind them came Jocko with an evil-looking revolver and Aunt Ruth with her shotgun.

Wayne hadn't seen them yet. Ellen shook her head, a let-me-handle-this motion they understood as only good friends can. They halted their advance, their faces registering everything from Joe's and Luca's gleeful approval to Razz's murderous rage.

"I guess I am, Wayne. I'm a pure bitch." Ellen laughed with such abandon her husband stared at her as if she'd grown two heads. "I'm Eve now, a tiger woman just itching for a chance to roar."

Ellen's fear drained out through the soles of her feet, planted firmly on the circus grounds. And in its place was such a vaulting freedom she actually pounded her chest and imitated a Tarzan yell.

"Come get me, Wayne. Come take me to our loving home, if you can."

"Good God! Who'd have you now?" He finally got to his feet, but as he stood there facing her, she realized he was no grizzly at all, just a coward hiding behind a clown mask. "Just look what they've done to you, Ellen. You're nothing but a pathetic-looking, scraggly-haired slut. Good-bye and good riddance."

He whirled around to march off and was suddenly face-to-face with Indian Joe.

"Can I take the bull hook to him now, Eve?"

"He's not worth your time, Joe."

Razz stepped so close he could have felled Wayne with one punch, and her husband turned the color of a bleached sheet.

"Say the word, Eve, and I'll feed him to the tigers."

"I wouldn't want to spoil their digestion, Razz."

"Let me and Jocko have at him." Aunt Ruth cocked and leveled her shotgun. "I been itching to blow his britches off."

Her husband's mouth worked like a fish, the evil words he'd meant to level at Aunt Ruth caught in his throat as Jocko aimed his gun straight for Wayne's chest.

"If you say one word against Mimi, I'll put a hole right through that empty spot where your heart ought to be."

"Wayne, do you want my advice?" Ellen grinned at the look on his face. "Well, of course not. When have you ever considered me more than a punching bag?" She continued in a manner that was chatty, almost friendly, and yet anybody looking at her would see a woman of grit and steel and fire. "Leave now while you still can."

He balled his hands into fists, but there was never any question that Wayne was in full retreat, a husband as befuddled and furious as if he'd been beaten within an inch of his life by a pet bunny rabbit. He got an even bigger shock when he turned his back to Ellen. The Great Giovanni had arrived, and with him a towering gray wall of elephant blocking all possibility of escape.

"Good God!" As Wayne floundered backward, Betsy snatched off his hat and Giovanni snatched off his clown wig. In full blue and gold regalia, the Great Giovanni was every inch the circus legend.

"Get out of my circus!" he roared. "And don't ever show

your face around here again. Eve Star is part of our family, and we don't tolerate wife beaters."

Wayne's face twisted in the kind of terror Ellen had felt for years. Finally he darted between Luca and Aunt Ruth and took off running, with Betsy and Indian Joe right behind him.

"Make sure he's off the circus grounds," Giovanni yelled after them.

Joe waved his bull hook and kept up the chase.

"Reckon Joe will catch him?" Giovanni was chuckling.

"I hope he does." Razz leaned on the fence and studied Ellen, his expression suddenly as soft as if he were seeing the first rose of summer. "Eve, you remind me so much of Lola I half expect you to steal my whip and show up in the big cat cage at the matinee."

"I'm not ready to tame tigers, Razz, but I sure do like being one."

"That's my girl," Giovanni said, winking at Ellen. "The coffee's getting cold, Razz."

"You planning to drink it in that getup, Al?"

"It wouldn't be the first time."

They set off to the cook tent, their voices melting in the gold of a summer morning. Jocko and Luca moved in closer to Aunt Ruth, as if they'd seen all along what Ellen had been too afraid to notice. In spite of her shotgun, Ellen's aunt was showing signs of being an ancient woman who needed to lay down her gun and her visions, then sit in the shade and rest for a very long spell.

"Are you okay?" Ellen asked her.

"Now that the skunk has lit out like his tail was on fire, I could kick up my heels and shoot poots at the moon." A spark of the fiery Aunt Ruth from years gone by showed through. "I was the one that got this lynching mob together."

"You knew he was here?"

"I seen his evil last night, but I didn't see nothin' about him in the signs. If I had, I'd a warned you."

"Then how did you know?"

Aunt Ruth glanced toward the flocks of blackbirds that suddenly took flight from the oak tree on the far side of the pasture. Then she winked at Ellen.

"You might say a little bird told me." She linked her arm through Jocko's. "Jocko, me and you's got cupcakes to bake."

"Cupcakes?" He looked puzzled till Aunt Ruth jabbed him with her elbow and nodded toward Luca, a not-so-subtle reminder of the man waiting by the fence as patiently as the ocean waits for the pull of the moon. "Oh, *cupcakes*? Yeah, that's right."

Luca waited until they were out of sight, and then he said gently, "Would you like some company?"

There were a thousand promises in those five words, and Ellen yearned for every one of them.

"I'd like nothing better."

With one easy vault, Luca was over the fence, wrapping his arms around her. She leaned into him, her feelings so complex she could only make out a giddy sort of triumph laced through with hope.

It was Luca who helped her with the rest. Tipping her chin up with one finger, he asked, "Does this mean I get to call you Tiger Lady?"

"Call me whatever you want. Just don't let me go."

"Not a chance."

His lips closed over hers, and the early morning sun was in his kiss, a warm promise of a bright day ahead.

JOCKO TARRIED AT THE trailer only long enough to ask Ruth if she needed anything.

"If I do, I know who to call."

"That's right. You and Eve can call me anytime. After what she's done for me, there's nothing I wouldn't do for that girl. I mean *nothing*."

He was just like Ray Boy, a proud man embarrassed by praise but pleased by the simple gesture, the small kindness. She put her hand on his arm.

"I know, Jocko. *I know.*"

After he left, she took the birthday cupcakes out of the oven and started spreading pink icing. She'd pit her cooking against Julia Child's any day, and she'd dare anybody to say different. She was icing the last cupcake when the faint outline of a tiger streaked across the living room.

The knock on her door didn't surprise her one bit. Nor did Razz, standing there in his baseball cap.

"I reckon I must be the queen of England," she said.

"How's that?"

"First the Great Giovanni invites me to sit in his box and now the man my sister considered a hero has come a callin'." She stepped aside to let him pass. "Come on in. The coffee's still hot and you can have a fresh cupcake to go with it."

She didn't know what surprised her most: that Razz took off his cap and smoothed back his uneven hair, or that he got watery-eyed. She turned her back and started fixing two cups of coffee so he'd think she didn't notice. What she'd learned about men had come from her granddaddy and Ray Boy, and that wasn't much. But neither one would have wanted a woman to see him cry.

Razz sat at the table, a small man who didn't have any trouble fitting, and wrapped his hands around his coffee cup.

"Lola said that about me?"

"In her letters. And in my visions, and I ain't ashamed to admit it." She got her own cupcake and sat down across the table. "I never did say thank you for looking after my sister. And my niece, too."

"How'd you know?"

"I got eyes. I seen you in the pasture this morning, and you and that tiger keepin' watch last night."

Razz shifted around like a man trying to get comfortable with his own feelings. When he sagged like a feather pillow settling into place behind your head, Ruth knew this was a different Razz from the one she'd seen before.

Maybe that's what age finally does to you: it takes away your sharp edges and gives you a gentler way of looking at things.

"I never thought I'd let it happen, much less admit it, but I've taken a liking to Eve." Tough old tiger-scarred Razz suddenly looked like a doting grandfather.

And that's what he'd have been if Lola had lived. Even though her sister hadn't told her the whole story, not yet at least, Ruth knew that as surely as she knew the white feather floating down from the ceiling onto Razz's shoulder was a sign he was going to be part of their family for a long time to come.

Suddenly Ruth started laughing.

"What's so funny?"

"It ain't you. It was the look on Wayne Blair's face when Eve stood up to 'im. Reckon Indian Joe ever caught that skunk?"

"He did. He was laughing about it at the cook tent a while ago."

"What happened?"

"He and Betsy played cat and mouse till they'd chased Blair all the way to his car. Then Joe turned the elephant loose and let her have some fun. She picked him up by his leg and dangled him in the air till he was screaming like a stuck pig."

Ruth didn't wish ill on people, but she wished she could have seen that. After what he'd done to Ellen, she wished Betsy had sat on him.

But the thing she wished most, had wished since her journey began, was to know the truth about her sister.

"Do you ever plan on telling me what happened to Lola?"

"I've carried her secret so long it feels . . ."

"Like a boulder settin' on your chest?"

"Yes," he said, and she nodded, then poured fresh coffee and waited for him to begin.

"She was sick the night Jim Hall found her, so sick she stayed behind in bed while I did the cat act by myself. It was raining, hard, and the minute I stepped into the downpour, I had this gut feeling I shouldn't have left her."

"But the show must go on."

"How'd you know?"

"Magic Michelle told me."

"It wasn't any trouble for him to find our train car. In those days, gold lettering on the sides of the cars told exactly who was in each one. Giovanni still likes the sign on his trailer."

"I seen it. I been thinkin' of getting one for me and Ellen. 'Mimi and Eve Star,' it will say. 'The Bravest Women on Earth.' Later, we'll add the baby's name."

"Is it going to be a girl?"

Longing and hope hung over his head like a yellow veil.

"Yes," she said. "But don't you go telling Ellen. I want her to be surprised."

"That'll be one secret that's easy."

Razz looked into his coffee cup, a man seeing not the swirl of dark liquid but the black clouds of a past he'd tried to hide. Ruth read him as easily as if he were a blackbird perched in her corn.

"When Jim Hall found Lola, he jerked the covers back and started beating her, and her with her hands up begging him to stop, telling him she wanted a divorce, begging him to leave." Razz scrubbed his hand across his face as if he could wipe out the painful memories. "I wish to God he'd listened."

Ruth had imagined the confrontation for fifty years. She'd pictured her sister grabbing a pair of scissors or going into the kitchen and getting a butcher knife. She'd even imagined a gun. Lola was a crack shot. Anybody brought up on a mountain who didn't know her way around a gun was just plain foolish, and Lola Hall had never been foolish.

But what Razz said next, Ruth would never have imagined. Not in fifty more years.

"What Jim Hall didn't know was that Sheikh and Rajah were sleeping in the train car, behind the curtain right by Lola's bed."

"Lord have mercy."

"She'd babied them, bottled them, and trained them. She was theirs. When a tiger defends his own, he takes the prey down from the back, then uses his claws to rip open the belly."

"That man who beat my sister black and blue every day she lived with him was gutted by two tigers?"

The justice of it settled into Ruth's bones—that the man who had struck fear into Lola every day of their marriage should in the end feel a clawing terror. And she'd dare anybody to make her feel bad about it.

"Lola tried to get them off, but she was no match for two full-grown Bengals on the kill. By the time I finished my act and got back to the trailer, she was near hysteria. And Jim was nearly finished off."

"You buried the rest of him?"

"I carried the remains to the lions. After they'd finished what the tigers started, they wasn't so much as a hair to show Jim Hall had ever been to the circus."

"I knew Lola didn't kill him. I knew it in my heart."

"She died a few months after that. And I've carried the secret ever since."

"You don't have to do that no more. If you don't mind me helpin' tote the load."

There they sat, two old codgers who had become unlikely friends because they'd both loved Lola, loved her so fiercely they would bury the truth and ignore the law to protect her. And they would do the same for Ellen.

The good news was that Ellen was now strong and brave enough to protect herself.

"If I was to ask you to help me take these cupcakes to the school tent, what would you say?"

"I'd say you were cagey and I was getting too soft to get in the cage with the big cats." Razz stood up and rammed his cap back onto his head. "Which side of that little bitty plate do you want me to tote?"

They set off across the circus backyard to the school tent where Ellen stood at the back of the tent with Luca, watching the children romp. April met them at the school tent door and hugged Ruth around the knees.

"Mimi! It's my birf'day, and I'm having two pahties!"

"Ain't that fine?"

"Yes!"

The little girl spread the wings she always wore and raced into the midst of crepe paper streamers and floating balloons straight into the arms of her teacher.

"Miss Stah, Miss Stah. Watch me fwy!"

April took off again, and the swirling colors of the party became a vision so clear Ruth could see far into the future: Eve Star and her daughter, Mary, dancing in the sunshine with Luca and Nicky while citrus blossoms floated around them as white as the muzzle of an aging tiger sleeping under the lemon tree. Sitting underneath the fragrant branches in lawn chairs, two old codgers looked on, grateful they'd lived to see another circus season and even more grateful the big top had been tucked away while they wintered in a state that promised plenty of sunshine and lots of hugs from the child they both considered their great-granddaughter, a little girl with Lola's blue eyes.

Turn the page for a look at Peggy Webb's literary novel, written as Anna Michaels, which Pat Conroy called "an unforgettable story told with astonishing skill."

THE TENDER MERCY OF ROSES

On sale now!

NEAR THE TENNESSEE-ALABAMA LINE

*I*T DON'T TAKE NO *high school education to figure out I'm in a pickle.*

First off, there's cow shit on my boots. Dirty boots is a sign of a shoddy upbringing. Since I mostly brought up myself, I can guarantee you I ain't no low class woman.

I ain't no fool, neither. The good Lord give me plenty of brains, then shoved me out of the womb a-buckin' and a-rarin'. I come into this world with my eyes wide open and I ain't shut 'em in twenty-six years. I aim to see what's coming my way, and if I don't like what I see I'll dodge or run or dig in my spurs and beat the living shit out of it.

But I sure didn't see this coming. How did this happen? Did I blink? Is that how I ended up flat on my back in a bunch of piney woods not being able to feel a thing, not even my own skin and bones? I'm laying here with my eyes wide open under one of them cloudless skies the good Lord strews through Alabama in the summertime and I ain't got a single urge in my brain. Not even to get up and saddle my horse.

Since I can't figure out no reason for all that, I might as well lay here till the good Lord gives me a clue.

Now, I ain't no religious nut, but me and God come to a under-standing thirteen years ago.

I was setting in Doe Valley Baptist Church listening to the preacher shout, "The road to redemption is straight and narrow," after which he passed around the collection plate. Dollar bills began dropping like faintin' goats. Then Brother Lollar commenced hollering about tithing, which is just a fancy way of asking poor folks to part with their butter and egg money. Twenties began drifting into the plate, and it looked to me like the road to redemption was paved with greenbacks.

I just about resigned myself on the spot to eternal damnation. Then lo and behold the preacher waxed eloquent about a option called endowments.

Now, I had two of them suckers setting on my chest. I knew on account of my science teacher. The week before, he'd invited me to his house to look at the stars through his telescope. While I was on his back porch trying to find the man in the moon, he sneaked up behind me, told me I was "well-endowed," then proceeded to try to feel both of 'em. I run back into the kitchen, grabbed the nearest weapon and whacked him over the head with his own corn bread skillet. He's the one ended up seeing stars.

Be that as it may, setting in the Baptist church with sweat rolling into my endowments, I figured that finally me and redemption might make a nodding acquaintance.

As soon as the shouting was over, I asked the preacher how I could use the gifts nature bestowed on me for the Lord. After he got his jaw back in the right place, he laid his hands on my head and prayed for "the soul of this pitiful, unfortunate orphan."

I ain't no orphan—I got a daddy—and I sure as hell ain't pitiful. I walked out and marched myself back up Doe Mountain and never looked back.

Daddy found me sulking in the hayloft. "Pony," he said to me, which is my name on account of being so little everybody said I reminded them of a Shetland pony, "ain't no use fumin' at God. He didn't see fit to give you no riches, but He give you a brain and plenty of grit. What you do with it ain't up to that preacher, it's up to you."

Me and God had us a understanding that day. I promised if He'd understand why church was gonna be nature from here on out, where ain't no bird nor tree ever looked down on me, I wouldn't never let Him down about using what He give me. I reckon God was okay with that bargain, because I done proved my daddy right a million times over.

Now, I ain't what you'd call a woman of the world, but I done traveled a good bit and seen how things is north of the Mason-Dixon line. And let me tell you, I ain't seen nothin' I can't handle if I set my mind to it.

I try wrapping my mind around laying here stiff as a poker, but don't nothing come to me except the scent of Cherokee roses—seven star-white petals, seven tribes of displaced Cherokee, the tears of a grieving nation turned to flower. I feel a rushing across my skin like the flow of cool blue water, the kiss of greening spring winds, the brush of a starling's wing. Right before my eyes a wall of roses springs up in the piney woods, blankets the trees, swings from the branches and covers the ground.

This ain't happened but once in my life—the day I kicked free of my mother's womb, the day she died. His heart split in two, my daddy took his chain saw and cut down my mother's climbing Cherokee roses. She was Morning Star and she'd planted them roses as a reminder that half the blood running through her veins was Cherokee. Daddy raved through the woods like a madman till there wasn't nothing left standing but him and the trees stripped of scented vines.

Satisfied there wasn't a single rose left to remind 'im of his loss, he marched out of them woods with tears streaming down his face. The midwife laid me in his arms, a screeching bundle of kicking wildfire. When he turned back around to show me that we was starting over— just me and him—ever' one of them Cherokee roses had sprung back to life.

As I watch now, the Cherokee roses start dancing, a-swinging and a-swaying like a wild wind's shaking 'em. But the air is so still *you can't see nothing move except them roses, not even the wind over a eagle's wing.*

My heart strains upward, trying to rise, and rose petals drift down and cover me like snow, like stars, like the tears of my ancestors.

I figure I must be dead.

If that's the truth, there ain't nothing I can do about it. I might as well hang around and see what happens next.

The WALLS BETWEEN Us

Present

The walls between us are as high
as the mountain ranges.

—*Chief Dan George, 1899–1981*
GESWANOUTH SLAHOOT
COAST SALISH, BAND OF THE
TAKIL-WAUTUTH NATION

One

DOE MOUNTAIN, TENNESSEE

TITUS JONES STOOD IN the middle of his tobacco patch, lifted his hoe from the hardscrabble earth, and listened. What he was listening for, he didn't know. Pulling a blue bandana out of the left back pocket of his faded overalls, he took off his straw hat and wiped the sweat from his face.

Nothing stirred, not even a crow's wing. He glanced toward the flock of pesky birds that had landed earlier in the blackjack oak high up on the ridge above his fence line, and that's when he knew what he was listening for.

Five minutes earlier the mountain had bustled with sound—the soft hum of sweat bees seeking a place to light, the skittering of field mice along the edges of the fence line, the mocking call of the blue jay. Now there was nothing. Just Titus and the mountain and the silence and the ever-present scent of Cherokee roses.

Pulled by forces he didn't understand but had learned not to question, Titus left his hoe in the middle of a tobacco row and walked toward the split-rail fence that separated his farm from the deep woods that belonged to the mountain. All of it did, really. He'd learned that from Morning Star. The land belonged to the universe. He was just a caretaker, that's all.

He'd learned other things from his beloved wife, as well—the magic of roses and totems and signs that would tell you everything you needed to know if you practiced the art of stillness and listening with your heart.

He was listening now, and he was listening hard. As he approached the fence, the roses came to life. He couldn't have told you how or why, but the flowers started glowing, sending beams of light so powerful the white petals looked like deep snow under a blazing sun. Scorched by memories, blinded by pain, it was all Titus could do to remain upright.

What fresh hell did the roses have in store for him? He knew it would be useless to cut them down. He'd tried that when Morning Star died, but roses with a message refused to be destroyed.

Undefeated, Titus shook his fist at the roses. "You ain't beat me yet." His voice cracked apart like heirloom china smashed with a hammer. In his heart, he knew. He *knew*. Still, he defied the roses. "Bring it on. I can take whatever you got."

Transfixed, he saw a wolf emerge from the roses. Pure white, the kind not found on this mountain or any other save for the frozen confines of the Arctic Circle.

Pony's totem.

The wolf stared at him with beaming yellow eyes, his message so clear Titus could see a new pathway opening beyond the wolf and the trees, even beyond the sky, a path that spoke of harmony and bravery and freedom. But it also spoke of loss and death, the passing of a remarkable soul from the earth.

Titus understood the wolf's message as few men could, understood because he had loved and learned from a Cherokee woman, because he lived with a mind wide open. Staring into the eyes of the wolf, Titus would have given his life to be like the rest of the world, dismissive of events that couldn't be explained, blind and deaf to miracles.

But he understood how you could be transformed in a twinkling from joy over the birth of your child to despair over the death of your wife, and how the roses you'd cut down only a moment earlier could spring back to life when your red-faced, squalling daughter was placed in your arms. And when she wrapped a tiny fist around your finger and hung on, you knew: it would be just the two of you from that moment till the end.

A story foretold by all the signs. If only you knew how to look.

From the direction of the stables, the Appaloosa whinnied. With a stillness born of living in harmony with nature, Titus watched as the wolf turned his majestic head toward Pony's horse then vanished. As the Arctic wolf slipped through the ominous jungle of roses, the petals flew loose and covered the ground—an elegy in white.

The wind picked up, then, crying and howling his daughter's name, lifting Titus's thinning gray hair and chilling his bones, though it was summer and already hotter than any northeast Tennessee summer in his memory. The weight and sorrow of the signs broke Titus, drove him to his knees. He joined his voice to the wind, pleading for God to strike him dead.

Under a sky so hot and cloudless it felt like a burning blue bowl turned over your head, there was a tiny sound, like the cracking of a nutshell. But it was not a black walnut or a Southern pecan that made the sound. It was Titus Jones's heart.

Pony was dead and there was no mercy left anywhere in the world.

HOT COFFEE, MISSISSIPPI

IN HOT COFFEE, WHERE blueberries grow when folks said it wasn't possible—they'd never survive the Mississippi heat—there's a feeling along the twelve-mile stretch of Highway 532 that anything can take root and blossom. Even hope.

The feeling is so pervasive, it attaches itself to blueberries, seeps into coffee, dives deep underground to permeate the aquifer that supplies drinking water. In farmhouses and businesses loosely connected by the legend of an 1800s inn that was the last stop for travelers going to Mobile, Alabama, it's possible to dream with your eyes wide open.

Possible for everybody except Jo Beth Dawson.

On a blue and gold summer morning, while fairies sipped dew from the cups of wood violets and sleepy-eyed citizens ate blueberry muffins with their morning cup of coffee, never knowing the dark java was the source of hope taking root in their bones, Jo Beth lay in her narrow bed under the covers, hating the sun. Soon the intense light would make it impossible for her to hide in the deep caverns of sleep.

She pulled the sheet over her head but the insidious sunlight crept under the ill-fitting trailer door, slid through cracks in the venetian blinds, and pierced the percale.

There was only one place left to hide. Holding a head already pounding from last night's encounter with Jack Daniel's, Jo Beth stumbled into the kitchen and searched her cupboard. Scotch, vodka, Kentucky straight bourbon whiskey, Baileys Irish Cream. All her old friends were there, all of them empty.

Dragging out the garbage can, she stood in her bare feet smashing bottles. Bits of colored glass flew over the rim of the can and rained over the floor like heartache. Jo Beth didn't even flinch when the shards pierced her skin. What were a few drops of blood on her feet compared to the river of blood that drenched her soul?

Glancing at the clock on her kitchen wall, she tried to judge whether the liquor store would be open, but the edges of her vision blurred. Did that signal a need for glasses? A hangover? At forty-eight, it could be either. More than likely both.

She thought about throwing on a trench coat and driving to

Bob's Package Store to wait for the door to open, but she didn't want to add to the talk. *Hot Coffee's newest resident sighted on the hottest morning in June wearing nothing but a full-length coat and her underwear.* Only six weeks in a podunky town you'd miss if you blinked, and already she had the reputation of being eccentric, unsociable, and stark raving mad.

Which was fine by Jo Beth. She didn't put down roots. She was a turtle, traveling with her home on her back, a 1968 Silver Streak camper-trailer bought dirt cheap after her divorce and held together with baling wire and determination. A pity you couldn't do the same thing with a life. Or maybe a blessing. She hardly knew the difference anymore.

Jo Beth shrugged into a T-shirt then grabbed a pair of denim shorts and tried to get into them standing up. She ended up perched on the edge of her mattress, a skinny-legged migratory bird ready to take flight at the least change in climate. When her cell phone rang, she almost fell off the bed.

If she continued fooling around with Jack Daniel and Tom Collins every night, she was going to have to turn the ringer off. Fumbling among the empty potato chip bags and candy wrappers on the end table—last night's supper—she plucked the phone and checked the caller ID. Maggie. The only friend she had left in Huntsville, Alabama. Maybe in the whole world.

"Jo Beth, in case you've forgotten, the rodeo starts day after tomorrow." Maggie never said hello. "When are you coming?"

"I can't come."

"You promised."

Maggie had known her for twenty years. She should know better than to trust Jo Beth. People who made that mistake ended up dead.

"Jo Beth? Are you still there?"

"I'm here."

"You can't avoid Huntsville forever."

She had for ten years, and she saw no good reason to go back.

Except one. Maggie was the only person who had stood up for her when everything she had was stripped away—her gun, her badge, her honor, her pride.

"I'll be there, Maggie."

Jo Beth's promise sucked all the air out of the trailer.

Huntsville—the city of her disgrace, a city of accusations, ghosts, and severed ties.

The rodeo—her history, her love, her long-lost safe harbor, full of forgotten dreams.

When she was a child the rodeo had been home to Jo Beth. Her grandfather, Clint Dawson, had organized a vanishing breed—the American cowboy—into the first professional rodeo. It symbolized the father she'd barely known (a rodeo cowboy), the grandfather she loved, and all the sawdust stories of her childhood turned to stardust because Clint Dawson made her believe in miracles. If a bowlegged, one-eyed cowboy could wrestle to the ground a steer so mean daffodils forgot to bloom the year it was born, Somebody in Charge could bring her daddy home so she'd have a regular family. If a rodeo clown in baggy britches and floppy shoes could outrun a bull as big as the four-bedroom house on Madison Street where her mother sang in a kitchen smelling of gingerbread and Maxwell House coffee, then Whoever Was Up There could put a baby sister in her mother's belly so Jo Beth would have a little girl to play with, someone better than her phantom friend, Grace, who rarely suggested games and vanished so completely in chairs, people tended to sit on her.

Sometimes her mother cried in that house, though. Once when she'd been eight, Jo Beth had asked her why. And Cynthia Wainwright Dawson, displaced Boston blue blood who'd left dreams of Juilliard for a rodeo Romeo named Rafe Dawson, had looked at her with eyes as sad as faded pansies, eyes that held the story of a man who'd promised her the moon then given her a child to raise by herself.

"Because that's what adults do, Jo Beth."

Rejecting her mother's sorrowful viewpoint, Jo Beth grabbed two cookies and went back into the yard to resume her game of cowboys and Indians with Bob Houston. He was her best and only friend, partly because he lived next door, but mainly because Jo Beth was such a tomboy the neighborhood girls didn't want to play with her.

A few Madison Street mothers tried to push their daughters into playing with her till Jo Beth overhead Mrs. Claude Upton refer to her as "poor little rich girl with a no-good daddy." Though she had been only six at the time and hadn't seen her daddy in two years, Jo Beth lit into Mrs. Upton like one of the wild bulls Rafe Dawson used to ride at the rodeo.

"You take that back! If you don't I'll have my granddaddy hogtie you behind a mean bull and drag you all over Tupelo."

Then she'd spat on Mrs. Upton's Etienne Aigner shoes. Jo Beth didn't cry till she got home.

The truth was she didn't have a clue about her daddy. He was mostly absent with the rodeo the first four years of her life. And then he took off for good.

The only true thing Rafe Dawson had left her was the Legend of the Wisdom Keepers. Sitting on the edge of her bed, he'd explained the magic of trees and rivers, stars and flowers, birds and animals who were more than they seemed, who appeared in unexpected times and places, who knew things ordinary mortals could not, who would tell you their secrets if you invited them in.

"The Wisdom Keepers will watch over you, Jo Beth."

Her daddy had told her good night, kissed her on the cheek, then walked out the door. That was the last she'd heard of him, except for an occasional card, until his death at fifty.

Still, she'd pushed pity aside in pursuit of the so-called normal life—college and a career. When she joined the police academy, her mother got a great deal of satisfaction out of telling the neighbors that her tomboy daughter had matured into a tough woman who could handle anything with a gun.

Her mother had been wrong. Jo Beth's facade hid a tender heart burdened by the need to keep everybody around her safe. After she started police work, the souls of the accusing dead started to collect over in Huntsville, falling like pollen she couldn't get rid of no matter how hard she scrubbed herself. They were the hard cases, the ones where she arrived too late to a distress call or couldn't put together a strong enough case to convict. For a while, she'd clung to a life raft made of memories of her grandfather.

"Jo Beth, your daddy's got a bit of wanderlust," he used to say. "But I'm here and your mama's here and we've got the rodeo. A girl who has all that and a red cowboy hat, to boot . . . why, the world's your oyster, just waiting for you to find the pearl."

Hope in a red hat. Clint Dawson had given both to her on her tenth birthday.

On her eleventh while she ate hot dogs and drank Pepsi, while Cherokee girls with bells on their skirts danced at the head of a rodeo parade, Clint Dawson dropped dead.

The newspapers said he died with his boots on. They said he was a legend, one of the last true American cowboys.

They said nothing about the scared child who had to be rescued by a cop with red hair and freckles on his hands. They made no mention of the little girl who had sat in the police cruiser while strangers paged Uncle Mark, her loss turning to a river of silver tears.

But while her mother had made an art of holing up in dark

rooms waiting to drown, Jo Beth learned that if you pretended everything was okay, you could swim in tears. You could float on their aching surface and hardly notice that underneath, deep in the shadows, lurked unspeakable things. Horrors whose names you'd discover one by one after you were grown, after it had all vanished—the grandfather with candy and optimism in his pockets, the father with his wild ways and big dreams, the mother who couldn't drown in tears but found a lake near a place called Witch Dance on the Natchez Trace Parkway to do the job.

Her mother's death had shocked Jo Beth at the time, though when she thought about it later, she knew it shouldn't have. The Dawsons lived in extremes—Rafe in Never Land, Cynthia on the edge of a precipice, and Clint in the clouds. Even the way they died was extreme—her father in the middle of a river, her grandfather in the middle of a rodeo parade, and her mother without witness at a place where no grass grew because legend said witches had once danced there.

There was no middle ground for the Dawsons. Jo Beth was living proof.

Faced now with the choice of returning to the ghosts of Huntsville or letting down the only person who could look at Jo Beth and still see something worth saving, she couldn't breathe.

Jo Beth plunged through the front door, leaned against the silvery shell of her movable home, and sucked in air. But it wasn't a fresh breeze that swept through her hair and coated her skin, twined around her feet, wound up her legs and buried itself in her heart. It was the scent of roses.

There were no flowers in this godforsaken trailer park. Why bother? The people who ended up here were not looking for beauty and permanence. They were looking for a rock to crawl under.

Shading her eyes against a sun so bright it bleached everything in its path except souls, Jo Beth scanned the uneven pavement, the scrawny pines that pushed through the cracks, the overgrown banks of the creek that rarely had water because of recent drought. High on the creek bank a rose bloomed, white with a golden center, a single blossom so fragrant the scent brought Jo Beth to her knees.

The only thing she still believed in besides the oblivion of vodka was the omens of the Wisdom Keepers. Bad ones.

That was not just any rose, but a symbol of the Trail of Tears—the legend of the Cherokee Nation forced to leave their rich green lands in the Southeast and embark on a killing journey across the Mississippi Valley, the tears they'd shed for their fallen touching the ground and turning to roses.

Kneeling in the trailer park with her face pressed into the dusty pavement, Jo Beth tried to pray. There was only one hitch: she didn't remember how.

For a reader's group guide to the book visit *The Language of Silence* page at **SimonandSchuster.com**

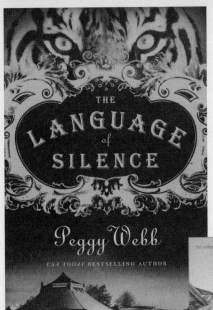

For more from this author,
don't miss her previous novel,
The Tender Mercy of Roses.

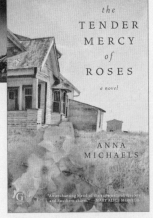

GALLERY BOOKS
A Division of Simon & Schuster
A CBS COMPANY